Thomas Gold Appleton, Susan Hale

Life and Letters of Thomas Gold Appleton

Thomas Gold Appleton, Susan Hale

Life and Letters of Thomas Gold Appleton

ISBN/EAN: 9783337135706

Printed in Europe, USA, Canada, Australia, Japan

Cover: Foto ©Raphael Reischuk / pixelio.de

More available books at **www.hansebooks.com**

OF

THOMAS GOLD APPLETON.

PREPARED BY
SUSAN HALE.

NEW YORK:
D. APPLETON AND COMPANY,
1, 3, AND 5 BOND STREET.
1885.

"... I am become a name
For always roaming with a hungry heart.
Much have I seen and known; cities of men
And manners, climates, councils, governments;
Myself not least, but honored of them all.
... Yet all experience is an arch where-through
Gleams that untraveled world, whose margin fades,
Forever and forever when I move."

CONTENTS.

CHAPTER		PAGE
I.	Biographical	7
II.	Boyhood. 1812–1825	14
III.	Round Hill. 1826	23
IV.	Round Hill Letters. 1827	38
V.	College-Life. 1828–1832	62
VI.	First Voyage. 1833	83
VII.	London. 1833	103
VIII.	Paris. 1833	123
IX.	Switzerland and Germany. 1833	142
X.	Florence. 1833–1834	166
XI.	Southern Skies. 1834	185
XII.	Two Weeks in a French Château. 1834	211
XIII.	Wandering Years. I. 1835–1844	232
XIV.	Wandering Years. II. 1845	252
XV.	Wandering Years. III. 1846–1854	270
XVI.	Oatlands Park. 1855	291
XVII.	Home Wanderings. 1856–1863	304
XVIII.	Commonwealth Avenue. 1864–1874	318
XIX.	Years of Repose. 1875–1883	335
XX.	The Last. 1884	345

CHAPTER I.

BIOGRAPHICAL.

THOMAS GOLD APPLETON was born in Boston, Massachusetts, on the 31st of March, 1812. His father was Nathan Appleton, a merchant of Boston.

The Appletons emigrated from Suffolk, England, to America, in 1635, and settled in Ipswich, Massachusetts. A part of the original grant of land held by them still remains in the possession of the family. Samuel Appleton, their ancestor, was a sturdy Puritan; he transmitted his principles and convictions to his sons, John and Samuel, who gained distinction in their time as stanch defenders of civil and religious liberty, by resisting the arbitrary measures of Sir Edmund Andros, the colonial Governor, in 1687, a period when such resistance entailed persecution and imprisonment.

Nearly a century later, Deacon Isaac Appleton, of the fifth generation since the emigration of the family to New England, went to New Ipswich, New Hampshire. Of his twelve children, two sons — Samuel and Nathan—became eminent men in Boston. The brothers were leaders in the commercial development of New England ; to Nathan Appleton is due, in a great measure, the first introduction of the power-loom into this country, with the foundation of the city of Lowell, and other enterprises establishing large manufacturing industries.

Nathan Appleton, born October 6, 1779, died July 14, 1861. He married Maria Theresa Gold, of Pittsfield, Massachusetts. Their children were :

1. Thomas Gold, died April 17, 1884.
2. Mary, married Robert Charles Mackintosh.
3. Charles Sedgwick, died 1835.
4. Frances Elizabeth, married H. W. Longfellow, died 1861.
5. George William, died 1827.

Mrs. Appleton died in February, 1833. In 1839 Nathan Appleton was married for the second time. His wife was Harriot Coffin Sumner, of Boston. Their children were :

1. William Sumner, married Edith Stuart Appleton.
2. Harriot, married Greely Stevenson Curtis.
3. Nathan.

Thomas was born in Boston, and there passed the greater part of his childhood. He was for some time at a private school in Jamaica Plain, kept by Mr.

Charles Greene, who is still remembered by the pupils who were under his care as an excellent and popular teacher ; he passed a year at the Boston Latin School, and in 1825, at the age of thirteen, joined a school established at Round Hill, Northampton, by Mr. George Bancroft and Mr. Joseph Cogswell. Three years later, in 1828, he entered the sophomore class at Harvard University, and graduated in 1831 ; he remained at Cambridge, in the law - school, during 1832.

Not long after the death of his mother, in the spring of 1833, Thomas sailed for Europe. This was the first of a series of voyages across the Atlantic, in the course of his life, during which he visited many lands, and became familiar with the languages, picture-galleries, and scenery of Europe. In his first tour, which lasted little over a year, he formed ties, never to be severed, with friends in England and upon the Continent ; and laid the foundations for the life of intellectual study and artistic enjoyment which he was destined to lead.

For many years following, either alone or with members of his family, he passed much of his time in Europe, drawn by the attractions of Paris to take an apartment there for a whole winter, or tempted to London by the society of his sister, Mrs. Mackintosh, who, after her marriage, was established there. He disliked the winter climate of Boston, and generally avoided it. He was, however, fond of the American summer, and not unfrequently suddenly recrossed the Atlantic, for the sake of the fresh breezes of Nahant, or the charms of Newport society.

Several years after her marriage, Mr. Appleton took a house in Cambridge, to be near his sister, Mrs. Longfellow, to whom, and whose growing family, he was warmly attached. As he approached the age of fifty years, even his ardor for travel and active spirit of observation were yielding to the wish for repose and the charms of a fireside. He thought of a more permanent establishment, and, buying land in Commonwealth Avenue, built the house in which he passed the rest of his life.

It was finished in 1864. Before it was ready to live in, Mrs. Longfellow's death occurred, followed a few days later by that of his father. The loss of these two, so dear to him, made a void in his life never to be filled; but his strong regard for his brother-in-law, Mr. Longfellow, his affection for his nephews and nieces, the children of so beloved a sister, and his warm interest in his half-brothers and sister, from this time forward fully occupied his heart; while the rest of his life was devoted, in a great measure, to the advancement of his native town in art, literature, and every form of intellectual culture. He had been a trustee of the Boston Athenæum from the early beginning of its modest collections in Pearl Street, and watched and aided its advance as it grew into the present Museum of Fine Arts. The Public Library was also an object of his care ; indeed, all schemes for the adornment and improvement of Boston found in him a ready advocate and worker.

In 1868, after an interval of several years, Mr. Appleton again went to Europe, this time in company with Mr. Longfellow and his daughters ; in 1874 he made the Eastern tour, passing that winter on the Nile, and the spring of 1875 in Syria.

This was his last foreign journey. With the exception of several excursions in America, and summers passed either in Nahant or Newport, the rest of his life was spent in Boston. In the winter of 1877, a fall on the ice caused an accident to his leg, confining him to his bed for many weeks ; the lameness which followed, although not permanent, rendered him cautious in his movements, more sedentary, and less inclined than of old to bodily effort. His mind, however, was never more active. He had already published several volumes of essays and reminiscences ; during the time that he was shut up in the house he wrote, by dictation, "Syrian Sunshine," containing his impressions of Palestine. An accomplished artist, Mr.

Appleton had devoted many hours in his life to the use of the brush and pencil ; these occupations now served to fill up the time and give pleasure to his friends. His poetical thoughts from boyhood found easy expression in graceful verse, plentifully scattered through his journals and among his papers. Some of these poems have been collected and published.

Mr. Appleton never lost his zest for travel, and, in the later years of his life, often ran on to New York and Washington in the spring, to vary the monotony of a long Boston winter. It was upon the last of these excursions that he caught cold ; and, detained in the Albemarle Hotel, New York, by pneumonia, he died there, after a brief and not painful illness of a few days, on the 17th of April, 1884.

Always industrious, even in the pursuit of pleasure, Mr. Appleton left ample journals of his earlier travels. It is chiefly from these, and from his full and frank letters to his father from abroad, that the following pages have been compiled.

Everything of a strictly private nature has been omitted, and much of the detailed account of buildings, picture-galleries, and scenery of foreign lands, which, wonderful to the enthusiastic young tourist, were set down with minute description for the benefit of untraveled friends at home. Such descriptions, with the glow omitted, to be sure, may be found now in the more hackneyed phrase of guide-books and countless books of travel.

Only such passages have been selected as should give the thread of Mr. Appleton's life, and present some idea of the wide circle of its observation and its sympathies. It would be, doubtless, possible, at some future time, to gather from the surviving correspondents of Mr. Appleton a full collection of his letters, but no such completeness has been now aimed at.

2

CHAPTER II.

1812–1825.

A HAPPY little boy, the son of devoted parents, making light of lessons, and working hard at play, popular with his playmates, and a favorite with his teachers, is the image called up by the earliest letters and the latest reminiscences of Thomas Gold Appleton.

He has described himself going to school in Pond Street (now Bedford), so called because there really was a pond in it—playing upon the wall which kept the sea from overflowing Charles Street; once jumping upon a scow there, and falling into the water, afterward taken home to be well warmed and well scolded. In those days the Common was a beautiful field of natural grass, where cows might graze, inclosed in a double fence of wooden rails. Mr. Appleton used to tell how the boys of his day loved to walk upon the top rail of this fence; and how one of them, engaged in this sport, slipped and fell, biting his tongue so that it had to be sewed up. He loved to recall the adventure of finding one day some money scattered on a path of the Common, which he supposed at first to be nothing but buttons; his joy in discovering they were really fourpences, and his decision to spend them for the common good of the boys in figs and raisins. The Frog-pond was a frog-pond then, with real frogs in it; the shores were muddy, and a willow hung over the water on the Beacon Street side. Thomas once lost a jackknife in the pond, and, to his latest day, often looked wistfully into its waves, as he passed by, in the vague hope of discerning this long-lost treasure.

In winter there was coasting, from the upper corner of Park Street across to Tremont, then, as now, the favorite direction for it. Tom's sled, named " Nimble Dick," is still remembered " by some old gentlemen," he says, " as the *ne plus ultra* of speed and beauty."

In those days a horse and chaise was a favorite means of pleasure-travel; with his father, Tom took long drives in the country, and learned his first lessons, by close observation, in a love of Nature, which clung to him all his life. One of these drives was to the Appleton pulpit in Saugus, where Samuel Appleton, an ancestor of the family, in 1687, exhorted his

listeners to resist the tyranny of Sir Edmund Andros. It is a pretty spot; a steep, almost perpendicular, cliff rises from a grassy base, with trees and
shrubs inclosing it. The flat top, at the edge of
the precipice, is a fine, commanding position for an
orator. Some years since, by Mr. Appleton's direction, a tablet was fastened on the surface of the
rock, to identify the place, and commemorate the
occasion.

Another object of their drives was Nahant. Mr.
Nathan Appleton was fond of the sea, and his son
inherited the taste. Driving across the long beach,
and watching the creaming waves, the boy talked with
his father on every subject. Many traces of these
conversations remained in his mind in later years.
There was from the beginning the closest companionship between them, and the warmest sympathy and
affection.

Mrs. Appleton, the mother of Thomas, was a lovely
woman, of great personal charm, a superior intellect,
and deep religious sentiment. An invalid for the later
years of her life, she impressed all who saw her, and
her children especially, with the purity of her character. Her memory was always treasured by her
son with a reverence and affection deeply pervading
his character. From his father, Thomas, even as a
little boy, received some knowledge of the Unitarian

views announced by Dr. Channing. A pew in Dr. Channing's church, in Federal Street, belonged to the family, and remained in their possession after the congregation migrated to Arlington Street, where, in his later years, Mr. Appleton was a constant attendant.

Two of his companions in early youth were Wendell Phillips and John Lothrop Motley, with whom Tom had a close intimacy. The dramatic instincts of all three sought development in a series of performances in the Motley house in Walnut Street, where the young performers, without audiences, used to strut and rant in impromptu costumes.

Dr. Holmes, in his "Life of John Lothrop Motley," has described this period. He says :

"His father's family was at this time living in the house No. 7 Walnut Street, looking down Chestnut Street, over the water to the western hills. Near by, at the corner of Beacon Street, was the residence of the family of the first Mayor of Boston ; and at a little distance from the opposite corner was the house of one of the fathers of New England manufacturing enterprise, a man of superior intellect, who built up a great name and fortune in our city. The children from these three homes naturally became playmates. Mr. Motley's house was a very hospitable one, and Lothrop and two of his young companions were allowed to carry out their schemes of amusement in the garden and the garret. If one with a prescient glance could have looked into that garret, on some Saturday afternoon, while our century was not far advanced in its second score of years, he might have found three boys in cloaks and doublets and plumed hats, heroes and bandits, enacting more or less impromptu melodramas. In one of the boys he would have seen the embryo dramatist of a nation's life-history—John Lothrop Motley ; in the second, a famous talker and wit, who has spilled more good things on the wasteful air in conversation than would carry a 'diner-out' through half a dozen London seasons, and waked up, somewhat after the usual flowering-time of authorship, to find himself a very agreeable and cordially welcomed writer—Thomas Gold Appleton. In the third, he would have recognized a champion of liberty, known wherever that word is spoken, an orator whom to hear is to revive all the traditions of the grace, the address, the commanding sway of the silver-tongued eloquence of the most renowned speakers—Wendell Phillips."

Some childish letters are still preserved, written on long foolscap paper, now yellow with time, the lines carefully ruled with pencil, the capital letters conscientiously formed, the sheet adorned with flourishes, and occasionally marred with blots. The spell-

ing in these early letters leaves something to be desired, and evidently called forth reproof from the
watchful father, followed by apology and improvement. This one, written on a visit, for the benefit of his health, in the country, shows a little
longing for the comforts of home :

NEW IPSWICH, 18*th July.*

MON CHER PÈRE : I now undertake to write you
for the first time. I shall put it in a sort of journal,
beginning—

Monday. — When you left me, I went into Mr.
Newell's, and read of the water - spout, etc., in his
book of curiosities. After breakfast, I drew a little
of that mill-view I got of Mr. Brown ; after which I
mowed a little with my host, Sam, and another, but
very poorly. After dinner, I helped them to get in an
exceeding large load ; going into the barn, my head
struck, very nearly, the beams, I being on top. I am
as yet well pleased with my host and hostess, and
hope to be contented.

Tuesday.—I went for the first time to-day to that
den of tyranny, a school. I recited a lesson in Sal-
lust, and was pretty well worn out before I came
home. This afternoon I stayed from school to write.
. . . I do not think school did me much good to-day,
and I don't want to stay there long. I long to see

you and the rest of the family, as I am rather tired of New Ipswich.

I remain, your

Ever-loving son,

T. G. APPLETON.

P. S.—I hope to come home before a month is out.

His next letter is more cheerful:

NEW IPSWICH, *July 25th.*

MY FATHER: You can not conceive what pleasure I felt in reading your letter. I have been much better the last two days, which I am sure you will be glad to hear. We had two very affecting sermons yesterday by a Mr. Danforth: the afternoon one was a funeral sermon; the text was, "And there is no hope." He gave a very animating description of the torments of the sinner in hell, for whom there is no hope, upon whom the dark waves of eternity roll, tinged with the bitter wrath of the Almighty.

On Saturday, I had a visit from Mr. Wallace, who offered to lend me any books he had, and invited me to come over and play chess with him, and showed *beaucoup de la politesse.* I read "The Absentee," by Mrs. Edgeworth, and am reading "Clarentine." I have drawn as yet three pieces, one of them, for Sam, a scare-crow. The dog-days begin to-day, and it rains, and I feel rather dogmatic. I did not go to school this morning, but expect to this afternoon, although it rains.

There is a postscript to this letter from his hostess, in which she says :

"I think Thomas's health is improving, and I should like to have him spend several weeks with us, as his company is very pleasant and agreeable. He submits to every inconvenience with cheerfulness, and I do not think it a task to have him here."

In the boy were to be traced the germs of characteristics which in manhood became strongly marked. Shy and sensitive, for fear of being laughed at, he said and did things to turn the laugh upon him, that he might laugh himself with the rest. An original mind, a keen perception of the differences and likenesses of objects animate and inanimate, a gift of comparing things most extreme, were born with him. His temper was quick, and his views of his own rights exacting, which put him at times at odds with his playmates ; but his good spirits and marvelous power of entertaining made him, even at an early age, a favorite companion.

Vanity was lacking among his early traits of character ; that love of praise and flattery, which leads boys to show off their accomplishments, was held in

check by a sensitive pride, born of fear of ridicule
and doubt as to success. At Mr. Greene's school,
however, and later, at the Latin School, he held a
good rank in his classes, showing early a turn for language which served him always in good stead.

CHAPTER III.

1826.

WHEN Thomas was thirteen, in 1825, he was sent
to the school at Round Hill, in Northampton, Massachusetts. He published, nearly fifty years afterward,
his reminiscences of this famous school, where he
passed three years. The fresh recollections he retained
of the place are a proof of the good system employed
there.

Two American gentlemen, Mr. Joseph Green Cogswell and Mr. George Bancroft, both scholars familiar
with the educational systems of Germany, determined
to attempt in their own country the experiment of a
school on the Fellenberg plan.

The institution of Fellenberg, at Hofwyl, in Switzerland, was intended to combine thorough culture of
mind with physical training. Situated within easy
reach of Alpine peaks, whose white crests indented the
horizon, it offered a perpetual promise of vacation
climbing after diligent study. Not only the fascina-

tions of Alpine ascent, but the severer home discipline of the gymnasium, secured development for the physical man, while careful attention was given to the routine of study through training by books.

Such double advantages to boys of mental and physical growth, inside the school-house and in the open air, these American gentlemen were determined to obtain. Drawn by the laws of association and external resemblance, they selected the beautiful eminence called Round Hill, near Northampton, for the site of the experiment.

Their prospectus drew, like a magnet, boys from all parts of the country; the school was opened in the autumn of 1823, and lasted about ten years.

It was a new thing, full of life and vigor, sustained by the proved scholarship and genius of the historian Bancroft, and of the large staff of officers under him; while its success was due, in great measure, to the singular combination of admirable qualities possessed by Mr. Cogswell. He was a man who united the characteristics of the man of study and of action. His head, filled as it was with the learning of America and Europe, could not overbalance his generous large-heartedness; he won completely, without attempting it in any manner, by the direct display of his own character, the respect and confidence of his scholars. At one time the boys must have num-

bered as many as a hundred and fifty ; they came
from almost every State in the Union. Not war, not
distance, not time, could break the bond between
them ; and the clasp which held them all was their
reverence and affection for Mr. Cogswell.

The relation of Mr. Cogswell with his scholars
was peculiar. He was not by nature fitted for the
austere duties of the schoolmaster. There was very
little of Dionysius the tyrant in him, whose relish for
the sufferings of young people intrusted to him has
survived in nests of cruelty of the type of Dotheboys
Hall. In fact, in no sense was there much of the
mere schoolmaster in Mr. Cogswell. He regarded
details of book-learning and study as but accessories
to the larger intention of making the man and the
gentleman. In the school-room, as on summer excursions, where he led off the procession, he was one of
the party—a boy, though of larger growth and maturer experience ; by no means a Jupiter Tonans,
frowning upon the rest from his raised platform.

Indeed, his relation to the boys was scarcely even
that of a teacher. He was the organizer, manager,
and father of the community ; his department was
that of affectionate moral influence ; besides which,
he was head farmer, builder, gardener, and treasurer
of the place. He loved his school, his boys, his
Round Hill ; and pursued his plans of expansion

3

and embellishment in every direction, without much
thought of profit or personal advantage.

These duties were enough for one man, without
the fatiguing details of instruction and recitation,
which fell to the share of a large staff of teachers—
German, French, Italian, and Spanish, as well as of
young men fresh from our college-training—all under
the able general supervision of Mr. Bancroft.

The indirect influences of education are often
overlooked. Many a scholar, many a noble genius,
has contracted the habit of devotion to letters, with
deficient love of the outer world. The outside influences of Round Hill were, perhaps, the best part of it,
and are certainly what its scholars loved and remembered the best. Let any one visit the lovely situation,
and he will readily imagine how the converging influences of such scenery acted upon the boys.

At the foot of the eminence, shining through or-
chard-bowers, was the then stately town of Jonathan
Edwards, and over the rich distance were seen
glimpses of the indolent circuit of the Connecticut
River. Mount Holyoke, one of the few real mountains of Massachusetts, of noble outline and sufficient
height, was ever encamped over against Round Hill,
to stimulate imagination with desire and mystery.

The area of Mr. Cogswell's domain was something
like three quarters of a mile square ; its borders were

known as "The Bounds," beyond which it was a pleasant wickedness to pass. The scholars were sorely tried, and did not fail frequently to violate the laws of limitation, for, on one side, under the hill, nestled hospitable roofs, and shops of succulent attraction for growing boyhood; on the other, were noble woods peopled with game — squirrels of all colors, woodchucks, rabbits, and even, very rarely, wild turkeys— to be hunted down leafy alleys, under majestic trees, which opened, to the ardent fancy of the boy, like vistas of the "Faerie Queen," where possibly a Una might be hid—one where surely glamour and enchantment reigned.

Though limited usually by the bounds, the boys were permitted excursions both in summer and winter, sometimes with Dr. Graeter, an eccentric German drawing-teacher, to sketch the lovely scenery which abounded near the Hill. It was a delightful afternoon's occupation, frequently leading the young artists as far as the banks of the Licking-water. Sometimes the doctor, as the boys called him, would leave them to sketch by themselves for a time. On one occasion a boy (perhaps Tom himself), profiting by this liberty, had enjoyed, with a party of his companions, a glorious swim in the river. The only sketch which he had to show later to the doctor, as the result of the afternoon, was the drawing of a palm-tree, which happened to be in his book. In broken Eng-lish and with much solemnity the doctor desired to be conducted to the tree. After taking the good man some distance, in the vain hope of tiring him out, the boy said the palm-tree was so far south, he feared they would not get back in time for supper. "I should dink so," remarked the doctor, without mov-ing a muscle of his face, and they returned without visiting the palm.

To bathe in the Licking-water, though it was, of course, not equal to the sea, was a great delight. So lucid was it that the bottom was everywhere visible. The sprays of over-arching trees touched and made music upon its surface, birds flew and sang overhead, scarcely was there a sign of man visible, and all seemed poetry and enchantment. Nor was the charm of the river diminished in winter, when, beneath the flawless ice, as through glass, were seen the pebbles below. To make a first impression upon its surface, to carve their initials with the sharp steel of their skates, was rapture to breathless flights of skimming boys, each seeking to outstrip the others.

In midwinter, the boys were expected to study from six in the morning till breakfast-time, by candle-light, coming from warm beds to break ice in the pail for washing, often grinding their young cheeks against slabs of ice, as if they were so much soap.

The zeal of Mr. Cogswell for his school led him to provide horses for the exercise of the boys, and in a cloud of cavalry they scoured the plain to the distant banks of the Connecticut. Señor San Martin, the Spanish teacher, who accompanied them, was an accomplished horseman ; he rode, well seated, with depressed heel, and had all the look of a true *caballero*. This professor had the typical pride and irascible temper of his nation. He was watchful for insult in certain mistranslations affected by the boys ; and when the Spanish word *todos* occurred, which he feared to hear rendered *toads*, the expectant passion in his face was a wonder to behold.

One of the great pleasures of the boys was a garden, a considerable bit of ground where many infant lessons were gained in farming. Most of the boys were as awkward with the roots of their flowers and vegetables, handling them in defiance of the laws of patient development, as they were with those tougher roots which fill the soil of Greek and Latin culture. An impatience of the growth of pease and peppers, cucumbers and melons, has always characterized the young farmer. The willingness of youth to see whether his bean or nasturtium may have taken root is the cause of a metaphor applying the process to the more tender sprouting of the affections ; officious friends have been accused of pulling up many a half-rooted attachment, in hope of discovering whether it was really fixed in the soil of the heart.

A greater pleasure than the garden to the boys was the unexpected bliss, through the generosity of Mr. Cogswell, of being co-proprietors of a boy-town, not to be found on any map, which received the name of Crony Village. Its site was a sloping hill, running downward to a brook. Bricks and mortar were furnished, beams and boards, and the little colony was constructed by the boys themselves, generally divided into families of two. Soon the evening smoke ascended from many hearths, round which the inmates of these happy homes were seated, reading or playing friendly games, or devouring, with a relish no after-meals could give, Carolina potatoes drawn from the ashes—each an ingot of pure gold, with added gold of butter; game, such as squirrels, the spoil of the bow, or rabbits caught in traps; to which were sometimes surreptitiously added pies and doughnuts, brought in mysterious raids from distant taverns and farm-houses.

All such delights have but their day. After a time Crony Village was found not to work well; the raids for pies and doughnuts were regarded with disfavor by the authorities, and the boys heard with anguish, from Mr. Cogswell's lips, the agonizing words, " ' *Delenda est Carthago*,' Crony Village shall be no more ! " A committee of destroyers, chosen from among the boys themselves, was appointed by Mr. Cogswell to do the work. With heavy hearts they proceeded on their fatal errand, under the magnificent chestnuts, which seemed to wave in sympathy with their woe, and soon all the work of their hands was destroyed. So deep was their reverence and respect for Mr. Cogswell that even this great calamity was accepted as a thing not only inevitable, but just ; and they could bear to see without flinching the carious hollows along the hill where their dwellings had been.

Mr. Cogswell's theory was one of guidance. Such occasional departures from right as became human nature were punished by loss of privileges, deprivation of play-time, or degradation to a lower form in the school-room, even by expulsion, but never by violence : he occasionally threatened, when the sinful element predominated, to bring the boys into the slavish routine and military subjection of West Point ; but it was only a threat, and the boys knew it. There was in use, however, one mysterious punishment for Titanic breaches of authority which impressed the school through its grandeur. This was the " Dungeon," in which the most refractory subjects were sometimes put. Through accident and infirmity even the most beloved and orderly boys would sometimes manage to get in, under some strain of their irrepressible natures, in which, according to the Calvinistic belief, as in bottled ginger-beer, a thousand original sins were always ready to pop forth.

In the main, the male sex predominated on the Hill. The masters were men, the boys were little men, and woman was a *rara avis in terra.* But one room there held two functionaries without whom no boy's life can be complete.

Mrs. Ryder supplied to him a little the place of his mother ; by her cozy fireside he found something of the old home feeling, and could ease the choking homesickness that at times must rise in his throat. In her room were no turbulence, no competition, only woman's sympathy and tender care. Mrs. Ryder may well have wondered why the boys loved her so much, but she half understood it at least. She felt expanded in her motherly nature until she could embrace with something of a mother's tenderness so large a family, and this well-spring of affection made green the waste places of her life. In her room was the boy allowed to sit, and say and ask those things which could not be said elsewhere. In her hospitable shovel could be run the lead for the tops of feathered arrows, and hatchets whose edge was not of the finest. She could say nay to no wish of the boys.

Behind, in the background, her rosy daughter stood for them all as an ideal of womanhood. She had less to say to the boys than her mother, but distance and withdrawal did not lessen their devotion. Once the elderly woman was taken with a fever, to the great grief of the school. Daily messages of love were sent to her which the daughter returned through her tears. Just as she was expected to die, Mrs. Ryder had a vision of one of the boys standing with a glass of soda in a certain place by her bed. The boy was told of it, procured the soda, and gave her, standing as the vision indicated, the refreshing draught ; after taking it, she immediately recovered.

The organ of nourishment is something marvelous in its demands. The man looks back upon his youth-ful appetite which is a part of the boy's ardor, in-nocence, and activity, with reverence and envy. In young puppies, and other browsing and feeding ani-mals when young, he sees something of the energy of that youthful mastication. In the boy, as in the pup-py, food seems instantly to be converted into fresh life, so that there is always a yawning void which no amount of ordinary meals can fill up. In vain does he throw into the abyss peanuts, maple-sugar, and all the foreign fascinations of the grocer's shop—*semper atque recurrit.*

Nothing could be less like Mr. Squeers's table than the generous board of the Round-Hillers. It was one of the habits of the school to prescribe occasionally at meals conversation in various modern languages ; but over that trivial barrier the hound-like appetite of the boy could easily leap. No Spanish difficulty in rendering " doughnuts," or apple-pie, kept him long from those dainties.

Twice a week there was cake for tea. The boys, in playing marbles, after losing to cleverer players their superb "blood-alleys," would pledge in advance on the issue of the game their cake of many cake-days ahead. It was distressing to see these victims of bad luck or skill surrendering to one haughty victor the cake of weeks !

This not morbid, most healthy, and animal hunger of the boys found a dangerous gratification in parcels of goodies placed by naughty carpenters and workmen, willing to accept money from the boys, in *cachets* agreed upon beforehand. Sometimes, too, the simplicity of a boy would induce him to procure from a town friend a box of fabulous attraction : guava, heavy and luscious in its filmy boxes ; prunes, purple and pretentious, with mystical French titles upon the corks ; gingerbread — with tenderness and aroma ever decreasing, until it became but a chestnut sawdust ; preserved peaches, huge fans of raisins, looking like those of Eshcol. Such boxes were always seized by the authorities and confiscated on their way to the person whose name they bore. Too often, with heavy heart, he would be allowed to look beyond the lifted lid upon the treasures that were denied him. At the end of the term he was allowed to recover his spoil, and to divide it among his friends. This was mostly a funereal pleasure, as only a few of the things, such as squares of chocolate, were none the worse for keeping.

The most distinctive element of the school, borrowed from the Fellenberg system, was the annual journey of the boys. They went with horses and wagons, "ride and tie," not to fatigue the weak ones. Cities were visited, villas of friends admired and examined, rivers crossed, until at last the little army found itself encamped upon a great water, Long Island Sound, at Saybrook, being usually the farthest point reached. A comfortable fishing-smack was provided for them, and many were the specimens of marine life that flopped and fluttered upon its deck.

All sorts of sports were encouraged as well as fishing, and the woods around Round Hill furnished an abundance of wild creatures for the exercise of skill in shooting. The huge chestnut-trees literally swarmed with squirrels, red and gray ; the chipmunk, or, as the Southern boys used to call him, "fence-mouse," was too tame to be counted as game. In summer evenings the flying-squirrel might be seen floating from tree to tree. Rabbits and woodchucks were to be trapped ; but the birds—robins, blue-jays, woodpeckers, among

them the superb yellow-hammer, and kingfisher—fell
before the arrow.   The bows were made of ash, with
arrows of hickory; their heads, tipped with steel points
or sharpened cones of tin, would often go clean through
a squirrel or a robin.   Much of this game served for
the repasts of Crony Village.

Mixed with this dawn-flash of animal spirits, behind these bounding pulses, unspoken of, were working outward the religious, immortal germs of inner
life.   Many a journal, blotted by tears, received the
heart-agony, the aspirations, the longings which none
suspected.

The respect and reverence which the boys felt for
Mr. Cogswell were entwined with a feeling, softer and
tenderer, of true affection.   Many years afterward all
the surviving scholars of Round Hill were summoned
to meet at a dinner in honor of their beloved teacher,
given at the Parker House in Boston.   Several of the
instructors of the school, and all the "boys" who
could come, were present.   Again the old sunshine of
the master's countenance beamed upon his children,
and the old memories were revived.   Old anecdotes
of boyish pranks, old nicknames, came to the surface;
gray-bearded men were again restored to boyhood by
the spirit of the hour.

After Mr. Cogswell's death, which occurred in
1871, his surviving scholars united to erect over his

grave a simple monument, in affectionate remembrance of their teacher. In speaking of it, Mr. Appleton says :

"As they look across that grave, from the sunset of their lives, they will see through the interval of years, bright with success or dark with sorrow and bereavement, their old master, their old school-days, themselves moving through the dilation of the crimson mists of morning. Everything then will be idealized, and that unfulfilled promise, which earth can not keep, may be to them dearer than the conquests which years have won for them, or the fugitive successes of life's arena."

4

CHAPTER IV.

1827.

DURING the three years he was at Round Hill, Thomas wrote regularly and with great frankness to his father. Many of these letters have been preserved, their style advancing from that of a child to one of maturer thought.

In the first one he describes his masters and studies, and then adds :

"I am building a house, which makes a pretty respectable appearance, in Crony Village. . . . I have been perfectly well since I came. As to my spirits, I am in as good as I could expect away from home. I want my sled, and I want all of you to write me often."

He was not long to enjoy the house. He writes :

January 15, 1826.

. . . Just before I wrote this, Mr. Cogswell declared that which will materially injure the happiness of the boys, which is, that our houses, or caverns, as he terms them, must be abandoned, and destroyed immediately. The reason is this : Mr. C—— has frequently observed certain boys to be absent from meals. He soon suspected something, and at last discovered the whole affair, by his cunning and sagacity, which is this : The boys, for their greater accommodation at their houses, have by stealth purchased sundry articles of the people in the neighborhood, and thus became acquainted with them, and went to their houses. Some of the articles were these : sausages, flour, potatoes, apples, etc. He stated that he considered it inconsistent with his duty to permit them to do things that he knew their parents would disapprove, and to prevent which he took them under his charge, and he made quite a long speech to us in the evening. Mr. Cogswell has a penetration and knowledge of human nature, with the like quality I hardly ever saw any man endowed. He possesses a wonderful awe over the boys, and there is hardly any boy who can conceal a lie or deceit from him. I have several instances of his cunning. I will relate one : One unpleasant and moist evening he told the boys he thought that it was unsafe to go down to their houses, and therefore forbade it. Some few, either not understanding him, or from a motive not so good, went down there. He, although one would think he would be detained by

some more important business, and the unpleasantness
of the weather, but still under the bare chance of finding some, went, and surprised them all in their holes.
In one of the houses they were enjoying themselves
on a pudding of their own make, little expecting such
a visit. Hearing him knock, and thinking he was a
boy, they opened the door. How greatly he and they
were astonished, and how soon the pudding went under
the bench, I leave you to imagine. Saturday evening
presented a dismal sight. About thirty houses were
utterly destroyed from the face of the earth, and their
inmates sent forth to mourn for the loss of their prop-
erty. The destroyers came, and that which was before
a flourishing village, rapidly increasing in houses and
inhabitants, was soon reduced to nothing but a heap
of ruins. And all this destruction was perpetrated by
only two emissaries of Mr. Cogswell, except those
houses that were destroyed by the voluntary despair
of their owners. Here one could see the remnant of
a roof, and there a smoking pile of boards. The axe
and club first demolished the houses, and then fire
was applied to consign them forever to oblivion. But
enough of this.

In the same letter he tells what he is studying :

As I believe you have not heard much concerning the books that I study, I will now inform you. In

Latin I am advanced about six sections in the second Catiline oration; in French, I study Louis XIV and Mr. Hentse's 'French Reader'; in arithmetic, I am half through Colburn's 'Sequel'; and in Spanish, I am getting along pretty fast, studying 'Colmena Española,' *que es un libro de las piezas escogidas de varios autores Españoles, por F. Sales.*

As the cold weather prevailed, T. G. was still anxious to have his sled "Nimble Dick" sent to him from Boston. His father seems to have made some objections, for the son writes:

February 5, 1826.

. . . I do not think your arguments against sending up my sled are very powerful. In the first place, you say it is not worth while to send *wood* into the country; but you must know that what most constitutes a good sled is the *irons*, and that it should run several years to be as good as mine; therefore, you see that we boys can neither make *irons* nor good sleds; as to the skates, we can not get good ones up here, as they are all quite low and poor; and my poor skates have received a mortal blow beyond repair, as both the iron and wood are broken. So I present my petition a second time, hoping that you may pardon my boldness.

He goes on :

I am rather surprised at your not mentioning anything about coming up yourself ; nevertheless, I must
remember that "*patientia omnia vincit.*"

This school has done a good deal of good to me
as to my manners, etc. ; for, as you know, it is composed of boys from all quarters of the Union, as we
have some from almost every State ; and, on that
account, the customs, phrases, and appearance of us
Yankees seem strange to them ; as likewise the flat
dialect and strange pronunciation of the letter *a* by
the Southerners seem disagreeable to our ears. On
account of these dissimilitudes we are constantly quizzing one another ; but I am sensible that the poor
Yankees have the worst of it, as the whole school,
masters and all, are constantly mentioning our faults
—for instance, the pronunciation of been, *ben*, while it
ought to be pronounced *bin*, the adding the letter *r* to
several words that want it, and not pronouncing the
ing in participles, and many other Boston peculiarities.
The effect these things have had on me is to mend my
pronunciation, cause me to walk straighter than before, and pay greater attention to neatness, which I
am deficient in.

Your affectionate son,

T. G. APPLETON.

Here is the whole of a letter written at this time:

March 12, 1826.

My dear Father: On Friday evening I received your much expected and wished-for packet. I could not read it as soon as I wished, as a rather ludicrous circumstance was going on; for two boys were tried by the other boys for whispering, and convicted, and as in the evening their punishment was to stand up half an hour, the uproar the boys made prevented me from its perusal then. But when I did it was with the greatest pleasure, as the cash was sufficient, and the matter good.

At first I could not imagine what the packet could contain, and I was much gratified in seeing what it was (and, indeed, I wish you would send me more newspapers and pamphlets than you do). I have read a good deal in it, and think it excellent, just as I should think Mr. Channing would write. I think the first half is the best; I mean by that what I understand the clearest, and written with most spirit and beauty. I like very much his comparison between Johnson and Milton, and his description of " Paradise Lost," which I intend to read.

On Friday the sun shone for the first time since eleven days, awakening me from my drowsy slumbers rather earlier than usual, and by its cheerful smile exciting in every heart mild feelings of buoyancy and delight, which the former dark and dismal days had suppressed.

It was a fine day, and all the boys valued it the more, it being so rare to have a pleasant Saturday. Now at six o'clock, where three months ago we needed lights, the sunshine is as bright as at midday.

I have performed a feat worthy of being undertaken by Hercules, for I have asked Mr. B—— that question you desired me to about the elephant and the serpent ; for the other day, as we were going from school to breakfast, I lagged behind to meet Mr. Bancroft, and when I asked him he smiled (this shows, by-the-by, how near his brain is to the end of his tongue), for, before I had hardly finished, he said : "The author, I believe, is Pliny ; but," said he, "I will write your father about it." But I doubt if he will. For my part, I can not see anything applicable to our question in Pliny, unless he refers to the immense serpent, supposed to have been a boa, on the coast of Africa, that obstructed the passage of Regulus and his army : the snake was so tough and large that Regulus was obliged to bring his battering-ram and machines against it, as in besieging a city ; at length he vanquished it, and sent parts of it to Rome as trophies.

I can't help giving you an account of a walk I took yesterday afternoon, the most interesting I have had

here. With three other boys, as the day was beautiful, and the balmy air and waving trees, together with
the holiday, invited us to walk : we set out over the
back of the Hill ; we crossed fields verdant with ever-
green and rendered pleasant by the warbling of the
birds and the beauty of the distant scenery, till at last
we arrived at a beautiful wood of pines, and there we
started the project of walking to the Licking-water.
'Twas no sooner proposed than undertaken ; we crossed
fences and woods, till at last we scarcely knew where
we were, leaping brooks, and pushing through thick
woods. After about half an hour's walking we began
to think we must be near the stream, and presently we
ascended a small hill and saw before us a steep bank,
and could catch through the waving pines glimpses of
the river. We descended the bank by the assistance
of twigs and decayed trunks, overthrown by some tem-
pest, till at last we found ourselves on the brink of
the river, enjoying one of the finest scenes I ever be-
held. I sprang on a rock to enjoy it better. We could
trace the river with our eyes to some extent both up
and down, rolling over rocks with a harmonious sound
which together with the sweet sighing of the lofty
pines, agitated by the gentle breeze, formed such rav-
ishing contrasts that it seemed as if I could sit forever there and enjoy the enchanting scene. The picture was beautiful, the water here tumbling over the

rocks in small falls, there hurrying along over a smooth
bottom, sometimes green, at others of a dirty hue ; now
and then a huge oak or pine rooted up by the mount-
ain-blast lay across the water, forming a natural
bridge, or draggling in the stream that foliage which
before had kissed the skies.   I could fill a letter with
the account of this walk, but as, unfortunately, my
paper is full, I remain affectionately your son,

THOMAS.

May 28, 1826.

The gardens come along pretty well, and every
day the old saying of "ill weeds grow apace" is proved
to be true.   Mr. C—— says he does not remember
the time when weeds and ants did so much damage ;
and it is true, for my melons, radishes, pepper-grass,
everything is prostrated before the gripe of this ruth-
less invader.   The whole artillery and strength of lime
and ashes thunders impotent upon the head of the
common enemy.   They continue to advance, and unless the hand of Providence quickly brings relief, there
will not be a vegetable fit to be seen in the whole
garden.

I expect to begin to ride before long, for now almost every Saturday Mr. Cogswell takes some boys
to ride with him.   The bow is now the principal im-
plement of play among the boys, and almost every

one has one. Bathing is one of the things I like best of all the summer amusements, it is so cooling and— I must stop, for the sounds, " T. G. !" from the mouth of Mr. Bancroft, vibrate upon my ear. It is very strange that twice lately, just as I was finishing a letter, I should have been interrupted by the agreeable summons—" A letter for you, T. G. !"—but so it is.

The summer vacation was passed at home, and a second school-year entered upon. Thomas writes :

January 21, 1827.

It would seem, dear father, that the late cold weather had frozen the communication between us, as neither of us has written or received any letters for some time. The cold here is extreme, the sleighing is remarkably fine, and has been for some time. . . .

Lately I have got very high in Mr. Bancroft's favor, and he has given me many flattering testimonials of it—taking me sleigh-riding with him, inviting me to his room, with many other marks of favor. I think I can trace it to my themes. He told me the other day that, as I wrote so well, he wanted exceedingly to make me a perfect writer ! He also asked me to write him a poetical theme ; and I have written one, but there are many lines of false metre. I have a good mind to send it to you, but you must remember that it is not finished off yet.

THE AMERICAN EAGLE.

I.

Proud bird of my country, to thee I sing;
　　To the Muses I call for aid.
Thou art borne aloft on the whirlwind's wing,
　　In thunder and darkness arrayed.

2.

Undaunted thou look'st on the sun's red glare,
　　And viewest the earth with scorn,
As thou sailest on high through regions of air,
　　Or dartest gayly along.

3.

Thou buildest thy nest on the mountain's cliff,
　　Or skimmest along the main ;
And hailest afar the adventurous skiff—
　　Forever thou art the same.

4.

When war's crimson hand our land bathed in gore,
　　Oh ! then thou left'st thy repose :
When foreign invaders encumbered our shore,
　　And slavery threatened its woes :

5.

When kindred met kindred in battle's rude shock,
　　Thou hovered over our head ;
Then thy broad wings were our nation's firm rock,
　　Or a shelter to the unfortunate dead.

6.

When Mars, red with blood, had quitted the field,
　　And Britain had recrossed the sea,

Victory by your presence you joyfully sealed—
  Oh, joyful may victory be !

7.

And now the strife's over, our vows we will make
  On the altar to Liberty's form ;
And long in our memory may thy look live,
  Which watched us in battle and storm !

My new clothes please me very much. They are made very well, and the color suits me to a T.

Your affectionate son,

T. G. A.

This juvenile, patriotic effort is ornamented by a huge penmanship eagle, such as is the delight of the writing-master, the admiration and terror alike of the unskilled pupil.

February 8, 1827.

DEAR FATHER : Mrs. G—— has arrived. After supper at her house, as we were alone, I suppose she meant to give me a verbal chastising. She asked me if I had read Mr. Channing's sermon in New York (which, by-the-way, I want you to send up). I replied in the negative, but said I supposed it was excellent, as the rest of his publications are. She smiled, and said she liked the style, but not the sentiments. She seemed to think Mr. Channing a bad man, who did not act conscientiously. This led to religion ; her argu-

5

ments seemed to lead to disputation. I had to reply, and as they were such as are generally objected to our sect, and such as, in our conversations on the sub-ject, I have often heard you refute, I found it easy to answer them ; and I fancy her victory was not so easily obtained as she expected, or rather she ob-tained no victory at all, for I answered all her argu-ments, and even asked her to explain some passages, till at last the entrance of some one put an end to the conversation. She seemed to think that a good Indian, who, guided by the light of nature and of conscience, did his best, would not be rewarded; and that no conscientious Christian of another sect than her own would be saved! She pardoned all other sects but the Unitarians ; she said they sapped the root of Chris-tianity, that they took away all hope, etc. And what surprised me most was that, while she was complain-ing that Mr. Channing railed at her sect too badly, she herself was caviling us terribly. Do not think that I mean this as a display of my vanity, but to fill up the letter, and make it altogether *entre nous.*

Mrs. Ryder was extremely pleased with her gown, and praised it above all the other presents she had ; and was quite surprised to hear that it was an Ameri-can production. I was really glad to see the joy tes-tified by the old lady. It must have come in good season, as the doctor's bill would require all her spare cash, and make it rather inconvenient to buy gowns.

The illness referred to here made a deep impression upon the boys, all of whom regarded the matron with an affection transferred in part from their mothers' share.

March 18, 1827.

Mr. Bancroft has had a fine ball, of which I suppose you have heard. He invited two hundred people ; but not so many came. Out of the school-boys only about eight were invited, but I was among this favored few. But the worst of it is that, while every one was congratulating me on my good luck, I had the fate to be racked with a wretched headache which incapacitated me from going. So I had to sit down in a corner of Mrs. Ryder's room, moping while the sounds of joy and revelry rang in my ears, of which I might partake if it were not for my headache. Nevertheless, the quiet of the old lady's room soothed my pains and before long it almost went off. . . . Mrs. Ryder told me her husband was the most industrious of three brothers, yet he was always unfortunate, and they prosperous ; to use the old lady's expression, his brothers would put a fourpence into their pockets and go to sleep, and in the morning it would be a bright ninepence ; while her husband would put a fourpence in his pocket, and work, and yet lose it !

I shall depart hence, I believe, a week from next Wednesday. Huzza ! Your affectionate son,

T. G. APPLETON,

with a fine flourish. His writing was much improving at this time, and already bore the characteristics of his later hand.

July 6, 1827.

Our 4th of July was a very pleasant one. Our mathematical master, Mr. Walker, was the orator of the day. His speech equaled if not excelled that of Mr. Bancroft, and he was warmly congratulated by his friends on his success. He committed the whole of it to memory (*O labor, sudorque !*), but Mr. B—— read nearly all his. In the evening we took tea, as is customary, in a meadow shut out from vulgar gaze, and decorated with arbors lined with cakes crowned with flowers, and glittering with gold and sugar, the voluntary labor of the village matrons. Mr. B—— was gay and Mr. W—— "bore his blushing honors thick upon him." From lack of acquaintances, we Round-Hillers were rather taciturn. We drank our coffee in haste, fearing the coming shower.

" Sky lowered and muttering thunder, and some sad drops
   wept,"

at our festivity. We, however, escaped to the hall, furnished for a ball (to which I also was invited), before the rain fell fast. I danced a little, but soon got out of partners, and went home rather early, the night being as dark as pitch.

I received a letter from L. Motley lately, and he states that they have about got through their studies at his school, and that the vacation will begin in about three weeks, which he fears will be a great bore! I have not so poor an opinion of mine, I assure you.

P. S.—Tell mother I have finished "St. Valentine's Day," and like it very much. I was surprised it agreed so much with history.

It was the custom at Round Hill to give holidays in the spring, and many of the boys went home at that time for a joyful visit to their parents and families. Traveling from Boston to Northampton in those days was not without its difficulties, as is shown by the following letter, describing the return to Round Hill:

April 26, 1827.

We have, my dear father, been neither killed nor wounded, and yet we have experienced all the evils we well could have met with. We went as far as Worcester, as you know, with the Governor, and the only evil we had till then was that it rained; but my bag was not wet, as it was under cover. We had a tolerably good dinner at Brookfield, but after that misfortunes were showered thick enough. In the first place, as we were packing the stage, my box being treated rather roughly, swelled with rage, the effect of which was that the top came off, and out fell a pair of shoes *et alias res.* I had to leave it at the tavern, to be sent on by the mail next morning. When we got agoing, we underwent the miseries of a full stage (it containing twelve), a hard rain (which wet my bag, it being on top, which I could not prevent), a muddy road, and lazy horses. I believe I saw a beaver, and Mrs. Watson corroborated my opinion. We plodded along as well as we could and reached Round Hill about eight. As we entered the gate we gave three cheers, which were echoed back by one hundred roaring boys. Looking out of the window, I could discern nothing but heads, and the air was rent with shouts. Charles, on descending the steps of the stage, was greeted with a stare and " Who's that ? " so that the poor boy was very much amazed. We put everything in order that night and this morning, and though it rained all the time, Charles evinces no symptoms of homesickness, and we are perfectly well.

Charles Sedgwick Appleton was two years younger than Thomas. This was his first appearance at Round Hill, where he now shared the room of his brother, and soon became initiated in the routine of work and play.

The next letter from Thomas contains a confession :

June 17, 1827.

DEAR FATHER : I have nothing pleasant to communicate, and the reason I have written this before the time is, that I have an occurrence to relate, viz. : R. Apthorp has sent me a box, by my wish, containing sundry articles, *pour manger*, etc., which the boys have often received before, and Mr. C—— has made no objections. But he took this in great dudgeon, and said I should not have the box ; and, I believe, said he should send it to you ; so you may expect it in a few days. . . .

June 24, 1827.

I have received yours of the 19th, and I admit all you said concerning my recent adventure to be perfectly just. I own I acted very foolishly in sending for *them ;* but boys are apt to do in one minute what they repent of the next. But, if you were here, you would allow that it is very agreeable to have a few things to satisfy that hunger which I often feel, without being able to allay it.

This must have been the box which, fifty years later, Mr. Appleton still remembered vividly enough to describe in his Round Hill reminiscences.

July 22, 1827.

My dear Father: . . . You asked me to write you concerning my studies. In Latin, I study Virgil, Livy, and "Elegantiæ Latinæ," each two days in the week. I am well enough in this department. In mathematics, I have reviewed Colburn's "Sequel," and now study Legendre's "Geometry." If I am to go to college, I ought to review Euler's "Algebra," which I shall not have time to do. In Greek, I am only half through Greek "Reader," and, to go to college, I ought to know all that perfectly, and something of the Testament. I study Spanish, but not French any longer, because I have to give more time to college-studies. Dr. Graeter takes his scholars in drawing now and then off the Hill, to draw from Nature, which is very agreeable. I have taken one or two views, and shall take several more. We are going to have an exhibition, at which I am to speak.

To this year probably belongs an (undated) letter written in Spanish, well expressed and fairly grammatical. At the end of it he says:

"No debes considerar esta carta corta, car hé ocupado mucho tiempo en escribiendola, y me ha causado *scabere caput* como dice mi amigo Horatius. Tenemos ahora un veritable Francese, maestro di danza quién antiquamente deba lecciones á las hijas del gobernador del Canidad ; piense que es abajo su dignidad de tocar el violin su mismo ; por este razon ha alquilado un negro para tocar en su lugar."

The question of entering college was now under discussion. It would seem that Mr. Bancroft advised Thomas to try for entering in the autumn of 1827, although he had not been preparing for examination through the year. His intimate friend John Lothrop Motley was to go to Harvard, and Thomas strongly inclined to begin his course there at the same time. In the end, however, he stayed another year at Round Hill, studying for examination at Cambridge, to join Motley's class—the class of 1831—in their sophomore year.

Accordingly, he returned to Northampton after the summer vacation, with the usual mishaps *en route.*

ROUND HILL, *September* 9, 1827.

The first part of my journey, my dear father, was by no means agreeable ; for, in the first place, before we had got out of Boston (for it took an hour to get out) the transient (or transle) bolt broke. We soon remedied that, and we were going along rather slowly, when suddenly, crash ! down came the stage, and the wheel rolled across the road. We were an hour fixing it, for the man had to go back to the last house, and get flax and twine, etc., to tie the wheel up with.

After some time we proceeded, with fear and trembling, four miles, when we got another stage. We were going on at a brisk rate, to make up for lost time, when suddenly, crash! down we came from our elevation, and we found that the main beam, passing under the stage, was shivered. The driver carried back this stage, and returned with the one we had before. These were all the break-downs we had, and these happened within fifteen miles of Boston. They were caused by the immense quantity of baggage possessed by a lady going to Albany.

The winter of 1827–'28 was devoted to hard study, especially in Greek; "dashing on," he says, "in Homer at the rate of eleven knots an hour—blinding Miss Polly Phemus, sacking cities, falling in love with goddesses with the greatest celerity."

Exercise was not neglected:

Mr. C——, in his bounty, has put me in a class which rides every other day on horseback. This recreation to boys of my age is particularly pleasing, and, I assure you, I take no little delight in it. Although I have not practiced, save on our White Mountain pony, yet I found I could ride well enough. The horses here are very good ones, and, though they have thrown three or six fellows, yet they have slain no one.

P. S.—Mr. Cogswell has made an invention quite ingenious—squirrel-power. Two gray squirrels turn a wheel, which communicates with another which turns a coffee-mill! In this way he grinds all his coffee. Quite a snug device, is it not?

The last letter preserved from Round Hill is dated

July 27, 1828.

DEAR FATHER: A growling thunder-storm, accompanied with his noisy and glaring attendants, kept the night in continual uproar, to the detriment of light sleepers. Notwithstanding the commotion of the preceding night, all Nature received rising Aurora with sweetest smiles, and everything promises not only a fair, but, I fear, even a hot day.

At the beginning of the past week a bright galaxy of wisdom and learning was assembled here. Dr. Ware preached, and Mr. and Mrs. Kirkland stayed here several days. Mr. Bancroft invited *us collegians* to his house Monday evening, where these and many more *literati* were assembled to be introduced to the *interrex*, Dr. Ware. We found the object of our visit and our host absent, and we were introduced by our fair hostess to the ex-president, but got no chance of being introduced to Mr. Ware.

You want to know when I shall come. At the

soonest in a fortnight from last night, perhaps a few days later.

You, thinking yourself rather in the dark as regards my *errorem*, demand, and shall have, a little more light on the subject. Transgressing the bounds (never assigned to us) has not been punished or noticed for a long time. Seeing everybody round me continually practicing it, and seeing and hearing no notice taken of it, I naturally concluded that it could be nothing very sinful, for the vice through frequency lost half its ugliness. I feel that I can plead "upon this argument." If it be a sin, it is one of no very dark complexion. Mr. C—— has a custom of making rules he never tells us of, and I have committed several of these petty crimes. Having thus shown that I committed a sin whose heinousness I was ignorant of, one that has been commonly practiced and commonly winked at, I will leave the subject, stating only that I think the picking of berries by one unconscious of crime is pardonable, and I hope it will be so to you.

I think of sending my books down before my own appearance ; so you need not be puzzled by the arrival of an old pine chest and a rat-eaten trunk next week. Love to all, and pleasant times.

I remain, yours, affectionately,

THOMAS.

P. S.—Father, if you stumble on a room that I can have, out of college, I should be agreeably surprised by your engaging it when I return.

Here the boy-life ends, with the close of the Round Hill period. Thomas entered Harvard in the autumn of 1828. The full letters he had been in the habit of writing to his father stop here for a time, as Cambridge was too near home to make correspondence necessary.

6

CHAPTER V.

COLLEGE-LIFE.

1828–1832.

THOMAS entered Harvard College as a sophomore in the autumn of 1828, joining the class which was to graduate in 1831. He found already on the field several old Latin school classmates, and some of his Round Hill friends, who had entered, freshmen, the year before.

The greater part of his college course was passed in rooms in the old Brattle House, still standing, but his first room was in another place. His first establishment and subsequent removal are spoken of in his letters to his brother Charles, who had returned alone to Round Hill for another year.

CAMBRIDGE, *September* 8, 1828.

. . . I will try to give you some idea of my room and situation at present. Figure to yourself a large, neat, well-papered, four-windowed room, in a light retired house, on the second story, and you have a picture of it in its naked state. Fill it up with a table covered with a green cloth, a desk, and divers books, novels, etc., spread over it in scholastic confusion. A crimson-cushioned rocking-chair rolls tranquilly before the table, and other easy-chairs occupy various parts of the room. A neat bed in one corner is balanced by a secretary full of books in the center of the opposite wall. Those two water-scenes I drew at Brown's occupy a station over the mantel-piece. Washstand, trunks, dumb-bells, pitcher and tumblers, mirrors, fill up and ornament the chamber. I shall soon have a carpet, fender, tongs and shovel, and more pictures. There! do not you call this a prime abode? I have not a very laborious life. Reading, studying, visiting, and eating alternately, fill up my time. . . . I went to Nahant a short time since, and killed plenty of peeps, four at one shot and three at another.

November 16, 1828.

The circle of my employments here is not confined as on the *Colline Ronde ;* if there is not a lesson to recite, there is a duck on the river, or a play at the theatre. . . . There is no news, except such as : Jackson is elected; Miss Sales is sick of the croup; Mr. Quincy has had a wound from the fall of a ladder; Doc. Pop is down with a cold, and such-like. So good-by.

It was perhaps at this time that Thomas executed
for a friend, who still retains it in his possession, a
likeness of a celebrated professor, on the cover of a
snuff-box.   He was responsible for a drawing, a front-
ispiece for the catalogue of the " Med. Fac.," a secret
society already popular, of a skull and cross-bones with
the somewhat questionable motto :

" Nil desperandum Satano duce."

The next spring he changed his room, of which he
thus writes :

May 26, 1829.

Charley, I have changed domiciles ; the other
house was to be sold, so I had to " cut a stick," and
am now lodged at Uncle Sam's old farm, do you remember ?   Finest location in Cambridge ; trees, pond,
peaches, cherries, etc., in abundance.   My new room
presents the same brilliant appearance as the other,
only its glories are somewhat tarnished by smoke, as
my chimney ejects the aforesaid article voluminously.
I learned oil-painting, as I suppose you know, in the
vacation ; and have had my apparatus conveyed hither,
for the purpose of whiling away an idle hour, as you
express it ; maidens, horses, and landscapes dazzle
around the beaming apartment, and the very air is
tainted with oil and varnish.   The government is as
savage as thunder.   Sent off J. L. Motley, Binney,

Harris, and Devereux last week. Think of that—a little while ago, Motley was second scholar.

" Oh, what a fall was there, my countrymen ! "

But, after all, college is a splendid place. I live here at my ease, near Boston, and possess everything to make a man as happy as he can wish. . . . Josiah Quincy is chosen for our next president. The inauguration will take place next week.

In Dr. Holmes's memoir of Motley, already referred to, is a reminiscence, by Mr. Appleton himself, of his life in the Brattle House :

" Motley's room," he says, " was on the ground-floor, the room to the left of the entrance. He led a very pleasant life there, tempering his college duties with the literature he loved, and receiving his friends amid elegant surroundings which added to the charm of his society. Occasionally we amused ourselves by writing for the magazines and papers of the day. Mr. Willis had just started a slim monthly, written chiefly by himself, but with the true magazine flavor. We wrote for that ; and sometimes verses in the corner of a paper called the ' Anti-Masonic Mirror,' in a corner of which was a woodcut of Apollo, inviting to destruction ambitious youths by the legend underneath :

' Much yet remains unsung.'

" These pieces were usually dictated to each other, the poet recumbent upon the bed, and a classmate ready to carry off the manuscript for the paper of the following day.

"'Blackwood's' was then in its glory, its pages redolent of mountain-dew in every sense ; the humor of the shepherd, the elegantly brutal onslaughts upon Whigs and Cockney poets by Christopher North, intoxicated us youths. It was young writing, and made for the young. The opinions were charmingly wrong, and its enthusiasm was half Glenlivat, but this delighted the boys. There were no reprints then, and to pass the paper-cutter up the fresh, inviting pages was like swinging over the heather arm-in-arm with Christopher himself."

A manuscript book remains, containing the literary effusions of college-life, in which, among poems, sketches, stanzas, snatches of rhyme, in Mr. Appleton's handwriting, comes the following in another hand :

SONNET TO T. G. APPLETON ON HIS INIMITABLE POMES.

BRATTLE MANOR.

As, in the room where Shakespeare first saw light,
  Travelers ambitious write their humble name,
  Tracing the hour when, pilgrim-like, they came
To make the Orient home of luster bright,
Whose beams have lit the raven wings of night
  Until they shone with a time-spurning flame—
  So I, in limping verses, dull and lame,

Here reverently my name and tribute write
  Within this book, the curious birthplace
  Of your quaint thoughts, that, " after many days,"
When, looking on this place of its location,
  My humble name with yours I'll see entwined,
  Like Galt's with Byron's—and, like him, I'll find
I've gained an " amber immortalization."
J. L. M.

DEAR TOM : If you swallow that without straining, the camel will go down unbuttered.

January 23, 1831.

A short extract will suffice from a long poetical letter from Thomas to his brother :

January 26, 1830.

How comes it, dear Charlie, we write one another
So rarely of late, although brother and brother ?
For, though all the rest of the folks get a plenty,
Me miserum I do not have one out of twenty.
However, *n'importe*, as the French lubbers say,
We ll not retrograde, but write more from this day.
. . . This winter in Boston has been very gay—
They've had bachelors' balls and loud times, they do say.
Aunt William herself undertook, *magna arte*,
To perpetrate a most delightful large party ;
Where coxcombs were strutting and belles looking bright,
And with mirth and dancing vexed the ear of night.
Miss Marshall there looked as fair as any peri,
And flashed around lightnings from out of her dear eye.
There Juniors sported their crow's-feet, and Seniors
Outrivaled town-bucks, though outvied by the Juniors.

And so on.

In the vacation of his senior year Thomas took a trip to the Canadas, etc., of which the account is preserved in a journal, the first of a series which he had the good habit to keep up for several years. The ink is faded and yellow, but the handwriting has all the characteristics of his later years. It is decorated with many flourishes and little vignettes. Half the book is filled with poems, chiefly original, some copied from Shelley and the favorite authors of the moment. The journal is preceded by this quotation :

" A word on the spot is worth a bushel-basket of recollections."—*Gray's Letters.*

His companion was his cousin, Isaac Appleton Jewett, of the class before him in college, just graduated. They went first to Burlington, Vermont, and thence by boat to St. John, where he had letters of introduction.

" 29*th.*—Went with my new acquaintances and Jewett to see the Gray Nuns ; we were carried round by the famous one-legged John. Bought a pin-cushion. Struck with the face of a young nun, whose portrait would make a capital Madonna. Did not perpetrate any verses on the occasion."

They went all the way to Quebec by water, enjoying the fine scenery, and stayed there several days. Their first expedition was to the Falls of Montmorenci :

"It is the most beautiful fall and display of natural beauty I have seen yet. It seemed to me as if a mass of the purest smoke was bounding downward, in opposition to its seeming lightness, from rock to rock."

"*August* 2d.—I got a soldier of the last war to carry me to the Plains of Abraham. He was a loquacious fellow, and told me many stories of his experience in the last war. He was in the chase of the Constitution by the British fleet. It was a beautiful evening, and I enjoyed my long-cherished wish of standing upon the Plains of Abraham. I could easily perceive the rashness of Wolfe's attempt, and conjecture pretty nearly the disposition of the two armies."

"To say a few words upon the Canadian character. They are spirited, but mean; slovenly to a proverb; ignorant and prejudiced, thinking their own country the finest in the world, and themselves worthy possessors of it. They are avaricious, and seem to think the merest service worthy a pecuniary recompense. Though, from this cause, their frankness and even kindness may excite suspicion, I, for my own better enjoyment, and the dignity of our species, am determined to look always on the bright side, and, in a doubtful case, to believe that which does most honor to the agent."

"We set sail—abominable bull! we left—Quebec

at eleven o'clock, with many regrets and lingering looks behind. It was a glorious moonlight, and everything united to produce a novel and pleasing effect. The gleaming waves, the variety of costume, the discordant voices, the merry cheering of neighboring sailors, the receding towers of story-hallowed Quebec, the distant watch-fires, the glorious moon, and last, not least, the society of a pretty miss among the passengers, irresistibly combined to render me happy."

This was retracing his steps on the river. They reached Montreal early the next morning, but passed on, without stopping, to Burlington, where they had letters, and were lionized for a couple of days.

" *July 7th, Whitehall.*—On the steamboat the night was hot. Haunted by the boot-black, who said at last, with a simper : ' Sir, ahem ! perhaps you are not aware that sixpence is the perquisite of my office.' In the morning, fine weather; we saw Ticonderoga dimly, and longed to go on shore. Scenery around both grand and beautiful. We ought to have got out at Ticonderoga and gone up Lake George, but the other steamboat had struck upon a rock ; so we had to go on."

They drove from Whitehall to Saratoga over a sandy road :

"Went all day at the rate of three miles an hour. Mem. : Avoid that road in future. It grew cool and sunny as we approached the Springs. We found every house full. So many strangers never known there since the memory of man. We boarded at Union Hall, but were 'colonized' at a private house, and that a mere rat-hole, between us two. We looked in, in the evening, at a hop at the United States. Lots of beauty!"

They found many acquaintances, and joined in the current gayeties.

"Scared the old Quakers by using a cue at billiards. Thirteen left the room in hysterics. In the evening went to a grand ball. Van Buren was there. He looked to me like a little, waspish, withered, cunning diplomatist, but developing more of the littleness of the fop than the dignity of the statesman. Mrs. Otis was the belle; she had on a kind of crown, with a tiara of feathers, and was habited in gold and purple."

"*July* 12*th.*—Took leave of Jewett and bustling Saratoga—the last place in the world one would think an invalid would be stationed at. His nerves are perpetually shattered through the day by the rattling of wheels, the tramp of hurrying feet, and the discordant jargon of a hundred tongues; and, in the night, the

murdering of a hundred tunes by a hundred instru-
ments."

From Albany, Mr. Appleton went down the Hud-
son to New York; probably this was his first visit
there, as railways had not yet made communication
easy from Boston.

"*July* 19*th.*—Spent the morning at the splendid
English Gallery of Paintings. Murillo's piece pleased
me the most, also a landscape by Claude Lorraine
and a Van de Velde. In the evening went to the
Bowery. Sam Hackett played 'Rip Van Winkle.'"

"20*th.* — Lounged about — admired the Battery
and Castle Garden; hardly ever saw a scene equal
in variety to the view before me, a complete panorama.

"Started about 4 P. M. in the Chancellor Living-
ston. I found a pleasant circle of acquaintance on
boat, and had a delightful sail up to Newport. We
passed rapidly through Providence, and reached Boston at three minutes of three o'clock. Five minutes
earlier I could have taken the boat for Nahant, where,
as I learned to my disappointment, every one of the
name of Appleton in our street was then vegetating."

Not much more is to be gathered, out of the forgotten past, of the three tranquil years of college-life.

After graduating, Thomas entered the Law School in Cambridge, in pursuance of the wish of his father.

Mr. Nathan Appleton took his seat in Congress in December, 1831. His absence from home, in Washington, gave occasion to his son to write to him, and the letters for two winters following are full and frequent, showing that, while at the Law School, Thomas devoted himself with diligence to the study of the law.

CAMBRIDGE, Mrs. Parker's, December 10, 1831.

Here am I with a musical fire wasting my nether extremities, while Jack Frost, in the rear, careers on a dozen blasts from a dozen cracks, in a knightly tilt against my back and shoulders. I have a huge pile of Blackstones, Rawles, Ricardos, etc., as a barrier to his attacks, but, alas! subtle Jack has no fear even of the law ; and though this mound may slightly protect my lower man, the advantage is compensated for by the double numbness of my ears. Certainly to roast and freeze at the same time is a torture surpassing even the ingenious miseries of a Dionysius.

I am now beginning the fourth book of Blackstone. Oh ! that the musty mazes of the law were all as classically garnished as those I have just trodden with Sir William ! But, alas! I see in the ample vista of the future the melancholy ghosts of Illuminated Dullness, prosing Pedantry, and tumid Technicality. I see the

Sahara of Learning, the level expansion of tedious Drudgery, where never streamlet glittered, bird never sang.

It is such fun to be euphuistic. I mean only to say that, from all accounts, Blackstone is the most elegant and delightful of law-books, and that Reports and other duller details show themselves ahead. . . .

I am reading Rabelais. What a quaint, humorsome old wight he is! Sterne evidently transplanted his flowers largely.

I am very tender of writing long letters, and know your dire aversion to them. But, father, where the heart is full, the mouth speaketh. One could write for aye to those one loves. I am in perfect health. Have you battled with your cold?

Hark! the bell chimes! the paper is o'er blotted!

Beso á usted los manos.

T. G. APPLETON.

This was but the often-repeated expression of his affection for a father who, he used to say, "was loved more than five hundred fathers were ever loved."

BOSTON, *December*, 1831.

DEAR FATHER: To keep your mill a-going, I will now add one to the stream of epistles flowing almost daily, I believe, from our family. I have had, for the last week, what is called Thanksgiving vacation, and, barring the influenza, I have had little positive amusement besides sketching. We are, it is true, just now an ailing family, and yet as well off for fun and comfort as ever, bating your loss, of which we are hourly reminded. Alas ! the key-hole now waits in vain for the tinkle of your wonted key. Your capacious arm-chair now remains unfilled, and the blooming turkey weeps through her oysters for the skillful weapon of its departed carver. . . . We get along as well as I expected since your sun set, but the immediate effects of the consequent gloom were a later bed-leaving, more gravy spilt on the table-cloth, a slight assumption of dignity, and a general influx of bills.

CAMBRIDGE, *December* 12, 1831.

As you say you like to receive a letter every day, there can be no harm in my writing you again. I have been at home the last two days, and am returned here to-night. Just as I got back, I met Wendell Phillips, who told me that, on account of the influenza and a want of coal for the students, the vacation was to begin this week, instead of next. I therefore have got, as soon as possible, to "brail up my duds," and race back again.

We had to-day, in the morning, a fine, masterly sermon from Dr. Channing. I would like to give you a sketch of it, if I had room. The text, "God careth for us," was most philosophically illustrated, and God's providence ably vindicated. It was one of his most thoughtful, and connected as a train of reasoning. The house was quite full. The doctor, at the beginning, requested all the young folks to refrain from talking, as far as possible. . . . The boys have been catching ducks in the Frog-pond daily lately. An interesting Scotch family have just come over. Aunt Sam had the children at her house the other night, and they danced beautifully. There is another Scotch girl just come—a confectioner, named Burns McDonald—quite a beauty. All the Appletons patronize her hugely. Her "Walter Scott snaps" are all the rage.

BOSTON, *December* 25, 1831.

DEAR FATHER: We all wish you a very merry Christmas. A right merry one, no doubt, you will have, banqueting with the great ones of the land; but, after all, Christmas is essentially domestic in its character, and its services are never so sacred and endearing as when its altar is the family hearth.

. . . In your letter you mentioned the service that letter-intercourse is to young men, and proposed occasional topics, etc. Now, if I take you aright, you seem to advise for me a little more correct, Addisoni-

an style than generally comports with my humor or
choice. Familiarity, colloquialness, and a rambling
ease are, as I think, the life of such an intercourse.
They are, to writer and reader, the "heart of the mystery," and therefore I have generally avoided anything
like composition-writing. To write fine in a letter is
to me to be tedious, and who, in a family, would walk
on stilts ? However, I dare say I have misinterpreted
your meaning, and therefore I cry your clemency, and
promise to suit you to the best of my "gifts." We
have been once or twice to the theatre. But we have
done with Burke. No one can eat honey forever. He
has had good houses, but makes little sensation.

CAMBRIDGE, January 8, 1832.

DEAR FATHER : My first act of duty, after perus-
ing a chapter of Kent's "Commentaries," I find to be
to reply to your last letter. It is in a very thoughtful
and retrospective spirit. Your sentiments on the New
Year are mine also. Heaped over as the cup of bless-
ing to us ever has been, we certainly should allow no
family to go before us in acknowledgments of favor,
and in a return of piety, for with sincerity I know no
one family that has been blessed so exceedingly in each
other as we. The hand of sorrow has not touched us.
Health, affection, prosperity, and honor are the gifts
with which we are favored. I pray Heaven we may

none of us dispel this charm of happiness by any unworthy return for such benefits. . . .

Mr. Ashmun, I am sorry to say, is in delicate health. As our studies are interrupted by his illness, I have provided a canvas, as a relaxation. I contemplate painting "The Dying Alchemist," a fine subject. Be not afraid I shall waste my time. I am, to be sure, not a little peculiar, in notions and practice, yet as to time I am orthodox. I hate to be idle, yet I do not like all employment. I never could make a drudge, yet, when interested, I do not feel weariness. I will not give up my mind to what I feel to be useless or of doubtful excellence. I study, as I do everything almost, to enlarge my mind, to multiply my ideas, to give a wider range for thought. But I own I am sometimes restive under some of the discipline which may be necessary. I am rather too fond of variety, too fond of mental excitement, too fond of the end, to be patient under the means. I think a good deal, but rather unmethodically. I know something, yet am ignorant, from lubricity of memory, of many common things. I am very variable in constitution, sensitive to weather—yet with all these faults hope I shall do well.   T. G. A.

CAMBRIDGE, *January* 9, 1832.

I have been alone all day, and am now just in the humor for a social chat with a friend. Would that I could transplant you to my rocking-chair, and have you enliven the monotony of solitude with the persiflage and fun of the Capitol!

The gift of ubiquity would be a glorious one—it may be among the attributes of our future eternity of happiness. To be at the same time in the presence as well as the hearts of our dear friends, to feel space no barrier, but to pervade the universe, and wherever there is a throb of affection for us to be present to enjoy it, would make life indeed glorious and every moment golden.

I am again reading "Boswell"—how capital, is it not? I am nearly through. I wonder I never finished it before. It is, I think, the most delightful as well as the most instructive book I ever read. Nor do I think so meanly of Bozzy as I expected. He certainly was knowing, polished, and affectionate. I love the Doctor as much as Bos. did, certainly. He was a noble fellow, saturated with knowledge; a magazine of satire, a powder-house of wit. Talking of him and his dictionary, as, you know, he despised the Americans, I will supply a few terms he probably overlooked:

CONGRESS. A place where business is evaded, originating probably in the Jews' synagogue. (See Bedlam.)

REPRESENTATIVE. Member of the above body;

consumer of the King's English, and of the Republic's pens, paper, etc.

PRESIDENT.   A national butt ; head-waiter at the Tennessee Hotel ; his only vails, abuse and removal.

January 25, 1832.

Mr. Ashmun has begun a course of lectures, of which we had one this afternoon, on testaments, and very interesting.   The professor seems to be in better health than I expected.   We have opened the term with great spirit, have already finished the first volume of " Kent," and begun on the second.

But I must stop ; on looking at my watch, I find that I must hurry to a debating society, that meets to-night to moot the question, " Were our ancestors fair and honorable in their treatment of the Indians ? "

These extracts give some idea of how the young law-student filled up his time.   It was not all work or solitary application.   A dinner club of six or eight men, classmates and friends, which lasted for a long time, was then formed.

In the spring vacation of 1832, Thomas escorted his mother and sister to the South, the main objects of the excursion being Mrs. Appleton's health, and the pleasure of joining the husband and father in Washington.   The journey was taken by easy stops, with a pause at Baltimore, from which Thomas writes to give warning to his father of their approach :

May 17, 1832.

We arrived here after a rather long but very delightful ride, about a quarter of six last evening. We have exceedingly good rooms, and are housed to our satisfaction. Soft crabs are here in all their glory, and we have them for dinner regularly. No wonder Crabbe was a poet ; every one is full of poetry—so full, that eating them inspires me, and hereafter I cut the Nine, and woo these armed bards of the ocean for inspiration.

The happy life, without break, so keenly appreciated by Thomas, was destined not to last beyond the close of the year whose commencement had his notice of so much family felicity. The health of Mrs. Appleton became a cause of anxiety. In the autumn of 1832 she began to fail more rapidly, and, before spring opened, Mr. Nathan Appleton was summoned home from Washington by her death, which took place in February, 1833.

On the 1st of April of that year, Thomas sailed for Europe. The sailing-packet Philadelphia left New York with a merry set of passengers, many of them already friends and acquaintances, who went from Boston to Providence by stage-coach, and to New York by the Sound.

Mr. Appleton was just twenty-one when he thus left America for the first time, his birthday coming on the 31st of March. Well equipped with an inquiring mind, the advice of wise counselors, the good wishes of warm friends, and a moderate balance to his credit, the young man started on the first of those voyages across the Atlantic which for many a year formed an important part of his career.

The next chapter is occupied by extracts from a journal of the voyage, written day by day on board the packet.

CHAPTER VI.

1833.

LIST of passengers in the Philadelphia, Captain Champlin :

<table>
<tr><td>Mr. Grey,</td><td>Mr. Baker,</td></tr>
<tr><td>Mrs. Grey,</td><td>Mrs. Hills,</td></tr>
<tr><td>Mr. Whitwell,</td><td>Mr. Lane,</td></tr>
<tr><td>Mrs. Whitwell,</td><td>Mrs. Lane,</td></tr>
<tr><td>Dr. Bigelow,</td><td>Mr. Hammersley,</td></tr>
<tr><td>Mrs. Bigelow,</td><td>Mr. Cook,</td></tr>
<tr><td>Mr. Foote,</td><td>Mrs. Boott,</td></tr>
<tr><td>Mrs. Foote,</td><td>Miss Boott,</td></tr>
<tr><td>Mr. R. W. Hooper,</td><td>Monsieur Larague,</td></tr>
<tr><td>Mr. Blanchard,</td><td>Mr. Guitshow,</td></tr>
<tr><td>Mr. O. W. Holmes,</td><td>Mr. T. B. Curtis,</td></tr>
<tr><td>Mr. G. M. Barnard,</td><td>Mrs. Curtis,</td></tr>
<tr><td>Mr. T. G. Appleton,</td><td>Miss Mary F. Curtis,</td></tr>
<tr><td>Miss Barker,</td><td>Mlle. Victorine (maid),</td></tr>
<tr><td>Mr. Berry,</td><td>Mr. Young.</td></tr>
</table>

Fifteen steerage-passengers.

JOURNAL. *April* 1, 1833.—At ten o'clock, on the morning of the 1st, were assembled on board the steamer Hercules the passengers of our ship. The day was most enchanting, and a very large crowd of friends were on the wharf, to be in our way, and to bid us farewell.

The air exhilarated, the waters sparkled, and the bell rang. Handkerchiefs waved, hands were kissed, and we were off. The weather was so fine that the little steamer was filled with a delightful party of girls, ladies, and other passengers.

We had soon reached our ship, which was at anchor in the Narrows, and, as the little wind there was was not favorable, the steamboat was lashed by the side of the ship, for the purpose of conveying her beyond Sandy Hook. The plump little Hercules did not belie its name; it took our majestic ship under its arm, and bore it off from the smoke and clamor of the city at a rate that made us wish for a longer acquaintance with steam than we had a prospect of. There was something ridiculous in the coolness and ease with which the Hercules bore us off; as Dr. Holmes said, it reminded him of Mr. and Mrs. K——, sweeping down Beacon Street — she all paddle and steam and smoke, he all dignified inertness. As we were dashing along there was a hurried rush; all eyes were strained to windward, and the fearful cry of "A man overboard!" rose from the quarter-deck. I sprang upon it, and saw a bluff sailor, with open mouth, blanched cheeks, and waving arms, swept by me into the ridges and froth of our track. I thought it was all over with him, as he was borne, like a straw, far into the distance. Some of us tossed the helm-cover overboard to him. It floated presently within his reach. He clung with a hearty good-will to it, and soon was in a position that required only patience to insure his safety. We held our breath until we saw him safe in the boat sent out to him, and were rejoiced that an accident, which would have been ominous on our starting, turned out so well.

The North American, a rival packet, sailed side by side with us, and we supposed she would be our consort for half the way at least; but presently her hull began to sink beneath the horizon, and not long after not even her mizzen-pennant was discernible above the ocean view.

(Here let me enter my protest against pens called "*Perryan.*" I abjure and despise them; they are vexatious, scratchatious, and detestable. I throw mine to the winds, and henceforth vow, tailor-like, to stick devotedly to my goose.)

After reaching and passing the bar, our visitors were regaled with a sumptuous collation, and soon after took leave of their friends. A simultaneous

cheer broke from either vessel as we parted company.
We held our course, and soon a strong and favorable
breeze wafted us out of all sight of fatherland. We
ran at the rate of ten knots an hour. In the evening
the moon rose full and cloudless, the sun setting in
the west in a sheet of crimson. We conversed and
promenaded till eleven, and then retired to our
berths.

April 2d.—After a delicious sleep, I rose and ran
up on deck. The breeze had died, and we were rock-
ing in a sea of silver. It was calm for the rest of the
day, with the exception of part of the afternoon, when
we held our course prettily. Breakfast at nine o'clock
is, I see, on the water, the key-stone of the day, being
most excellent, and sauced with an outrageous appetite. After it, I took a walk with Mrs. Boott on the
deck. She told me she had been very sick, but the
calm had restored her. Though all day we did little
better than roll in the trough of the sea, I passed the
time most agreeably. I felt nothing of that do-little,
drowsy *ennui* that I had expected. I varied my
amusements, and found them all delightful. I talked
sentiment with Dr. Holmes; then flirted in bad French
with Victorine; soon joined with Mr. Curtis and our
two doctors in a cannonade of puns. This, by-the-
way, is our *forte*, and we keep it up, each made nim-
ble-witted by the quickness of the others, till we have

to desist from side-ache. Then I took Shelley into the jolly-boat, and read—

> " Our boat has one sail,
>   Our helmsman is pale," etc.—

or rather, for sympathy—

> " Our boat is asleep on Serchio's stream."

And right sound did our lazy ship sleep all day ; but, thanks to her light build, did not snore, as some do.

At twelve we have lunch ; and, at four, dinner ; tea at eight, and, quite marvelous, no supper. Dinner went off famously ; the dullness of the weather had drawn forth the social capabilities of our company, and we found ourselves admirably supplied. A constant succession of stories kept us in a roar, and thus killed an hour and a half without our noticing its decease. We came to the conclusion that the elements of social happiness were distributed among us with very unusual good fortune. There is no sulky, cross-grained vagrant to mar our merriment. Though incongruous as the details of the witches' caldron, we all assimilate into a capital sea-broth, and seem likely to keep always a-bubbling.

Mrs. Hill and Miss Lane, both uncommonly proficient and enchanting musicians, played for us all the evening, without the painful process of supplication ; and an admirable voice in the steerage gave us a suc-

cession of stirring ballads, singing, with a full chorus
of bass voices—

" Britannia rules the waves."

We had a cloudy moonlight, which we enjoyed in
the round-house, entertaining each other with ghost-
stories and conundrums.   Monsieur Larague was unusually frisky this evening, and we had some awful
punning at supper.

April 4th.—On rising from bed, I found myself
pitched nearly head-first through the window of 'my
state-room, and, having succeeded in dressing, bruised
and battered, I went aloft.   Clouds were trailing along
the horizon, and a gale was blowing.   It was a most
magnificent sight.   The waves soared around our bows
in a very fiendish manner.   The poor chickens and
ducks were chattering in terror ; the captain was
shouting pithy orders through a trumpet, and everything presented a lively picture of animated nature.
All the still-life of the day previous had undergone a
sea-change.   The sailors stood at ridiculously acute
angles with the deck, and the first movement I made
was to throw myself in an ecstasy of fondness upon
the bosom of the first mate, who, in a sort of fireman's
cap, and a picturesque overcoat with moony buttons,
was eying the spars aloft from the opposite side of the
vessel.

Few were there at breakfast, and fewer at dinner. Only ten out of the thirty appeared, the rest being employed in "shooting cats," as the captain calls it. Dinner was the most absurd operation. With no heart to eat, we had to be wary to prevent the dishes from forcing themselves on our acceptance. There might be seen an avalanche of turkey, with its vortex of gravy, sliding into the bosom of a *monsieur* taking wine with his *vis-à-vis*, who pours his claret into his waistcoat-pocket, instead of his *verre de vin.* All this was amusing to me, as I have not in the slightest degree suffered from sickness; though, while I write, my stool slides from under me, and the dinner-table jingles with the rolling glasses. . . .

April 5th.—The worthy passengers begin to recover from their troubles. Almost all were at dinner.

April 6th.—The sea a most beautiful sight; lying in shifting light and shadow, "deeply, darkly, beautifully blue"—that blue which I had heard of, but never saw before. The water hissed and simmered as we clove its ridges, running off from the sides in long, undulating sheets of foam, with partial breaks of the most exquisite beryl tint. I have leaned this morning hours on the taffrail, gazing at the stir and tumult, the many beautiful shapes of the wreathed spray, or watching the effects of light and shadow—light which makes the distant billows look like a twisted and wrinkled strip of tin-foil, and shadow that gives to the sharp edge of the horizon the hue and outline of a hacked carving-knife. Excuse the romance of the similes, for their truth.

This morning we lost a hen overboard. Mr. Curtis thinks she will meet foul weather. . . .

April 6th.—A most delightful evening. The moon showed but a lurid disk, and that was soon lost behind the brown-black volumes of a long curtain of hanging cloud. It was glimmering darkness, and our sole spectacle was the water. How magnificent that was! The ship appeared trampling the powers of darkness, and their faint anguish and smothered cries hissed up from their livid lips as we dashed above them. The vessel was every moment apparently on the borders of night and chaos. It was almost fearful to see her stepping off into what seemed a pitchy void. The ocean was ink, the foam faint crimson, illuminated and living with insect phosphorescence, and we left a trail of vivid and whirling light. The dim sails were as wings that fluttered our sea-bird over the deep. After exhausting the intoxication of the sight, we unromantically scrambled down-stairs to a penny game of *vingt-un*.

April 7th.—This day is the Sabbath, and, though no church-going bell pealed us to worship, we felt we were in a nobler temple than we had ever before

offered up adoration in. I felt more fully than ever
the glory, grandeur, and mercy of the God of the great
sea; and I needed not other impulse to render devout
heart-worship to him to whom I nightly pray for those
far away, whose prayers I feel are nightly offered up
for the absent one.

We have all been on deck this morning, the air is
so fresh and the day so seductive. Many of us were
sunning ourselves on the windward side, when, slap !
a sea broke over us, and salted us all dismally. Such
a running, screaming, shaking, and laughing !

We have all day run to the south, partly because
the captain wished to avoid ice, and partly because
he could not help it. We have not thus far been very
fortunate in our winds, but, as we are one third over
on our seventh day, if we are lucky, we may make yet
a shortish passage. The days begin to slip away almost unperceived, and without incident.

April 10*th.*—This morning is delightful, the warmest we have had. Every one, I believe, appeared at
breakfast, which was very excellent, as usual. We
have always fresh eggs, and often hasty-pudding ; and
to-day, in addition, an unusual appetite.

. . . What an odd, good-for-nothing life we lead !
A prolonged morning nap, jokes, and a wire-drawn
breakfast ; a turn on deck, a sluggish conversation, a
book held in the hand for an hour or two, another

turn on deck; the bell sounds—we dash to dinner; three courses, laughter, candles, tea, and the moon. And, *voilà*, the elements of ease and pleasure! How character is drawn out and made familiar! We are all inevitably brought in immediate contact. We are one family. I already feel as if I had lived always with these messmates. After tea to-night the shrill and joyous *fanfaron* of a rooster sounded from behind the mizzen at table. A hoarse and continued bray rejoined. Geese shrilled, turkeys gobbled, horses neighed, pussies mewed, lions roared, etc. We were the ark, or a traveling menagerie. Each imitation was furiously applauded. Victorine, the French maid, must have thought the "*tristes* Yankees" had become Bedlamites, as the cabin rang with the discord of a hundred animals.

April 11th.—Mr. Curtis got out a chart, and we found that we were within a degree of the spot where the packet that last crossed saw vast islands of ice. The night was utterly dark; you could but just discover the horizon-line. This all frightened us pretty considerably, and I could not get to sleep for hearing, in fancy, the crushing of our ship on an iceberg, and for seeing the pale and terrible splinters of an iceland. About one, the captain thought he saw the lights of a passing ship, and put up his own to keep us from hitting. It was so dark he could see nothing farther. At breakfast we had a good laugh at our poetic, romantic captain, who, it appears, had been passing compliments with the moon !

April 12th.—I got out of bed in a hurry to ascertain whether we had perished or not in the course of the night. The captain says we are now out of the region of danger.

While gazing over the railing at the seething caldron about the ship, I had a fair sight at that most poetical of ocean-rovers, the nautilus. It was spinning round in the foam, in shape like a sculpin, with a many-colored and semi-transparent body, and two beautiful azure, gauze-like wings or sails. I saw no oars. It was whirled instantly out of sight.

April 15th.—. . . We have progressed famously, and sanguinely expect to see English ground in four days. Looked over Carter's letters and Mrs. Cushing's " France and Italy"; came to the conviction that there is no book that may be made so dull as a book of travels, and take a hint therefrom as to my own management of the matter.

In the evening we organized a lottery with reference to the day of our arrival. Tickets were a crown each. Mine fell upon the 29th of April, from 6 A. M. till noon—this being the last in time ; so, as the rule is that I have the benefit of all possibilities of arrival after this date, I stand a pretty good chance. This occupied the evening very pleasantly, and gives some of us a divided interest in the matter.

April 16th.—A calm began about nightfall, and we found it still holding us this morning. This, of course, has affected the price of stocks, and I have had offers at a high percentage for my ticket, but would not sell. We have regular exchange-hours, and Hammersley is now having auction-sales overhead. Mem. : To call him at dinner the Knight of the Hammer.

I had written thus far when I heard from the deck the cry of " Whales ! " I rushed up-stairs, and, with the rest, breathlessly strained my eyes over the bulwarks. Close by the ship the surface parted, and a broad, black, and smooth-looking snout was slowly and gracefully evolved from the still water. A fountain of foam shot into the air, accompanied by a blowing like the letting off spare steam of a steamer. There were about us four whales at least, and of the largest kind. They appeared to be about sixty feet in length, and left a wake much longer. Two of them were lovers; they swam on in company, rose together, and sympathetically poured forth their souls in a simultaneous blow. They proceeded in magnificent disdain of our ship, showed themselves once or twice very near, and the next we saw of them was their long backs and vaporous spout at the distance of a mile and a half. Immense as they are, they positively look smallish in contrast to the boundless pond they swim in.   Seen in museums, they had to me always looked gigantic and out of all proportion ; but here there is a sense of fitness to their element.   What would I not give to straddle one of these fellows, hold on to his ears, and be borne down to his sunless cells and his waving meadows of sea-weed !—to leave my card for all the mermaid belles, and call on some old Triton at his coral country-seat, paved in the court with pearls, fenced with sea-wrecks, and lighted throughout with one moon-like carbuncle ! If the old fellow was rude enough to give my charger a twitch, and, whizz ! to be spun back to the insipid regions of air and daylight.

I heard this morning from deck the cry, " Sail, ahoy ! "—ran up, and discovered on each bow a brig running with the wind.   It was a fair race between them.   I should have been glad to have my canvas and brushes with me, as the sea and clouds were of an excellent kind for a picture, the waves being short and high, with lucent transparence of clear green, and their tops blown off, like smoke.   Here's a sonnet about it :

> With sudden birth, from forth the murmuring west,
> Before mine eye a glorious phantom grew
> To instant beauty from the vacant blue.
> A faëry creature, in bright colors dressed,
> Like some fair angel on an errand blest,
> Of mercy, with soft, floating wings it flew.

> Most silent and most swift, through the dropped dew
>   Each wave holds trembling on its silver crest.
>   A hundred prayers shall follow it with tears,
> And anxious wishes round its path shall fly.
>   It shoots before my eye, and now appears
> In gray relief against the troubled sky.
>   Behind the ocean-rim it disappears,
> And now 'tis sunk beyond it utterly.

This shows the advantages of poetry. I have taken no less than two egregious poetical licenses. In the first place, I have called her a ship, when it was only a brig ; and, in the next, I have made her come out of the west to get to America! because, forsooth, *east* only has rhymes in *yeast, beast*—both evidently unsatisfactory.

April 18*th.*—The night was very uncomfortable to all of us, the ship rolled so much ; and dinner was a little more angular than it has been heretofore. I was to windward, and consequently had nothing to do but to hold on to my plate ; but, to leeward, many a waist-coat and shirt-bosom reeked with the good things of our larder, and the table literally ran with milk and honey.

April 19*th.*—The breeze this morning left us, and we were all out sunning ourselves, looking like a pack of *lazzaroni*, and listlessly watching the flapping sails of a brig about half a mile to starboard—

> " As idle as a painted ship
>   Upon a painted ocean."

About an hour before, she was sailing down on us in fine style, when we were rolling in a dead calm. She kept on, all sails set, like the Flying Dutchman, till within half a mile. Then the calm struck her, and there she stuck. She then let down her boat, and it is bounding over the gray to us. . . .

There were six grim and rusty-looking seamen in the boat, and a handsome fellow held the helm. At last it reached our side. A painter was thrown out, and the steps were lowered. The man at the helm ran up, and bowed to the crowd of inquiring faces on our deck that met him as he stepped over the bulwarks. He was one of the handsomest *subjects* I have ever seen. Curling and tremendous whiskers hung around a cheek bronzed by an equatorial sun. A blue roundabout, with round bullet-buttons, covered a pair of square and very broad shoulders. The black cravat was loose about his neck; and his black, crisp locks curled close about his smooth, wide forehead, surmounted by a neat straw hat, worn with a nautical cock. His eye was blue, small, and restless. Good-humor and drollery curled from the corners of his handsome mouth. Add an open manner and the free swagger of a sailor, and you have a picture of as pretty a fellow as ever walked a ship's deck.—That is, I flatter myself, quite in the style of Cooper, and, if I were in the humor, and the ship did not roll in such

9

a shameful manner, I might cover a ream in the account of this visit, and get to the end of my book before I had returned my hero to his vessel. This chap was the mate. He said they were sixty days from Sierra Leone, with a cargo of African oak, and that they were out of provisions, but had water. We gave them nearly a barrel of beef, a barrel of biscuits, a bag of potatoes, another of rice, and a drum of figs. Some of the passengers added a box of cake and a lot of cigars for the captain. The rusty sea-dogs in the boat grinned a hungry satisfaction as the good things were successively lowered down to them. The mate offered to pay, but the captain declined. The poor fellows looked heartily grateful for his generosity, and I make no doubt toast us to-day as they dine on our liberality. It was quite a pretty incident, and. helped off the morning capitally.

. . . Grey is a good romance-killer. Hearing my enthusiasm about Italy, he told me he doubted if I ever could get through it; he had attempted it, and failed; that the only way to get through Italy was "from a sense of duty." "It was impossible to relish anything, the *lazzaroni* were so importunate." *Credat Judæus!* When will men leave off measuring others by their own foot-rules?

April 21st.—This is our third Sunday, and, God willing, our last. Mr. —— borrowed my Bible and

Channing's "Sermons," one of which I was in hopes he would give us ; but self-love supplied instead an indifferent one of his own.

April 22d.—We now begin to flutter with anxious eagerness for land. We are within soundings, the water having changed its blue to a dull gray, and the fine beryl tints just under the foam are lost in a turbid white. The first actual symptom of land was the visit of a pretty little blackbird, fluttering about us with weary wings, yet fearing to alight.

So, at last I am within hail of Old England ; and, after all, what is the trip across? As Dr. Holmes said, with truth, the worst part of the voyage is the ride to Providence ! If a man is not sea-sick or impatient, it is as if his parlor was wheeled off with him ; or, as if, like the man in the Eastern tale, he sat on his carpet and was wafted everywhere.

April 24th.—I have a faint recollection during the night of hoarse cries and the rattling of blocks, various symptoms of an increasing wind blending pleasantly with my sleep. I was awakened by hearing screams through the cabin of " Get up, get up ! Pilot coming on board." His little boat was dipping about just astern of us, and a violent, favorable wind blowing.

The pilot is a good specimen of the Bull people. He has the ingrained ruddy cheeks, the heavy build, and the cockney accent, never to be mistaken. He has been out a fortnight, an easterly wind having prevented many vessels from getting up the Channel. He says that, if the wind holds, we shall be carried to Portsmouth in twenty hours.

After breakfast a cloud to the north lifted up, and we could see very distinctly the land. It was the Lizard—a point of Land's End, at the south—and its two lighthouses were quite visible.

The captain considers the voyage as over, as he has resigned his command to the pilot. He says we have made a passage of twenty-three days—fifteen head-winds, three days' calm, and five fair wind.

The morning was truly English. Clouds overhead, and a haze hanging over the long, purple line of coast. The wind is very fresh, and the scene about us most animated. Hundreds of little things—fishing-boats, pilot-boats, and the like—are scudding to the shore with the violence of the gale. They seem, being wholly black, without any white strip, like a flock of ravens hovering over the water. Once or twice larger boats have come so near as to show everything in them distinctly; they dance hither and thither like acorn-cups in a basin. We are running in a most delightful manner, and the captain says he expects to wake us all, by six to-morrow, to go ashore. We have passed one or two promontories, and my eyes have

delighted themselves with the green fields of Old England. There is a haze over the shore, yet we went
near enough to see the trees and checkered meadows,
cottages, and a church, whose spire stood forth, sharp
and gray, against the white clouds. Mrs. Curtis said,
by-the-way, that it must be the Church of England.

In the evening we had a horned moon and a brilliant sunset. The frequent lighthouses stood, like sen-
tinel stars during the darkness, before our path ; but
we saw nothing of that " sea-built tower the engineer
smiled at," owing to the fog.

April 25th.—I went to bed early last night, expecting an early stirring ; and Mr. Curtis, as his head
was on his pillow, no doubt heard the lottery-money
already jingling in his pantaloons ; but, I make no
doubt, was as regretful as I was delighted, on finding
my sleep and his unbroken till the usual breakfast-
hour.

The wind has come round easterly, and within
sight almost of Portsmouth, with the white cliffs of
the Isle of Wight, tall and tree-crowned, on our lee-
bow, we have to beat up, with the prospect of not
getting in for three hours or more.

Berry will win the prize in the lottery—seven
pounds. We have drawn up and signed a polite letter
of acknowledgment to the captain, and are all muster-
ing on deck in our land-gear. Black pantaloons are

hanging, damp and wrinkled, round many a leg of late familiar with tar and what not; and the unusual neckcloth painfully takes precedence of the careless stock.

Farewell, good ship! Adieu, kind captain! May we meet you both again, and, till then, may storm and calm, land-sharks and water-sharks, spare both! I shall not, Philadelphia! readily forget thy luxurious quarters and flying wake. Kind captain! not readily forget thine eyes' mysterious twinkle, thy stories, and thy fun.

The voyage was over. The journal goes on, however, to relate the adventures of several of the passengers.

CHAPTER VII.

LONDON.

1833.

LEAVING the Philadelphia, the little party went on board a small sloop which conveyed them to Portsmouth. As they approached the city, their eyes were busy in catching the first points of interest in this new world. The journal continues :

"Partly the long confinement and exclusion from the world, and partly imagination, gave to every individual thing a wonderful newness and oddity. The tiled roofs, the salient angles of grotesque towns, pinnacles and house-tops, the many colors, the multitude of beings and novelties, all in a jumble, dashed upon our stagnant spirits and excited the blood, till I almost jumped out of our boat with delight.

"It appeared to be washing-day, for clothes were hanging to the water's edge on every shed. It looked like a Dutch painting. I was not prepared for the picturesque look that everything wore. I had heard

Portsmouth was a dull place, and did not imagine that sea-life could have made me so in love with the stupid as I find myself. In fact, I have had to pinch myself often to-day to make sure I am awake. It was not till a drive in the afternoon that I fully realized I was in England. We got a 'fly,' a sort of carriage that throws open like a barouche, and four of us drove off with a 'coachee' in white top-boots. I was staggered, stunned, and exhausted with the rapidity and violence of new emotions.

"We turn a corner—sheets of living green appear deeper, richer than we have in America—oaks, with rooks cawing about their rookeries. Another corner turned, and we were whirling along a road smooth as if leveled by a roller, and studded with villas, and rows of cottages nearly touching—each different, and each as it succeeds challenging preference. The farms are like gardens, and the men like the costumed heroes of the drama. We were at once struck by the fairness, ruddiness, and full habit of the English in general. We Yankees must look like a continent of consumptives. I returned from our drive, having enjoyed more than was before ever compressed into the same space in my life.

"After tea we visited the rest of our party at another hotel, and found them all preparing to scatter to the four winds."

The next day was spent at the Isle of Wight and Carisbrooke Castle, where they entered by "a door like iron, of old oak, dented with the knuckles of centuries. An awful bell pealed, and a benign old gentleman opened the door. We were by him chaperoned."

Everything was new, and every detail noted. As they left the hotel finally, "on the steps a respectable-looking stranger announced himself as Boots; the maid soon simpered up after him for their *vails*, after which we started. There are two universal phrases, as I have already discovered, in England: First, all servants end everything with 'If you please,' touching their hats if they happen to have them on; second, on starting, or on getting over any difficulty in a stage-coach, the guard universally cries, 'All right!' A coach once running over a pig, the driver thought it was a child, and stopped. The guard saw it was a pig, called out, 'All right!' and on they dashed."

From Portsmouth they went to Southampton, and thence to Salisbury, visiting first, however, Netley Abbey. At Southampton they were delighted with their dinner: "Chickens, small and tender as pheasants; potatoes that crumbled under the suspicion of a touch; a sole that, for the first time, I could call my own; ale, a beverage such as Hebe never held; an omelet that lingered like fruit upon the tongue;

young radishes, English cheese, an English waiter,
and English charges."

At Salisbury they joined other members of their
Atlantic company, and compared notes :

"Conversation in a flood ; we are all full to reple-
tion with ideas which no one has time to digest—
none but an anaconda could—such is the glorious
rush of impressions we have received these last three
days.

"I came over in a Trollopian spirit, but my first
drive sank the cynic in the boy. I am in love with
this my fatherland."

The description of the cathedral, and of the service therein, as well as that of Stonehenge, and all
castles, picture-galleries, and the like, have been so
repeatedly given by other travelers, that they are
omitted here, in spite of the freshness of observation
which gives them individuality in the pages of this
journal.

Of such sight-seeing Mr. Appleton says thus early
in his travels :

"To tell the truth, the effect is hardly pleasant.
There is too much labor—one is distracted, dazzled,
tantalized, and fatigued. I prefer some one simple,
deep feeling to all this multiform and perplexing
pleasure. One soon wearies of just glancing the eye,
even at perfect pictures."

This is the end of the volume containing the journal of the voyage. The sheets were sent off by packet to give pleasure to the family at home, while the young traveler, with one companion, Mr. Barnard, set out for London. Of May-day he says:

"No merry minstrelsie, no holiday pageant, no garlanded May-pole ushered in the day in his Majesty's good town of Salisbury. The stalking-horse hid his diminished head, festivity was not, and the gaitered citizens, plodding through the fallen rain, thought not of the fun and merrymaking of by-gone years. A few filthy and miserable children mocked with dirty flowers and tawdry ribbons the custom they alone seemed conscious of; they danced about amid the iron-shod groups, vociferating for ha'pennies, the muddier at every fresh gambol. Alas for the days of old lang syne!

"On the 2d of May, Barnard and myself took our seats in the basket of the coach for London. The English coach has an inside, a box, and a basket, the two latter half the price of the interior; having engaged his place, one can not change it, as with us. Now, as the interior has only four seats, and as in this climate rain is the prevailing weather, it must strike any one that the coach is built expressly for the discomfort of travelers. We drove the whole way in the rain, on a seat of such construction that our attention was always occupied in holding on.

"The coaches are narrow, generally painted green, and lettered all over. At a little distance they look like our fire-engines. Straw is liberally distributed to pillow the constrained limbs, and a cloud of umbrellas rising from a heap of straw looks not unlike mushrooms growing under a stable.

"Twenty miles outside of London the pulsation of the great heart began to quicken. Men and vehicles became more frequent, and long before we had entered the city the road was lined with houses. We passed Hounslow Heath without the suspicion of a 'Stand and deliver!' The frolic-ground of Paul Clifford and his worthies is now almost built over, and no one would call it a heath nowadays.

"We saw Virginia Water, with a cascade, just on the road, and caught a glimpse, through the trees, of Windsor. We dashed at once into the West End, and found ourselves surrounded by palaces grim with coal-dust, looking as much like prisons as palaces, in spite of statuary and carving. Just as we entered London, on crossing a trifling stream, I thought I might as well ask its name; the reply was, 'The Thames!'"

On the evening of their arrival the two young men went to the theatre, and saw Mathews; on the next, to Drury Lane, and heard Madame Malibran in "La Sonnambula."

"Madame's face is oval, her features very regular and full of expression, her voice when speaking is quite similar to that of Fanny Kemble. Her acting is nature, her singing expression. She is as graceful as possible, though with largish feet. She is altogether a charming woman." Of the scene in Hyde Park he says:

"I will wager a sovereign that in this immense crowd there was not a smile the afternoon long. It was a sort of gaudy funeral. The perspiring footmen looked with long faces into the cloudless heavens, and even the silk-laced lap-dogs turned blue as they saw the fog-like faces of their serene mistresses." He writes, after two visits to the Academy Exhibition in Somerset House:

"I do not wonder at the fame of my countryman Leslie. He draws beautifully, and his coloring, though now looking raw, only wants glazing to be true. This morning I see all the wonderful merit of Wilkie. His scene in a Spanish convent is esteemed his very best picture, and indeed the best ever within the walls of Somerset House. It represents a monk at his confessional, and for breadth and force is perfectly Rembrandt. I can not admire Turner vastly: all his pictures this year are sea-pieces, with chalky gray for sky and water, and black and white for shadow and light, the sole force of the picture being in most cases an ochre sail. Ochre is his favorite tint, and he is often called 'The Ochre-Man.'

"There are pictures here which we should hardly admit into our Athenæum. Indeed, I am quite comforted in seeing so many bad pictures. Portraits occupy, as with us, an unreasonable space, and, after all, in proportion, I don't know but there are as many bad canvases as with us. . . .

"Last night I went to the Haymarket, to see Hackett in 'Rip Van Winkle.' The theatre is about the size of the Tremont, lighted with wax. The play was stupid; Hackett was poorly supported, and I have seen it better played in New York. No one here understands the naturalness of Hackett: all his characters are thrown away. There is a Yankee in the piece, played by a man who, because he talked quick and wore a straw hat, though in white-top boots, and using the cockney haspiration, was thought admirable."

After visiting Westminster Abbey with deep interest, he "stopped to see the Exhibition in Water-Colors. This is the glory of English art. It is their forte. I hardly had a notion of the richness and finish this work is susceptible of. At a little distance many of the pictures I should have mistaken for oils. But

that water-color pictures are so liable to destruction,
I think it might be equal to and as popular as oil."

They saw Pasta in "Medea." "Her figure is of
Siddonian proportions, her acting and carriage those
of the queen of tragedy. She is not in the least
handsome, but at times very terrible.

"After the opera, we had a ballet, in which Taglioni was chief dancer; though there were a hundred dancers in it, no one would ask which was
Taglioni. She is tall and slender, with a pretty face.
Words are not to describe the perfect ease of her
motions. Wheeling a wheelbarrow is with her as
beautiful as a pirouette. She seems often to assume
attitudes and perform steps expressly to show how
much ease and grace can be thrown into movements
which are in themselves awkward.

"*May* 11*th*.—Barnard and I at ten in the morning
met by agreement, at the Royal Exchange, a party of
about twelve, mostly Americans, to spend the day
together rook-shooting at an estate owned by Mr.
Pickersgill, the partner of Mr. Searle, who invited us.
I never enjoyed a day of pleasanter sport. Captain
Champlain and I sat on deck; the hold and basket
were crammed, and away we cracked.

"After driving ten miles through a beautiful country, where I was startled by finding again about me
all the balm and song and freshness of spring, we

stopped in a large court at the door of a sort of farm-house, at the threshold of which, in shooting trim, stood Mr. Pickersgill. He received us warmly, and with English hospitality insisted before we went farther upon our entering the hall and taking a bite of bread and cheese, and a flagon of home-brewed. That done, we arranged matters for the sport. We divided into parties of two, each party having one or two air-guns, and firing by turns. This rook-shooting is the only kind at this season of the year, and is esteemed choice fun. Immediately from the court entrance begins a noble forest, with slopes of bright green, here and there summer-houses and rabbit-burrows, and winding through all an osiered sheet of water, to which some two or three prefer to retire, acting Izaak Walton along the brink. The air was alive with cawing rooks, and out we sallied, a liveried servant attending to pump our guns when exhausted.

"The sport was most delightful. I killed my first three birds dead, and Mr. Pickersgill paid me the compliment to say he would back me against any of the party. The air-gun is a delightful instrument. It carries a ball as truly as a rifle, and without other noise than a sort of fatal whisper, and it has the advantage that when pumped it is good for a dozen shots. We rambled all over the grounds in high spirits; the day was most enchanting, and the woody scenery fine.

"When we desisted at five, after a long day, with a relaxation, however, from the sport to see the grounds, we found each party had bagged about two dozen rooks. I killed six or seven. Whetted sharply were our appetites when we sat down to a simple but good dinner in the long 'painted gallery,' so called from having no pictures, by the *lucus non* rule. I ate the better part of a rook-pie, which resembles pigeon, but better. Departing after dinner, we gave our host three cheers from the top of the coach. So much for a day of capital fun."

After breakfasting one morning with some English friends, Mr. Appleton was taken by them to the rehearsal of an ancient royal concert. "This is a very aristocratic affair; none but subscribers being admitted to the concerts, but they can bring friends to the rehearsals. It was not crowded, but select. There were plenty of noblemen—who in dress, look, and manners are just like anybody else—and several lovely girls. The Archbishop of York had two pretty daughters. There was the Bishop of London and the Marquis of Westminster, and, among others, the poet Rogers. The concert was rather heavy, though we had a magnificent orchestra and many distinguished singers. At the close of the rehearsal, Pasta came. I scarcely recognized, in the smooth, round, good-humored face I saw, the terrible Medea of an evening previous. She sang one bravura with Rubini, and two sweet arias, that drew audible bravos."

In the afternoon he visited the House of Commons. "It is just opposite Westminster Abbey; but how unlike! It is small and dingy, with a gallery running all round it like any chapel, supported by pillars heavily gilt at the top, the only pretty thing in it being the Speaker's chair, which is high and has the royal arms over it. Sir Robert Peel was speaking as we entered. He was in white pants, and rather witty. A terribly long oration followed from a Dublin University member, who denounced Althorp's bill, and was very statistical. After him Colonel French declaimed in a polished and easy flow, amid unnoticed 'hears' from the administration benches. Then, with a heavy step into the front row, down stepped O'Connell. He is of solid mold, tall and thick-featured, with a close, wiry head of hair. He gave a very spirited speech to back his honorable friend of the university. His manner is earnest, violent, and his deep voice has a rich brogue that gives point to many of his good things. He contradicted the administration men often flatly, and seemed little afraid of any of them. O'Connell's sarcasm called forth a shuffling and stammering explanation from Lord Althorp. His tones are those of a querulous old man, and when I leaned forward and saw the silken whisker, erect carriage, and dashy waistcoat of the noble lord, I could only conclude that too much politics had made him old in his prime. This 'hear' is peculiar. It often sounds like the cackle of a flock of geese when a stone is sent among them, and its constant chattering serves no other purpose than to deafen and confuse ; but a loud 'hear, hear !' when a fine speaker is in full swing of excitement, is to him as the shouts of the hunters to the lion. It calls the sparkle to the eye, and thunder to the tongue. . . . We walked up to Bentley's in New Burlington Street to get the new novels of Bulwer, James, and Disraeli, which we had seen announced, but ascertained that in modern English 'being ready' means 'not to be had.'"

The Tower, the Zoölogical Gardens, Astley's, Christie's, and St. Paul's, were all visited, inspected, and described, with the thoroughness of a conscientious tourist. Of the last he says :

"The whispering-gallery is only the base of the dome, and any circular wall would, I should imagine, give the same effect. To try it, I put my mouth close to the wall, and whispered to the guide, who was on the opposite side—

"'Who painted the pictures overhead ?'

"'Sir Christopher Wren,' came back, in confidential and mendacious distinctness. The poor man had but one answer for everything. They were painted by Thorndike.

. . . "Billiards are played with three balls, a modification of the French game. One evening I went into one of the billiard-saloons—a fine, showy hall. The marker offered to play me. It appears it is customary to bet something every game. I told him I should only risk sixpence, and, of course, should lose, as I never played their game before. Taking me for an Englishman, the man expressed surprise. I was in good play, and made some hits now and then, asking how to proceed, and beat him the first game. 'No gammon, my covey,' said he. 'You don't come the jerry over me ; you've played often enough. Anyhow, you're the best player that ever played on this 'ere table.' I blushed at the compliment, and, as I received his money at the end of the rub, I told him I was an American.

"*May 19th.*—This morning, while I was dawdling over a late breakfast, Dr. Holm, the phrenologist, was announced. I received him without ceremony. He dwelt with warmth upon Spurzheim, and our reception of him in America, lectured me long on his science, and offered to examine my head. Certainly, the character which he read off instantly from my skull is true in several points. 'You have,' said he, 'great affection ; where you attach yourself, you will love lastingly. You are cautious, and not hasty to accept new plans. You are very fond of natural scenery, and can remember and represent again any scene or view you may have seen. You prefer light and delicate to harsh and dark colors. You remember things and places, but are bad at dates and names. In music you have a bad *time*, but are fond of harmony,' etc., etc. There must be something in this phrenology."

Mr. John Lowell, in his cab, drove Mr. Appleton to Windsor, thence to Richmond, Twickenham, and Hampton Court. It was a little tour of a couple of days. After noting many things at Hampton Court, he says :

"We at last came to the cartoons. Here the crowd we came with hurried through, but Lowell and I remained as long as the patience of our guide permitted. Though the colors appear faded, the figures have fully retained their beauty of expression and design. The cartoons are water-colors on paper, and were intended to be transferred to tapestry. I feel all the high superiority of the divine Raphael. There are faces here that none but he could have conceived. I shall always bear within me their excellence as my standard."

These are doubtless the famous cartoons for tapestry designs which Raphael drew for Leo X, purchased by Charles I at the suggestion of Van Dyck.

. . . "At eleven, I drove to Mrs. Wiggin's ball, and found the first quadrille commenced. Madame, in a gold turban, received me at the entrance. I danced with the prettiest girl in the room. She pointed out to me the celebrities—among others, Lord Somebody, who traveled all over Europe as a Swiss female minstrel. I was introduced to an ugly damsel, with whom I went through the dance likewise. The party was lamentably like our own—the same over-dressed creatures, chattering and smiling about and at they knew not what; the same heat, the same affected conversation. The quadrille is an immense one, and the figures appear to differ somewhat from ours. Madame asked me if I *valtzed;* but I declined the grip of one of these stalwart Venuses. I got home by one, walking the whole way, through blind alleys full of rowdy characters. As I stepped into bed, it occurred to me that I had not dined, and instantly I became rabid with hunger."

A horticultural *fête* at Keswick, with Mr. Lowell, was the last excursion from London, and the month closed with the festivities connected with the king's birthday. King William held a *levée* at St. James's.

"The windows of the coroneted carriages were open, and fair creatures in jewelry and feathers, and grim warriors in scarlet uniforms, alternately smiled and glowered at us. The windows, verandas, etc., were alive with spectators.

"In the evening the illuminations presented a gay appearance. 'R. W.,' in vari-colored lamps, shone loyally; but it struck me oddly that the king should celebrate his birthday so long before it comes off. It looks as if he were determined not to be forestalled by Death of any amusement it might afford.

"Just before twelve Mr. Lowell called for me, in his cab, and we drove to Willis's Rooms, King Street, St. James's, for tickets had been applied for to the ball, and Princess Lieven had us upon her list. In a side-hall we presented our tickets, paying a guinea each, and were shown up-stairs to the grand ball-room— that *El Dorado* to the adventurers of *haut-ton*, that promised Canaan to the tribe of toadies, that spot of bitterness to the swarms of the disappointed, the holy of holies of the temple of Fashion!

"Quadrilles were just forming as we entered. It is a noble hall, profusely bright with wax-candles, and carved and relieved in white on a pink ground in a very pretty manner.

"This was a brilliant evening on account of the birthday festivities. I will describe the dress of one

of the finest women in the room, with a queenly expression of rank. Her face was Grecian, and the hair
close in front and on top without ornament, save a
broad, classical fillet of simple gold round the head.
A massive but simple gold necklace reclined on her
uncovered shoulders. Her dress was white, tastefully
embroidered with flowers in different colors.

"The dress of the men was, in most cases, an
unbuckramed, skin-like coat, long, and with broad
flaps, a stock, colored waistcoat, pants pyramidal to
the ankle, stockings open-work and high colored ; add
quizzing-glass, hat (not opera), cane, and mustache
à discretion, and you have the ball-costume of an
English gentleman, A. D. 1833.

" Waltzing and gallopades were oftener than quadrilles. Gallopade is a huge square, the figure apparently at the fancy of the dancers, taking care they
keep time. There were more young people—awkward lads with painfully correct hair, and unfledged
misses—than I expected. Mothers walked about with
their daughters, as it were to display their wares ; fat
old ladies waddled like moving phosphorescences,
each, like the toad, bearing a precious jewel in her
head. When the dancing struck up, a green cord was
held by the servants to dispart the dancers from the
rest. The refreshments were simple to plainness,
little else but coffee and sandwiches ; the cake what

we call 'President's biscuit.' The English affect French a good deal; one hears it constantly at parties.

"*May 30th.*—This morning we four parted, Barnard for the north of England, the Motleys for America, and I for France, by way of Brighton. Till I was off, the morning was agony, with bills and botheration. I took my place on the box of the Brighton coach with singular satisfaction, having shaken hands with my friends, and shaken off the waiters; at ten precisely we cracked away. The lion of Northumberland House held his tail stiffer than ever as we swept under it. The Abbey looked sad and solemn.

"Soon, with unstifled lungs, I was with delight looking back upon the smoke and hubbub of the great Babylon.

"In leaving London, I must say that hospitality of all sorts has been offered me. I have seen nothing of John Bull's *noli me tangere* spirit, but have found everywhere the reverse."

This was in spite of a *contretemps* which deprived Mr. Appleton of all his letters of introduction, among them those given him by John Howard Payne, who was in Boston the winter before, and who had received the hospitality of Mr. Appleton's dinner-club. Mr. Payne gave to Appleton and Hooper letters to many of his friends—O'Connell was one of them.

All the letters were seized on Tom's person when he arrived in London by an over-zealous customs official, and, although unsealed, were put by him in the post-office for their various destinations. For long afterward the unfortunate young gentlemen were hunted up from time to time by some of the more civil yet naturally irritated recipients of these letters, who knew not where to seek the persons so highly recommended to them. Mr. Appleton used to give an amusing account of these interviews, and the annoyance caused by his apparently innocent mode of sending the letters.

On the 1st of June, Thomas crossed the Channel from Brighton to Dieppe, and took his mental farewell of Old England—"bade adieu to her plump daughters and serious sons, her nectarian ale and her patrician turbot, her melting mutton, her velvet lawns, her roads, her coats, her cabs, her umbrellas, and, thank Heaven, her charges!"

CHAPTER VIII.

PARIS.

1833.

"PARIS, *June 6th.*—Why did I waste my substance —why did I lose patience, money, comfort, and time in the smoke of the island Babylon—when dear, delightful Paris was within a jump? Experience must be bought, and I have bought it. Would that all the money that London ravished from my pocket were there again, to circulate in the natural veins of Paris !

"Paris is as unlike London as fire and fog, yet some people ask me which I like best ! No money can purchase in London comfort ; in Paris, every sou returns a throb through the whole man. To come to details :

"In London, at breakfast, you have a little coffee-pot, little milk-pot, and little muffin. Here, *café au lait* brings a *garçon* to you, with a huge pot in each hand—one is for coffee, the other milk. He pours the *café* till you cry, '*Tenez !*' and then dashes the whole cup with hot milk. This is but one instance, to show that this people certainly understand the philosophy of living better than their fellow-creatures ; and all the wonder is that they are not universally imitated.

" I went into the garden of the Tuileries. In a moment I was as if in the melancholy of primeval forests. Embracing trees make twilight and silence, unbroken save by giddy bursts of sunshine and the song of birds. Pay a sou, take a chair, and read Béranger, as uninterrupted as in a desert ; or, if you have him not in your pocket, step from the wood, and as far as the dark, carved palace, and your eye is dazzled by sparkling water and gleaming marble. Here gold-fishes leap from their circular oceans to the sun, there Apollo strains the monster python. A hundred statues appear through the trees. I walked beside the banks of the Seine, passing many a noble bridge, till I came to the Pont de Concorde, lined with gigantic and exquisite statues of the French heroes— Bayard, Condé, Du Guesclin, etc. ; it is, indeed, noble in effect.

" *June 7th.*—Dined at the famous *café* 'Les Trois Frères Provençaux.' The quantity of glass in Paris is astonishing ; the houses are all open, and the frequent glass realizes the idea of every one's carrying a window in his bosom. Mirrors, that the Trojan horse might have seen himself in, reflect you at every turn.

A good *café* is all mirrors. My parlor is ornamented with a very elegant clock and three immense mirrors. I have a capital *salon* and bedroom in the Prince Regent Hotel—quiet, and but a step from the Tuileries.

"This morning my valet made his appearance, hat in hand. He is a spruce, lively fellow, and will be of great service in lionizing and conversation. He put my room to rights, and arranged my wardrobe in the most knowing manner."

Three of Mr. Appleton's friends (Drs. Holmes, Hooper, and Warren) were studying medicine in Paris, so that he had no lack of congenial companionship; and with them, or under the guidance of the valet, François, he went through a course of the lions of Paris, which, like those of London, are now too familiar to bear description. The Place Vendôme, the Louvre, the Luxembourg, Frascati's, the Gobelin tapestries, received attention on the first days after his arrival.

"*June 9th.*—As this was Sunday, I gave the lions a day's peace. I met Baker in the street, and went with him to visit á friend of his. What was my astonishment to find in this friend Sam Ward, with imperials, and the disguise of a perfectly French manner! No one would doubt he was French.

"After a dinner at Prévôt's, the medicals and I sat in the Palais Royal, and watched the gambols of the children. Though I was prepared to hear them speak French, they were the source of great amusement ; they dress prettily and oddly, have fine eyes and redundant hair, and play together like embryo Frenchmen.

"After amusing ourselves on the Boulevards, we dropped into a *théâtre des enfants.* The theatre is little, and the performers all children. They played with great spirit ; one girl did admirably. Mothers bring their good children here to reward them. A fine nest of young Burkes !

"At the Panthéon we were shown the tomb of Rousseau ; it is the real one, transported from its former place. It has reliefs on it. One, a projecting hand setting fire to a world, is very just. *Vis-à-vis* is the tomb of his arch-rival Voltaire. We saw the tombs of many of the generals of France, and should have seen more, but one of the party, John Bull, cried out, 'Seeing one is seeing a thousand—let's be off !' and as he was the majority, off we came.

"Yesterday, while I was dining at a *café*, a whole English family entered and took a table; as was presently evident, not one of them spoke a word of French. In vain did the polite waiter offer them the treasures of gastronomy, they could appreciate nothing. But, at last, in connection with *bifteck*, he mentioned *à l'Anglaise*, and the whole clump cried out, '*Oui, oui !*'

Miladi smiled on the waiter her broadest grin, and he hurried for *bifteck à l'Anglaise.* At the Opéra Comique the other night, in 'Fra Diavolo,' there was an English lord caricatured to the life. He has red hair, and an immense drab surtout, with huge buttons, long waist, and low pockets. It is a good *pendant* to Mathews's Frenchman.

"At the Café de Paris, the room was full of English, but there was one good specimen of the Parisian dandy. His hair was parted, and fell sleek to the neck, and there formed a ridge of curls round the head. His collar was turned over, and sustained by a complicated mass of black silk. He had a figured *gilet*, and large cossack; white pantaloons, very wide at the boot. His coat was huge, and the broad flaps were rounded at the end. Huge rings were on every finger. Moreover, he was young and handsome. It must be said that the men here do not dress with at all the taste of Englishmen; but the ladies—*mon Dieu!* they are simplicity itself!

"*June 12th.*—After dinner I took a parterre-seat in the Opéra Français. The house is large and handsome, and cut up into different portions, each with a different price. The pit is very nice, with velvet seats; and the utmost order prevails. *Gens-d'armes* at the door are ready to repress the least trouble; but none occurs. If one wishes to leave the theatre for a while, and keep his seat, he puts thereon his opera-glass and gloves, and, were he gone the whole evening, would be sure to find them untouched on his return.

"The opera was 'La Tentation,' and consisted in the devices of the evil-one to seduce a holy monk. The music is not very good, but the subject gives full scope to the wild taste for *diablerie* which seems at present to prevail. One scene in the crater of a volcano, where the fiend reviews his army, was magnificently terrible. There were full two hundred persons on the stage, and all as devils. The army marched to a full band of infernal drummers, and little fiends for pipers, headed by the *sapeurs* of hell. The *garde nationale* of the brimstone country, with horned heads, curved and hacked cimiters, and pale-green mustaches, appeared next; and in the rear followed a multitude of she-devils and young Zamiels. In another place we looked into the recesses of heaven, and saw afar a band of angels singing, with harp and lute, the praise of God. The cold, silver light falling on the purity of their robes, contrasted well with the devilish glare upon the evil army in the foreground.

"*June 15th.*—At half-past eight in the morning Warren and I took a gondola for Versailles; when there, after a slight breakfast, visited the palace. It is gorgeous as a lavish taste could make it. The pictures are not generally very good—that is to say, they are mostly French. The gardens are the perfection of mathematical beauty—

> ' Trees cut to statues, statues thick as trees '—
> ' Grove nods to grove—each alley has a brother,' etc.

It is all as Pope says, even to the swallows in ' Nilus' dusty urn,' for all the fountains were rusty for want of use.

"*June 16th.*—After the theatre the Boulevard was a gay scene. Thousands in merry moods throng the walks. The glass windows of the *cafés* reveal the blaze of day. Venders of all things invite at every step; here a thousand clocks of gold protrude into the gutter, and there rich prints strew the earth. Now a man pulls your arm to sell you a waistcoat, and anon another to show you his dancing fleas. Your eye glides over a gay mass of frolic. Here an image Turk turns his head in grave slowness up and down, and there a wooden Othello stabs a plaster Desdemona. All is fun, and *flaneurs* riot in the witching hour. In their mood, I stepped into one of the thousand *spectacles*. A man had a collection of wise birds. A lovely girl took a franc from me, and I found I had bought the best place in the theatre, while all the other spectators were behind me ; thus, unfortunately, I had to do all the card-shuffling, etc., for the company. The birds could pick marked cards from a heap, make out the names of towns by letters, etc.; but the poor things were rather too sleepy to work, and we were given tickets to come again when they were more awake. My position drew upon me several severe jokes.

"*June 17th.*—Holmes and I actually were at the Louvre this morning three hours instead of one, such was the seduction of the masters.

"O Salvator Rosa, thou king of the terrible; O Rubens, emperor of glowing flesh and vermeil lips; Rembrandt, sullen lord of brown shades and lightning lights; O Cuyp, magician of sunny twilights; Raphael, thou prince of painters; O Wouverman, thou Mars of tumult and battle-smoke; O Teniers, Thyrsites of the canvas; O Titian, thou god of noble eyes and rich, warm life; O Veronese, apostle of the Marriage Feast; and last, not least, Murillo, thou Burns of the cottage and the shed—when shall I repay you all for the high happiness of this day?

"In the evening I attended the most Parisian of *fêtes*, Tivoli. I was admitted to an extensive grove, brilliant with colored lamps and vocal with a hundred musicians. Laughing groups of well-dressed Parisians lounged under the trees, or to the music twinkled their pretty feet. Here it is that the fair milliner, the fairer goddess of the *café*, and the nonchalant do-nothing, meet in common revel. I wandered as chance guided.

A boat in full sail, holding a laughing party, whirled over my head on a circular cruise in the air. Quadrilles were performed on the turf, and lovers turned aside to the darker alleys of the wood. A man put a pistol in my hand; I pulled the trigger, a rocket shot through the skies, and, as it hit a metal bird, a shower of fire fell around. I pass on; pantomime rules the moment. Harlequin eats whole puddings at a swallow, and plays a thousand tricks. Café blazes before me in many-colored letters. A party is watching a game in which a Frenchman strikes his ball into a hole and wins—a flower. 'Blanche ou rouge?' asks the winner, of a pretty girl at his side. 'Blanche,' whisper her rosy lips. 'Excellent! c'est l'image d'innocence et de vertu,' he replies, and fastens the rose to her bosom with an insinuating bow. I try my luck at archery; lose thirty sous, but do not hit the target; the arrows are charmed. From a stupendous height the rope-swinger careers in air. He twists and turns till, alas! he falls headlong from the rope. A cry of horror bursts from fair lips. The rogue! he is laughing at them, while he holds the rope securely in one hand. *Vive la bagatelle!*

"*June 20th.*—We made a party and dined at the Rocher de Cancale, the crack eating-house described in 'Pelham,' and had a capital dinner. . . . Went to the Théâtre Français in the evening. Mdlle. Mars

played in two pieces ; her acting is nature, with those
little but true touches that belong to genius. She is
very quiet in manner ; her modulation is distinct and
delicate, and in verse you seem not to hear the re-
straints of rhyme, but only metrical prose. As she
manages it, I have no objection to dramatic rhythm.
Though not exactly looking young (she is fifty-seven !),
yet her fine face and figure supply the loss of youth,
and she has the pleasure of knowing she is an old and
established favorite.

"*June* 21*st.*—This morning I took my catalogue
and gave the statues at the Louvre a cool and thorough examination. I was all alone, save as at intervals I passed a rusty and pale student with his bread
and crayons. I enjoy this gallery as much as the other.
Surrounded by these triumphs of the Roman chisel, I
can easily picture in my mind all the splendor of the
imperial city. I see the Pompeiian circus that this gigantic Melpomene once guarded ; and the Appian Way,
gorgeous with these very statues of the emperors, runs
into white perspective to my eye. Here are the originals of the 'Diane à la biche' and ' The Fighting Gladiator.' How unlike the plaster copies ! The muscles
of the gladiator positively tremble with fatigue, and the
stain of centuries but deepens the haggard and weary
earnestness of his furrowed countenance. He seems
to spring from the pedestal. The busts of the em-

perors are most interesting. We are certain of their fidelity, and can fancy we see them live. Trajan has the lowest forehead I ever saw. Germanicus is the amiable and graceful youth I expected ; Nero, a handsome sensualist ; Nerva, admirably Roman.

"I went up-stairs and met Brown, just going to visit a private French collection, and joined him. The house was far toward the barrier, and the collection a famous one. The picture we were most pleased with is one by Constable. It is as fine a landscape as I ever saw, and wholly above those in the London exhibitions. There were also good Rubenses, Murillos, and Ruysdaels. We took a walk in the garden—very beautiful, with statues, grottoes, and water ; there we met the wealthy owner of this little villa. He expressed pleasure at showing us his collection, and proved himself a man of taste by his comments upon his own pictures.

"I dined with M. Henri, my French teacher, *en famille.* He has a pretty little daughter, from whom I dare say I shall learn more French than from any one else. Little girls talk faster and more prettily than men. As I paced the Boulevard, I looked in upon the wise birds, but they were not visible.

" *June 22d.*—I got from Galignani the 'Sketch-. Book' to re-read. How true Irving is in the narrative of the sea-voyage and the effect of 'land !' on an

American ! The poetry of the cottages and emerald fields of England was not lost upon him. I inquire here often for the Saint-Simonians. They are a discarded tribe. The only one I have seen is a student in the Louvre, with flowing hair, one-sided hat, and brown robes, the costume of their sect.

"*June* 23*d*.—After procuring a fresh supply of francs from my banker, I put one of my father's speeches in my pocket and went to call on Lafayette. Unfortunately, he had the day before gone to the country. Visited Percival, and we arranged plans for Swiss travel. At sight of the map, and Lake Geneva, I became furious to be off. I want to be among the glaciers, and to hear the cry of the lammergeyer. Percival carried me to the expiatory chapel of Louis XVI and Marie Antoinette. It is very beautiful, and the sad sentiments of Louis's will, and Marie's last letter, breathe from the storm into the tranquil chapel a pathetic solemnity. The chapel was begun by Louis XIII, and finished by Charles the Bigot, who put a finishing touch to every church he could find. . . .

"In the evening I went to the Gymnase, and was kept in a laugh the whole evening by Perlet, a capital actor, who was the life of two excellent vaudevilles. A *vaudeville* is a comedy interspersed with songs set to popular tunes ; it is very common with the French, and quite their *forte*, as the spirit and vivacity of their conversational language give a sparkle to every *tête-à-tête*.

"These French are a very strange people. It is easier to like than to esteem them ; yet all that relates to *bienséance* is irreproachable, and their *bonhomie* is universal. You ask a man the way, and he will go to the end of the street to show you. It is their politeness that prevents them from laughing at foreigners. There is no chance of meeting at a *café* that surly and grumbling tone so common in London. But the French are an ugly nation. The animal is stamped indelibly on their features. I do not think I have seen an intellectual head since my arrival. They dress badly. They are inferior in size to the English ; the soldiers are short, sallow, and look ill-fed. If by accident a man elongates into a grenadier, he is not stout and plump like an English one, but seems ready to break down under his mountainous cap.

"Whenever I see a body of these troops moving to its lifeless music, I can not help pitying it as a sort of animated corpse. The soul is fled. The voice that called to victory is still. Under One, the French soldier could dare impossibilities ; now he falls back into an ill-fed animal. These same troops, with Napoleon at their head, would be a terror to their enemies ; now they are harmless.

" . . . As I passed the Château d'Eau, the finest fountain in Paris was playing beautifully. These fountains are very numerous, and in hot weather are the most refreshing sights in the world. They constitute one of the chief beauties of Paris.

"I descended a flight of steps from the Pont-Neuf, the oldest bridge in Paris, with a fine equestrian bronze statue of Henri IV, to try one of the many baths of the Seine. They all consist of a large, open square, into which every one turns, having little stalls for clothes. The water was only up to the waist of the hundred bathers, and was too turbid to suit one accustomed to ocean freshness. On getting home, I found a packet of letters. I danced with delight.

"In the evening we went to the Cirque Olympique, as there was to be a *réprésentation extraordinaire*, and extremely so it was. The house not being full, the actors did not attend, and no piece was played after the first. There was an uproar, in the midst of which a fellow in the third row sprang upon the railing, and made a violent speech to the house upon the indecency of keeping the whole waiting, not to mention its stupidity and weariness. He finished his speech by offering his services to supply the place of the defaulter, who was to have given imitations; so saying, he ran down, crossed the pit, climbed the stage, and began, to the wonder of the artistes of the stage, who stared at him from behind the scenes.

"*July 1st.*—The Louvre again. What originality and genius there is in Poussin's 'Deluge'! I saw it suddenly lit up by bursts of light, and the effect was admirable. It seems as if the faint lightning shone between the falling sheets. The snake on the rocks seems actually to snore, and the upright suppliant in the boat has life. From studying Poussin's landscapes, I am satisfied that Allston has copied him; his early landscapes are very much in his style—the same hard, cold foreground, the pebbly water, the defined bushes.

"*July 4th.*—At six we were to celebrate the great anniversary at the hotel next Frascati's. We found the committee, with blue ribbons at their front, at the door to welcome us, and were ushered into a large anteroom, amid a crowd of fellow-countrymen. In a few minutes General Lafayette, his son, and grandson, entered and shook hands all round. The dinner was soon served; about eighty sat down, and the peculiar occasion, the gay table, and the splendid hall, made it most interesting. A large band—large, but not very good — stunned us at intervals. 'Yankee Doodle' made the table ring to the glasses, and was *encored*. It strung my feeling to a higher pitch of patriotism than I thought possible. Afterward there

were toasts and speeches. The hero, in broken English, finished his speech by a toast referring to our
late crisis : 'Public common sense, may it hereafter
always be the arbiter of all difficulties!'

"*July 6th.*—This morning I was up betimes. The
day before, smitten with the irresistible beauty of the
boy of Raphael leaning on his hand, I resolved to
copy it. For a trifle I had bought an easel, etc.,
written for permission to the director, and at ten this
morning I was at the door. I strode down the inter-
minable gallery like Napoleon, found the dear boy,
more lovely than ever, and *con amore* dashed him in,
in dead colors, finishing that part by four, the hour
the rooms are closed. This boy of Raphael is, perhaps, the sweetest thing in the gallery ; it is brilliant
with excess of finish, and, in my two or three days,
I can not expect to get more than a sketch, but it will
serve to remind me of the divine original. I found
that by returning to my old pleasure I obtained a
more active sense of the excellence of the pictures
about me. I had forgotten how difficult it is to
produce effects ; it carried me home to my dark
room and the hard, lifeless abortions of my pencil.

"*July 7th.*—Heard the celebrated Abbé Chatel,
one of the most eloquent preachers of Paris. His
church is Unitarian ; it was founded in the year 1831

by the abbé, and calls itself the *French* Catholic Church. The house is very simple, and similar to many of our plain Unitarian temples. After the *messe*, and burning of incense before the altar, the abbé began his discourse. It was extemporaneous, against dueling. The abbé is a fine-looking man, his voice clear, and his action animated. Though short, the sermon was sensible and eloquent. There are no pews in the French churches ; they are full of the same cheap chairs that fill the Tuileries and Palais Royal. The old lady bustled about for her two sous, and the chink of money did not help the religious effect. After the discourse, the abbé read portions of a new catechism he has published for young and old. It is his 'Creed and Reasons,' and, as it was curious, I bought one. The abbé believes Christ to have been a man, but for his excellence to be worshiped. He disbelieves in his bodily resurrection, and discredits the miracles. He told his hearers that, when they worshiped in a *Roman* Catholic church, they must not adore the symbols and images, but the Almighty ; all else was to receive but a formal and secondary worship. He thinks himself about identical with the English Unitarians ; but he seems to me to go further than we do.

" *July 8th.*—All my plans for presenting the good folks with a Raphael are dashed, for Monday no one is admitted to the Louvre, and losing this day ends the matter. I will leave the canvas till I return, and then perhaps finish.

"*July 9th.*—This morning François, whom I have taken into service again, packed my trunk and made things all ready to be off. He brought home my passport yesterday, having worked all day carrying it from one ambassador to another. 'There, sir,' said he, as he handed me the bestamped and besigned paper, 'I think there is not a country in Europe your honor can not visit now!' I have consigned my Raphael to Brown, and am quite anxious to be off; I have seen pretty much all one should see, and have no excuse for staying now but to eat good dinners.

"*July 10th.*—At one o'clock P. M. I should have been at the Messagerie Royale, but, by an aberration of the knowing François, found myself at the wrong one. As I reached the right place, I was told that the coach had just started, with all my luggage on it. After the necessary *sac-r-r-r-és*, I jumped into a cab, and told the astonished driver he must overtake the diligence before the barrier. Stung by money, he was successful, and by two I was rumbling over the rugged *pavé* in the *intérieur*.

"I have for the last month lived in the spirit of Béranger's 'Song of Jean de Paris'; with Jean—

> ‘Proclamant sur son âme,
>   En prose ainsi qu’en vers
>   Les tours de Notre-Dame,
>   Centre de l’univers.’

Whether I shall say ‘ay’ to his cry—

> ‘Reviens dans ton Paris ’—

I know not, but for the present I have, with Jean, got the traveling mania, and repeat with him—

> ‘Quittons nous cette ville unique,
>   Nous voyageons—Paris à dos.’ ”

Mr. Percival, who is mentioned here for the first time, was an Englishman, the younger son of an English nobleman, whose family name he bore. He subsequently joined Mr. Appleton, and they traveled together ; the friendship between them became warm and lasting. A little pencil-drawing in one of the sketch-books, under which is lightly scribbled the name “ Percival,” gives a pleasant glimpse of a thoughtful, genial face, in the turn of the head not unlike the pictures of Burns.

CHAPTER IX.

1833.

HAVING left Paris, Mr. Appleton, with his friends Mr. Russell and Mr. Percival, went by diligence to Dijon, where they took post-horses for Geneva, enjoying every moment of a journey of some days, which is now made so swiftly by rail that all details are lost.

"We walked the third day almost the whole of the first post. The pure air of the mountains was exhilarating, and, with Byron in my hand, I chased the goats from peak to peak. A thousand lovely, rare plants and flowers were under our feet. The delicate bluebell azured the cliffs, wild-pinks and the beautiful family of the mosses drew us hither and thither. I filled my hands with the variety of flowers.

"We had started at seven, and about two hours after, by an abrupt turn, the checkered mosaic of the Pays de Vaud, the blue crescent of Léman, and the brown roofs of Geneva, burst upon our sight. The Spirit of the Mist was not our friend. He drew his shadowy battalions before our eyes, and veiled in cloud the icy turrets of the monarch of the mountains, giving us but shifting glimpses of the lake and plain. The *coup d'œil* reminded me strongly of the view from Mount Holyoke. Lake Léman is fairly matched at a distance by the Connecticut. After winding a few miles through the softly wooded plain, we stopped outside Geneva, at a most neat and English-like inn. From my window I have a bit of the vivid blue of the lake, with nearer a broken foreground of rich trees, and can dimly discern afar the snow-streaked form of Mont Blanc.

"*July* 16*th.*—After shaking the dust from our habiliments, we entered the town and crossed by two bridges the whirling and deeply azure current of the Rhône, along which sheds of *blanchisseuses* make music with their bats."

They visited Ferney and the château of Madame de Staël; like all good tourists, bought *bijouterie* at Geneva, and made the tour of the lake, visiting Lausanne, Vevay, and Chillon, and then, with knapsacks and other preparations for walking, leaving heavy baggage to be forwarded to Milan, they went up to Chamounix.

"After dinner, having amused ourselves visiting a mineral collection and a live chamois, and buying

rings of chamois-horn, we walked to the glacier of
Bossons.   After tramping vainly over the fields, and a
toilsome march up a wooded hill, we heard `a tramp
as of wild colts, and, looking up, I found two men,
six or seven boys, and an old woman let loose on us.
One put an iron-shod staff in my hand, and they all
offered service as guides.   We insisted we should pay
but one, come who might.   This they heeded not, and,
as I looked round while we were climbing, I should
have thought we were a family of squatters.   Some
bore shoes for the ice, others axes, all poles, and the
old lady brandy on a waiter.   I asked one of these
intelligent citizens if they loved the king.   'Oh, yes!'
'What is his name?'   'I do not know that,' was the
reply."

The excursion to Montanvert, and the Mer de
Glace, was much like that of ordinary tourists, before
and since ; more exceptional is the account of a circuit of Mont Blanc, to take five days.

"*July 25th.*—We engaged Payot, whom we much
liked, to be ready at three that afternoon, with a mule
to carry our knapsacks.   After a lunch of bread and
gruyère, the common cheese of the country (full of
holes and not good), Russell and I started, bidding
farewell to Mr. Percival, whom we hope to meet at
Martigny.   As we left the valley, the air was so pure

and cloudless that we obtained an unusually fine view of the range of mountains. We took our mule alternately, and she, with astonishing sure-footedness, bore us by yawning precipices. In our gay caps and worked frocks we made, no doubt, a smart appearance, but one soon sinks the picturesque in the comfortable. As we advanced, the setting sun hung the mountains with scarlet robes, and gave the glaciers and *aiguilles* a delicate *couleur de rose*. The scenery was of the wildest character, but the path abominable, being often the bed of a running brook. At last we were housed in a nice inn at St. Gervais, the landlady being a particular friend of citoyen Payot—we having come at least twenty-five miles. Our guide has cheered us with the story of a German who has just been robbed by three banditti in masks, within an hour of St. Bernard. The rogues had carbines, and he nothing, with but a boy for a guide. They took from him six hundred francs, and returned him forty for road expenses, and his watch. We have heard since that the robbers were taken. They were three brothers ; they were detected somehow by the boy-guide, who knew them in spite of their masks.

" *July 26th.*—We started this morning at six. The first thing we saw was the Pont de Diable, under which, far below, a torrent howls amid fearful rocks. No peasant dares pass this bridge after dark ; the

13

legend relating to it I had from my guide. It appears the devil had the bridge made, with the proviso that he should have the first person that crossed. After consultation, the peasants sent a cat over, at which the devil was so furious that he snatched a stone from out the bridge and threw it at the cat. No other stone can be found to fit the place of this one. Before the devil could throw another, a priest advanced with *eau bénite* and exorcised him. With such tales our merry Payot beguiles the way. The day was most delightful; we passed half a dozen beautiful cascades, and one covered with a lively rainbow. All we did yesterday, however, was but play to to-day's work. We ascended, after four hours' labor, the Mont de Bon Homme, crowned with two castellated rocks—the good man and his son. For three hours we were wading in snow up to our knees; it was often red as if with streaks of blood ; just after crossing a bridge of ice, we came to the grave of three ladies who perished here in a storm ; below was that of their three servants, who dragged a little farther. We arduously ascended the Col des Fours to the very top. The guide assures us this is 'the finest view in the whole Alps.' I am sure I shall never forget it. We stood alone above the world; about us was the whole amphitheatre of the Alps, with all their garniture of cloud and glacier. On one side, as from an infernal gulf, boiled up fantastic and gigantic masses of vapor, at times sweeping over the view a momentary veil. It seemed, indeed, like chaos ; cloud, water, and earth, mingled in unorganized order. The sky overhead was a faint purple, and around us the most vivid blue. The air was so rare and pure that everything was seen in startling distinctness. When inhaled, it tickled all the throat, and seemed to pierce the pores as with fine needles. We took short breaths, and could not go far without resting. I felt a most new and delightful exhilaration ; it was the intoxication of the gods, looking down upon a prostrate world. The mountain is eight thousand feet above the sea. To fortify ourselves, we ate a snow-ball drenched with *kirschwasser*, and at last, with slow steps, left this heaven.

" The guide showed me where once he surprised an eagle carrying off a marmot, who, frightened, dropped his prey, and the guide took it home for supper. He knew no such bird as the lammer-geyer, and says the avalanche is never called the lawine ! Coming down, the hill would have made a magnificent 'coast,' and I felt the want of 'Nimble Dick.' We stopped in the valley at a little hut, the ideal of an Irish cabin. It is the worst place I ever was in. Into the parlor—the sole room—all sorts of animals have at times made entrance to greet us—pigs, goats, horses, calves, and cats. The air rings with the cries

of animals, broken only by the shrill treble of two or
three babe-lings in this one room.   The mother manages the baby in the coolest manner : the thing is put
into a cradle, nothing but its hand left out, and then
it is strapped down in primitive style.   Good milk,
which even here was boiled for coffee, and eggs over
which, according to rule, three *paters* had been said,
made a good supper ; I made madame dry the sheets
before the fire ere she put them on the straw mat-
tress.   Our hut is quite an original experience, one of
the sort of things one prefers to look back upon to
having present.

"*July 27th.*—It appears, the house is divided into
three apartments : the one we occupied and filled ;
another is the parlor, kitchen, and nuptial-chamber of
our hosts ; the third is devoted to the beasts.   The
walls, the floor, and ceiling, are all rough boards, so
that through the cracks we had a general supervision
all round.   Glad of any couch, we stretched out our
weary limbs on the hard straw in hopes of sleep.
Things promised well until some imp pinched the
child in the next room, which struck up a shrieky *solo*
instantly met with an *obligato* from every animal on
the premises.   This positively continued until dawn.
It was the choral song of fiends over a guilty soul.
Bells tinkled, mules brayed, goats baa-ed, pigs grunt-
ed, babes shrieked with varying misery, and at times

came a deep blow as if a school of porpoises were playing round the beds. At last, fatigue threw me into a sort of stupor, which, however, the first ray of morning dispelled, and I gladly left my Procrustean bed.

"We resumed our mountain-ascent. I found the copious supply of fleas and such small deer which had made park-ground of my limbs all night had materially reduced my strength ; but the guide, with the simple recipe of wine poured over a slice of bread, made us fresh as ever."

They reached Courmayeur about three, where they passed the night at an hotel " frequented by the first families of Turin," and started the next day on a descent, reaching Aosta before noon, and St. Remy before night. On the way, they heard that the report of the robbers being taken was a mistake.

"*July 29th.*—This morning, leaving St. Remy at half-past five, we began the ascent of St. Bernard. A Prussian count, with peculiarly straw-like mustaches, joined us. After about two hours the huge figure of the convent shimmered through the fog. It resembles exactly a cotton-mill, and the pond beside it preserves the resemblance. . . . The holy fathers were much scandalized by the cool robbery within an hour of their convent. They said they lent money to the victim, and had taken all means, but vainly, to catch the three rogues.

"In leaving, as we were to pass the very spot where it occurred, all thought it advisable to keep together; and doubtless it was our warlike front, and the curled mustache of the count, that lost for my journal a nice adventure.

"We saw the plain where Bonaparte gave his troops a grand dinner, and also the spot where his guide saved him from falling over the precipice. When fairly down the mountain, I could not but confess that the difficulty of Napoleon's passage was much exaggerated. Our companion, a Genevese, was in the army that crossed. He says that it was in May, with much snow, and avalanches sweeping off men and horses. With all that, to my notion, it is a feat that our Yankees would perform, and never think they had 'set the river on fire.'

"At Liddes we took a *char*, having a long pull to Martigny. A *char-à-banc* has seats sidewise, like a woman's on horseback, between the wheels, with the advantage that one looks away from the precipice over which he hangs. We rattled down stony hills, perpendiculars all about us, and only by the grace of God were we saved, for, just on entering a village, the front portion of our *char* gave way, and the rest ran off to one side, and, coming smack against a house, overset. If it had been five minutes back, we should have all been Sam Patches. By dark, at last, we reached Martigny."

Thus, sometimes walking, sometimes by diligence or *char-à-banc*, Mr. Appleton visited Interlachen, Vevay, Berne, Lucerne, Zürich, Schaffhausen, with a little tour including Flüelen, the falls of the Händeck, Grindelwald, etc. During most of this time he was alone, his traveling associates having left him to vary their tour. At times he joined chance companions. He was always observant of costume and national peculiarities of speech and character, and especially of the beauty of nature everywhere: always sensitive to the influences upon his moods of weather, sunny or rainy, and of solitude and society.

"My friends left me," he says, "to go to Milan. It was indeed with painful feelings that I parted with them. After we have for a month traveled pleasantly together, I am disturbed to lose them, and to become indeed alone amid a world of strangers. It is in such moments that the magical word 'home' has to the ear its full charm, and brings before the pining eye all the warm hearth-loves that have been the growth of a lifetime, with all the thousand little comforts we have lost—the cushioned arm-chair, the familiar sofa, the loved pictures, and, beyond all, the 'bright familiar faces,' the undeceitful smile, and earnest kiss.

"SCHAFFHAUSEN, *August* 22d.—I walked early to visit the falls.   They form a charming picture.   The whole body of the pure green Rhine, which even here is a wide, brimming, and noble river, shoots itself with roaring over a mass of shingly rocks, which in three or four little wooded islands stand up amid the fall. On one side is a turreted old château, and on the other an old mill.   I had returned to the hotel, when the well-known *bonnet rouge* shone through the dust of an approaching diligence, and in a moment Russell's hand was in mine.   I was tired of trusting to casual acquaintances, and right glad to meet him.   The next morning we started in the post-wagon for Baden."

Here they stayed some days, amusing themselves at the gaming-tables, a little on their own account, but more in watching the conduct of the typical gambler.

"I saw all those strange exhibitions of our nature that mature at the gaming-table—men and women, old and young, all following their own schemes of money-winning, till, as was often the case, stunned and irritated by ill-luck, they would dash from the only spot able to excite.   One old fellow, with a stoop and a sepulchral cough, was the model of a gambler. He never smiled or missed a point. His cold, quick eye detected the moment of decision, and his heap of silver each time almost invariably doubled. The landlord told me strangers of all nations had come here in a chariot-and-four and gone off in a *voiturin.*" They met there a number of friends. "We were thus a tremendous body of Americans, in all nine, and we created quite a sensation going in a body up and down the *salons de conversation et de jeu.*" Their next point was Heidelberg, which they thoroughly examined and enjoyed.

"Our guide was a sergeant-major by profession, rum-marked but merry. He professed to have fought on all sides in Europe, and to have been with the British in America at the burning of Washington, and in a skirmish on one of the lakes. He told us very coolly that the President of the United States was here last year, and that his name was in the book; but we saw it not. The pseudo-President was liberal of kreuzers, and told our friend the guide that he hoped, the next time he visited Washington, it would not be in a red coat, and sword in hand! The castle of Heidelberg is the finest in Germany, and the noblest ruin I have seen."

They went from Heidelberg, through Darmstadt, to Frankfort, where they arrived one evening.

"It was after dark when we reached the diligence-office. Six or seven vagrants seized our luggage, and each, carrying some trifling article, as we did not know German enough to hinder them, trailed after us in a mob, while we went to various hotels without getting in, all being full on account of the fair beginning to-morrow. At last we found a room in the *troisième* at a second-rate hotel. The next day we luckily succeeded in getting a good room on the *rez de chaussée*, at the 'Roman Emperor,' where we found the Edgar party.

"*September* 1st.—The town of Frankfort is a free town, owning some land beyond the walls. Its streets are wide and cleanly, and its buildings often look noble. We dined well at the *table d'hôte*, and ordered *sanglier* for to-morrow. We were told at Darmstadt that we might see any evening, at a certain place, the keepers of the forest feeding the wild-boars in great numbers. If so, they can not be very wild.

"At last I have letters—delicious and welcome they were, and put me in spirits, in spite of the rain.

"In the evening we went to the opera, as we heard there was to be something fine—a new one, 'L'Olympien.' But I was disappointed. The house was ill-lighted, and the opera stiffly classical. The only idea I received from two acts was a suspicion that one of the personages was Alexander the Great!

"*September 2d.*—This morning I was awakened early by the falling off of the confounded down-quilt, which is the sole warmth to the bed, universal throughout all this country. It is in no way fastened down, and is always slipping off at a kick. With the valet, we visited the small beginnings of the fair—a long avenue of shops, many of them for the sale of pipes, handsomely painted, or of clear '*écume de mer.*' We visited the Museum, which contains an extensive collection of pictures, neatly and well arranged. The Dutch and Flemish schools are better represented than at the Louvre. After so long an absence from art, I found these pictures gave me the keenest pleasure.

"*September 3d.*—This morning, after dishes of chocolate, we were off for Wiesbaden, in a *calèche*—four of us. It was shamefully cold, and, tired of the dreary view, we fastened down the sides of the carriage, flung ourselves back on the seats, and dozed the route through. We noticed only three interesting facts on the trip: First, that all the horses were blind in the neighborhood ; second, that the pigs have very long, and, third, the dogs very curt legs. It rained dismally, and we found things little better in our cold, forlorn rooms at the hotel at Wiesbaden. The only way I had of getting warm was to take a bath, as the clumsy *Kammer-Mädchen* had no success in lighting the stove. The bath was mineral ; the water, full of salt and iron, tasted like a sloppy *bouillie*. When I returned up-stairs after the bath, the fire was started, and the smoke with it.

" All the lamp-posts in Wiesbaden have a wooden snake, that, curling round them, lifts its head in air, and suspends from its mouth the lamp. It is pretty. We had remarked this mode also at Darmstadt.

"Wiesbaden seems to be a pretty town, but the rain spoils everything. In the evening I stayed at home, and amused myself with Scott's ' Napoleon.'

" *September* 4*th*.—We started at three for Mayence, in an excellent *calèche*, and arrived, after crossing the Rhine upon the bridge of boats. We are at a capital hotel, d'Angleterre, with excellent rooms."

Mr. Appleton at this time little suspected that he was destined, before many years, to make a more intimate acquaintance with this part of Germany.

" To our surprise, we saw many of the stiff Prussian and Austrian troops in the streets; since Napoleon's downfall, these two powers, with Russia, have held the citadel, as allies.

"O that Napoleon were again alive, to drive this white-legged vermin to its native regions! The Austrians are all in white, with black gaiters. It must be confessed they are stout-looking fellows.

" *September* 5*th*.—This morning, by the early hour

of five, we were upon our feet, and, half an hour later, on board the Europa, to enjoy the descent of the Rhine. The morning was not favorable, but, as day advanced, it grew warmer and the sky bluer. At first we thought the scenery inferior to our expectation; but, in a few moments, doubt was hushed in delight. The color of the Rhine here is not other than a turbid yellow, whirled in eddies, and sliding at a pace that makes the boat but one day descending, though two coming up. The scenery, as we found, in a short while burst upon us in all its famed beauty. It is unique, and should be compared with no other, as its castles, which are unrivaled, form the chief glory of the scene. They crown every crag, and the dashing boat gives them to the eye like the quick changes of a panorama. Crags and châteaux shoot up at every turn, as fantastic as ever falling cinders take shape of moat and castle, turret and drawbridge, before the dreaming eye. Ranks of vine, step over step, make green every patch that is not rock. But for the castles the scene would not be so fine; but they are all poetry and robber-wildness—all different, but all possessing a Salvator fierceness. We passed numberless towns and storied towers.

"All the fine portion of the river is between Mayence and Coblentz, with one solitary exception. Below Bingen we passed the Mouse-Tower, where the rats

14

devoured the miserly bishop. At Coblentz we had, on the right, the fine fortifications of Ehrenbreitstein. They are not equal to Quebec, but very fine and enormous in extension."

There they left the exciting features of Rhine-scenery. At Cologne the party separated ; Mr. Appleton, with Mr. Russell, passed, by post or diligence, through Prussia to Hamburg. There was some talk of going on to St. Petersburg; but the season was too late, and everything adverse: it was necessary, it appeared, that their names and intention of traveling in Russia should be published for three weeks before they could depart.

July and September were passed in Germany, chiefly in the large cities. Mr. Appleton does full justice to the Museum at Berlin, and the wonderful Gallery at Dresden. At Leipsic he inspected the famous battle-plain. The first Napoleon was an object of intense interest always to Mr. Appleton, and, throughout his life, he failed not to read every book written about him, and missed no opportunity of sifting and analyzing his character and course.

But Germany was not congenial. The language did not flow readily upon his tongue, so fluent in French and Italian. The "frog-like" French of the Germans suited him no better, and he never got used to the

German bed. The journal speaks well of the people, condones the food, and praises the galleries ; but it is but half-hearted praise, and it is to be noted that, with the exception of an enforced stay at Mayence some years later, Mr. Appleton never revisited the country. It rained all the time he was in Dresden, and weather was very apt to influence his impressions. On the whole, he was glad to be beyond the boundaries of Saxony, in an *Eilwagen*, on the way to Prague, on the 27th of September. "Before long," he writes, "we had entered Austria. Everywhere the double-eagle was perched, and all the turnpike-posts were now striped black and yellow."

He had fallen in with a chance friend, in whose companionship he traveled for some time ; he is at first always spoken of as "the merchant," or "my fat friend." He turned out to be the Swedish consul for Brazil.

The "shocking German bed" pursued him to Vienna, where he, at length, rejoices in "Christian sheets and a downy pillow."

He stayed nearly three weeks in Vienna, visiting all the monuments. He made the chance acquaintance of an agreeable Polish count and his fascinating countess, whom he frequently encountered at places of amusement. At Vienna he was much impressed with the mustache, a modern innovation there universally worn.   He says : "They are full half and half with smooth cheeks, and their variety is a philosophical study.   They may be reduced to four classes —amatory, savage, sentimental, and unfortunate—according to the twist given them by their wearers."

On his first arrival in Germany, Mr. Appleton was disgusted with the frequency of the pipe and its accompanying habit ; but, before leaving Austria, he had set up a pipe of his own, in deference to the custom of the country.   However, pipes were never much in favor with him, although he dearly loved a good cigar.

His Brazilian departed, Mr. Appleton found himself solitary in Vienna, and decided to make his way without further delay toward Florence, where it was his intention to repose for a while.   At Munich he found, to his great satisfaction, his friend Percival. They met there a Scotchman named Campbell, "stout, and about forty-five," who asked to join their party. "I am to do all the talking," writes Mr. Appleton, "and bargaining, as he is just from India, and speaks not a word of French."

Thus the three companions, on the 1st of November, found themselves driving through the Tyrol, and soon, to their delight, leaving the crabbed German tongue and slippery beds, for the softness of Italian speech and slumber.

Two weeks in Venice, a memorable day in Milan, looking at the "Last Supper" of Leonardo da Vinci, and rapid posting, brought the travelers to Florence, where, with feelings of profound relief, Mr. Appleton laid aside for a while the habits of the tourist.

"*December 8th.*—At last I am settled at No. 1159 Borgo di Santi Apostoli, with two little rooms in a central situation. I pay seven dollars a month, with ten cents for breakfast and thirty cents for dinner. I have wandered for a few moments in the Pitti Palace, but glanced only at the glorious affairs on the walls, to stand most of my time before the heavenly 'Seggiola,' with its earthly mother and divine boy. What unutterable sweetness and soul in the expression of the Madonna! It enters the heart, with the certainty of living there, while a thousand other emotions may vainly agitate it. The eye and the mouth Raphael stole from heaven.

"Mr. Percival found rooms in the same house; poor Colonel Campbell we have left aground, and, like a whale deserted by his pilot-fish, he rolls his huge sides in vacillating uncertainty. He will be landed ere long in an English *pension*, if he does not, as I prophesy, drift with the stream that moves Romeward.

"*Eh bene!* Is it not odd? Here I am scribbling

in precisely the position I have always looked at as *il Paradiso*, the horizon-star of my hopes, to paint at Florence! And I AM happy. I shall copy at the gallery, and make sketches from my travels—strike before the iron is wholly cold.

"Barnard is here, but only for a few days. Like old men, we sit and talk over our young enthusiasm in England, now dead and buried under the broad tide of events and emotions; yea, even in Florence, we look to the end of our career with pleasure, and, overleaping Rome, draw hopes of happiness from home, sweet home!

"We went, with Barnard, in the evening to the theatre. We could not get into the pit, so took a whole *loge*, for which the janitor asked fourteen pauls, and accepted eight. Such is this universal spirit of roguery, that one by instinct abates the half. I question not that, so strong is custom, a Florentine would dispute the toll of the angel that admitted him to paradise.

". . . Raphael is, on many accounts, the most wonderful artist of any day. He lived only thirty-six years, and yet his pictures mark a growth and maturity of genius that any one would suppose those of a long life. He, too, united all excellences and all extremes. With a genius that gave birth to the heavenliest, most ideal beauty man has conceived—his infants and his Madonnas — yet, in minuteness and truth, he equaled Teniers or Mieris. His portraits are the finest in existence. Then, too, how much contrast! From his portrait of his mother to Leo X! The first has more dryness even than Perugino, and the last matches Titian. His last works, indeed, are faultless. What might he not have done if his life had had the limits of the Evangelist's?"

Mr. Appleton was resolved to copy in the galleries of Florence, but it was a work of time, not only to decide upon a fit subject, but to obtain the necessary permission, and to fairly establish himself. Meanwhile he was sketching and taking Italian lessons, and his time was fully occupied in sight-seeing and observation.

"My opinion is made up as to the weather. The Florentines themselves allow winter to be bad enough, between the *tramontino* from the hills and the *sirocco* from the west. When it is fair here, the sky is quite blue; the air is bracing and chill, and one requires a cloak. It is to me very agreeable—like our fine October weather.

"My street, or rather lane, as we should call it, is so narrow, and the eaves lap over so much, I doubt if a sun-ray ever reached the pavement; it is wet, damp, and dirty. I have no light till eight in the morning,

and it goes by half-past four.   I have foolishly left oil
and wood to be furnished by my hostess.   However,
she says that Americans are *fini, con testi discreti.*

"We burn wood—no coal is to be had; and our
lamp is of a very antique and classical figure, with two
flames and a chain suspended.   Once a week Madame
Fiocchi places a fresh pot of flowers upon my mantel,
which retain their bloom by aid of water during the
interval.   Our furniture presents the usual Italian in-
congruities.   Beside a bureau, without locks, stand
chairs once fit for a palace, imposing in their tarnished
gilding and torn satin.   There is not much neatness in
our room, but of course one comes down to the Italian
standard.   My ceiling is a sky, in which birds are
sporting.   It retains its blue with vastly more con-
stancy than the fickle Tuscan heaven out-doors.   On
the whole, I am already at home, and like my surroundings.   I think I could live a year thus, and find
active occupation all the while.   As yet the days are
too short by half, and I hardly once a day find time
to smoke my dear pipe, the admiration of the ladies."

Here the manuscript-book of the journal was sent
to the hands of the book-binder, and thence was forwarded to America, with a warm greeting to the loved
ones at home.   The volume is dedicated, affectionately—

" To the eyes of the family circle ; to them, and to them only."

It is only with the full permission of the remaining members of that group, and with the license given by the lapse of so many years, that these extracts from its pages are given to the wider circle of friends.

CHAPTER X.

1833–1834.

"ONE bulky volume," writes Mr. Appleton, "in the hands of the book-binder, and now I am to fill another. A merry heart blots much paper; and so, with a prayer to our patron, the god Saint Mercury, I apply myself to the task, made pleasant by the hope that some future hour may owe its amusement to the piece-meal scrawlings of the present."

He was now pleasantly established for a couple of months in Florence, with his friend Mr. Percival, in an Italian family, of which the two daughters amused the young men by their easy talk and kind attentions. The society of several Americans, old friends, prevented Mr. Appleton from feeling lonely; and the relief from the hurry of travel, and the comfort of settling down to a methodical life, proved most agreeable.

He applied immediately for permission to copy in

the galleries, and was impatient of the long delay which attended the application. "I patiently (impatiently!) wait my day," he says. "Titian's mistress will soon be mine. As for the Pitti, only seven are admitted at a time; and an artist who is to copy some Salvators for Mr. Perkins has been waiting eight months. Pretty patrons of the arts! No art but that of procrastination." Meantime, always observant, he filled up his time inspecting all the treasures and curiosities of Florence.

"*December 20th.*—There are always in the Ducal Square two rivals, Punchinello and a charlatan. The latter puffs his drugs and elixirs from his old sulky with infinite variety of gesture and eloquence, and apparently does a good business with the soft ones of the town; but Punch draws the larger crowd and the loudest laughs. I notice that he differs somewhat from his relative in England, though retaining his usual character for gallantry and quarreling. He appears here in a black mask, and with a nose much more moderate than his English namesake, who, in vivacity and variety of adventures, certainly does not equal the hero of Italy. Bergamo had the honor of originating this Lothario, immortal and ubiquitous.

"My banker gave me a billet to procure me permission to copy the Seggiola at the Pitti. I have little hopes. On application, I was requested, with much solemnity, to wait a moment for the high and mighty *custode*.   In five minutes a servant came, took my cloak, and told me to pass to another apartment, and wait again.   In five minutes more the great man bowed himself in, and, after some solemn talk, told me that Monday, at twelve, I should know when I could gain my object. Gil Blas could hardly describe more courtly detentions.

"Last evening Madamigella Rosalinda was quite gay; she did up our hair in papillotes and laughed heartily at the effeminate figure I cut, and the Gorgonian one of Mr. Percival.

"The Italians are very fond of bonbons. There is an invaluable shop in my neighborhood, where soda and mineral water are also sold; it is always full of Italians filling their pockets.

"I am crawling through Sismondi's 'Italian Republics.' What poor stuff these Italians were, from the first! The soul sickens at the unvaried variety of the causes—quarrels and massacres of Bianchi and Neri —Guelph and Ghibeline. How many bloody rains have reddened the bases of these old churches! How many times has the affrighted Arno blushed an alien hue! As I walk under the Duomo, I fancy it living and musing upon the inconstant tide of humanity that has swept along beneath it, ever vain, ever busy,

'hasting to do evil,' with the passions, objects, of in-
sects.

"*December 25th.*—Christmas-day is one that should
be spent at home. I was fortunate to have friends
enough about me to give our dinner a Boston appearance, whose wit and geniality made a holiday indeed
of the flying hours. The day is kept by the Italians
pretty much as we keep it. The shops are shut, the
citizens lounge and drive along the Lungo Arno, and
retire early to their turkeys and mince-pies. Yesterday was kept as a sort of fast. No one ate anything.
Mdlle. Taquina quoted the proverb—

> ' Chi non jejeuna la vigilia di natale,
> Corpo di lupo ed anima di cane.'

"*December 28th.*—What miserably short days! I
can not do the half I propose, and have many affairs
of three days' neglect on my hands. I have bought a
full collection of prints from Bardi, and have consigned them to friend McCracken's portfolio, to be
sent to New York, there to await my coming.

"Yesterday, a Turk in full costume visited me.
What was my astonishment to hear him inform me, in
pure English, that he was a professor in my own *Alma
Mater!* He only meant, however, that at Cambridge
he had taught the Oriental languages to any one who
wished to learn. He knew all the professors ; he was

15

there in the time of Madison, whom he said he knew. He did not relish the high society he went into, it cost him so much in shirts and coats; and at the dinners he felt so uneasy he could not eat, and was obliged to entreat a second dinner for eating. On the strength of American associations, I bought of him a pound of Turkish tobacco, not quite so good as that I obtained at Vienna.

"To-night, as Signor Rosca (the Italian teacher) was taking his leave, he saw a lady sitting in the chair at the top of the stairs. With his usual courtesy, he bowed and wished her the felicitations of the season. There was no answer, and smothered laughter from down the corridor induced him to take her by the hand. It was a mere figure that the girls had prepared in the carnival spirit, amusing themselves with the mistakes of the passers. Gay folks these in our house, and yet they are always saying they are very miserable.

"Picture-dealers begin to find me out. A man came yesterday, and I bought of him a copy of Correggio's 'Madonna of the Tribuna.' It is very excellent, and I felicitate myself on the purchase.

"*December 30th.*—Spent the morning running about making bargains and paying bills. I fell in with the *famosa* stock-maker, and am advised to beware of her seductions. She is a Corsican, who, they say, has made as many conquests as Bonaparte.

"Went to visit the secretary of the Palazzo Pitti, to hear what chance I have of copying. To my joy and surprise he told me, with a smile, that I shall have La Seggiola for all the next month! I give up, therefore, my other applications; a careful copy of this touching Virgin will repay me for my lost time, and feed my future days with pleasant reminiscences.

"While walking through the rooms, I met Mr. and Mrs. ——. They were all Boston; and their northern salutation reminded me of the cold manners, half-forgotten, of my countrymen.

"*January* 3, 1834.—The third day I have been at my easel in the Pitti. I am much amused at the parties of English who, from behind me, express their various opinions upon the picture and my copy; not suspecting my English, they express their criticisms freely. I have been twice asked if the Madonna were original. From my platform I see a galaxy of genius. The 'Leo,' the 'Judith of Allori,' Rubens's portraits of himself, his brother, and Hugo Grotius, his masterpiece in this way; two Sartos, most delicious, and others, all admirable. If, while gazing upon these fine works with something of sympathetic love for the art, I in my vanity exclaim, 'Ed io anche son pittore!' I must be pardoned the presumption for my passionate admiration of these high names in whose presence I find myself. I paint better for the influence of their presence, and, far from being overawed, feel only warm ambition to produce a copy which may gain some admiration for the original Seggiola. . . .

"Last night, at the Cocomero, I saw 'Maria Stuart,' newly translated from Schiller. I could not pardon the want of beauty in the fair Mary, though she acted well. The costume was not ill generally, and great sympathy was manifested for the unfortunate Catholic, wearing a conspicuous golden rosary at her girdle. The queens are made to meet, and they scold like fish-women. Mary taunts Elizabeth so keenly that she is hurried off in a speechless paroxysm of rage. Unfortunately, this Elizabeth was much the prettier.

"*January 5th.*—We went to a little theatre, the Bourgonisante, taking Constantino to explain. These small theatres amuse me better than the larger; one finds more jollity and fun in the house, often more spirit and merit in the actors, and the drolleries of the supernumeraries, and the *naïve* remarks of the audience are very diverting. There are eight theatres here, and some where the tickets are eight cents! In the farce we saw a personage, new to me, but a favorite with the Florentines, who has ousted, it seems, from the public favor his rival, Arlichino, viz., *Stentirello.* This individual is a servant, dressed comically and painted with huge eyebrows, and wearing a party-colored coat. He

always misunderstands all remarks, and with his buf-
foonery, wit, blunders, and improvised songs, keeps the
house in a convulsion of merriment.

"*January 7th.*—All day at the Pitti. Finished the
head of the Virgin.

"*January 10th.*—Mild and rainy. In fact, this is
by all said to be a very mild winter. I have only seen
ice once, while last year there was a month of skating
on the Arno. All day, as usual, at the Pitti.

"Last night went again to Fenzi's *soirée*. La
Guicciola was expected, but, to my disappointment,
she came not. I have seen her on the Lungo Arno,
but not distinctly. She is not, however, so pretty as
she ought to be for Byron's good taste in selection.

"*January 14th.*—Yesterday I received a solemn
note from Ambrosi, saying that I must be at the Pitti
Palace in the evening, in *froc de ville*, at half-past
eight precisely, to be presented to the grand chamberlain and then to the duke. After long and unsuccessful efforts to make use of the white cravat
Linda has bought for me, I succeeded in dressing to
my mind.

"We entered the Pitti grounds at the side-gate, and
drove through the Boboli to the private entrance of
the duke. The approach was magnificent ; at every
few yards were candelabras blazing on either side.
These almost illuminated the gardens and the cy-

presses, and the statues, in mysterious number and
obscurity, gave a finish to the elegance of the effect.
Soldiers were stationed in many places ; as we
stopped, a servant showed us into the palace. We
wandered through many long galleries filled with ex-
otics, doubting where to find the presentation-room.
At last we came upon a large body of servants in
the livery of the duke—buff and crimson. The first
room was not large and few persons were in it. We
passed soon, however, to a large and magnificent
salon, where we found some other gentlemen waiting
to be presented. The French took one side of the
room, and we the other; the English were on the
right, and the Russians on the left. We formed thus
an amusing congress of nations, solemnly staring and
quizzing at each other. We Americans were almost
as numerous as any—not far from a dozen, I think,
with many ladies. Our three officers were in uni-
form. We were kept waiting a long while ; finally the
entrance of the duke was announced by every one
rising. He was simply dressed in a greenish coat,
with three orders. The duchess came with him, pale,
but richly jeweled. He glided through the crowds,
without ostentation, the chamberlain introducing him
to each person. They began with the Russians ; the
English followed, and we, having no minister, were
miserably left. The introduction was done in an easy

manner, with but slight remarks. At last he came to us. 'Voici les Americains,' said the chamberlain. We gave our names. The duke paid us some national compliments, and said to one of the officers, in English, 'The Americans do not fear the waves in the middle of the sea.' All this occupied about an hour and a half, when the presentation was over, and conversation and dancing began. The duchess took her seat in the center of one side, with the princesses about her, and her maids of honor behind. The duke opened the dance with Lady Seymour, the English ambassadress. The duke danced as though he loved it, but with the *gaucherie* of a backwoodsman. There was great variety of dress. Some old Russian ladies were almost in the Queen Anne court costume. Feathers were in quantities, and the blaze of diamonds, and moonshine of pearls, redoubled the splendor of the wax-candles which were in trees or pyramids to the ceiling. The different ministers of the Italian states wore orders, ribbons, and other distinctions. The Pope's legate was in a sort of cloak, with brown stockings ; he wore a little black skull-cap jauntily on one side of his head, and the expression of a *volpo soprafino*. There were any number of splendid rooms *en suite*. Many had card-tables, and some persons were pretending to play chess amid all the uproar.

"The supper was laid out on two buffets, in a room next the *salon de danse.* It was most *recherché.* Statues and a variety of little alabaster figures were interspersed amid *patisseries* and cakes, and two whole sturgeons were not among the least conspicuous of the dainties. A pyramid of champagne looked like the cone of happiness.

"We left before supper was announced; and I drove home to dream of jeweled duchesses and pretty English girls, at times nightmared by some monster of a sturgeon squatting with finny tail upon my melancholy bosom. . . .

"Rusca told me to-night a curious story of a snare laid for him by an antiquarian friend of his. This friend, it appears, was a profound rogue. He lived in Leghorn, and Rusca used him to hunt up antiquities for him. One day he told him he had stumbled upon some famous bronzes, outside the Leghorn gates, at the house of a fair lady. They agreed to go at the twenty-fourth hour (by the Roman calculation—i. e., sunset). Though rather surprised at its lateness, Rusca did not object, and forth they fared. When they arrived at the house, the man kept outside, and on entering Rusca found a most beautiful and agreeable woman, in whose society he soon became absorbed, forgetting his antiques in the charms of this modern specimen. The lady left him alone for a moment, when, hearing low and mysterious voices in the next room, the idea of a betrayal came suddenly upon Rusca, and, coupling with the circumstances suspicious things he had heard of his acquaintance, he gave himself up for lost. In this unpleasant state of things, knocks were heard at the door. The lady returned, and some female friends entered, which fortunately gave Rusca an opportunity to make off, though the lady was much displeased, and urged him to stay and examine the bronzes. He pleaded an engagement, seized his hat, and, without waiting for his 'friend,' made but half an hour's walk to Leghorn.

"He afterward learned that it was undoubtedly planned to murder him for the money he had brought with which to pay for the bronzes. His 'friend' was afterward exposed; and he saw the *lesina*, an awl with which this man used to kill men, by a sharp blow at the back of the neck. The victim hardly felt it at the time, it was so delicate, but bled to death when at a distance.

"*January 18th.*—To-day is Saint Antonio's day. He is the patron of animals: my hackman came running to me with a splendid bouquet, which he presented in the name of the saint. It is a sort of April-fool's-day with the people. They say to some one, '*Prestatemi un paulo*'; and when they have it, they say,

'*Ringraziate Dio e San Antonio!*' and run off, the poor lender having no right to ask again for his money.

"*January 22d.*—Went to-night to the duke's ball again.   It was in the same rooms, with the same style, and almost the same persons I knew there.   The supper was as distinguished.   Mr. Curtis and I were determined to try it this time; and when the eating began we slid up to the sturgeon and demanded a slice.   This fish is delicious, and deemed princely here.   Having heard the duke's pheasants were fine, we tried them, and finished with a beaker of kingly tokay, such tokay as Vienna could not afford, such as monarchs give one another, such as slides down the throats of princes.   Noble duke! his supper has bribed me to eternal praise.

"*January 24th.*—We dined at Madame Humbert's, at the invitation of Colonel Campbell, my quondam traveling friend.   After dinner I took a walk with the gastronomic hero, who was one of the guests, an Englishman.   His father paid sixty thousand pounds of gambling debts for him and disinherited him.   He is as rosy as the morning, and professes to worship no other god than his appetite.   He moves about Italy in the direction of good hotels.   He has never entered the Pitti, and stays here only for his good table; but soon goes to Naples, cutting Rome.

"*January 25th.*—Desirous of making some return

for the civilities of our friends, Percival and I gave out invitations to a dinner for to-day, at Marché's. Marché did his duty, and served us a most exquisite dinner. We were all in spirits, and laughed and talked till near eleven.

"I found Professor Pacciani in the parlor at home. We began a conversation; the professor was very polite, and ended by offering me most excellent letters to Rome, Gibraltar, and other places. He is a queer person. Distinguished for his literary attainments, one moment he is pulled by nobles, and the next carousing with vagrants. He dresses at the north and south of decency; now in brocade, and now in rags. A philosopher, he turns a deaf ear to the solicitations of his high-born patrons. He avoids the court, and prefers to sip his *vino comune* with his own valet, to kissing cups of tokay with the duke.

"We are drawing near to a close of our sojourn here. My visit to Florence has been delightful, and I am indeed sorry to break this studious quiet, and recommence gyrations. Mr. Curtis thinks he shall not take his own carriage to Rome, but is desirous that we should all go together in some large conveyance. This is charming. His servant, Gretano, is now on the lookout for some such 'carry-all.'

"*January 26th.*—The Carnival at its close gets a sort of sickish vivacity. Rusca says he can recollect when it brought every one into the streets in masks ; now for ten years it has inexplicably languished.

"The Corso winds, in a long file of carriages, from Santa Croce to the Annunciata. All the windows, roofs, and streets are crammed with spectators, with a plentiful sprinkling of masks. Crowds of wigged doctors, Rinaldos in beaver, cuisses and waving feathers, Swiss girls, etc., and more than one redoubtable *Arlecchino* in spotted clothes, jostled along with much less vivacity and life than I should have expected from an Italian masking. At Santa Croce, the bright-colored crowd on the steps was a brilliant sight, like a frozen rainbow—many pretty faces shining amid the gay shawls. There were several fine-looking peasants from the environs, inheriting more of the old Italian features than the town people, the pure type, as Pacciani says, of the language, preserved in greatest purity away from the cities, where it is corrupted.

"The duke was present, with ten dragoons behind him ; many of the nobility with liveried servants, and I noticed one shining negro, magnificently turbaned and shawled, with a crooked sword by his side.

"*January 27th.*—Finished to-day my picture, and fairly to my satisfaction, with extravagant compliments from others. In catching the expressions, and the old, rich tone of the original, I have not been wholly unsuccessful, and these are the points in which most of the copies I have seen fail.*

"*January 28th.*—To-day is charming. I have always had a childish impatience to see the statue of the Apennines, as I have looked at it when a child in my 'Wonders of the World.' So to-day Percival and I took a *calèche* and drove to Pratolino, six miles to the north. The landscape was lovely, with many Doughty-like effects upon the sun-smitten hills.

"We found the garden in the English style, like a beautiful forest, and wandered through its Cretan intricacies till, at last, we came to the sheet of water where Pater Apenninus 'se tollit ad auras.' This statue is by John of Bologna, and curiously constructed of masses of rock and brick plastered over. It did not seem sixty feet high, as asserted, but Mr. Percival, sitting on one of the feet, was scarcely bigger than one toe of it. There is much poetry in the idea; the genius looks so reverend with time and hoary with sleet and snow, his stony beard sweeping to the ground, and his matted locks overhanging his ancient visage. Water trickles from the mound on which he rests. His face is painted to imitate life; the rest looks as gray and grim as it ought. We ascended be-

* The copy of the Seggiola made by Mr. Appleton is now in the possession of his brother, Mr. Nathan Appleton. It hangs at present in the gallery of the Museum of Fine Arts, Boston.

16

hind, amid the braces which bind the statue, into the head, and, looking out of the eyes, enjoyed a fine view of Fiesole and the valley.

"*January 29th.*—A thousand things to do—bills to pay, neglected sights to kill off, cards to leave, and clothes to pack. I went with Madame Curtis to see my Seggiola in its frame. We both were pleased with the *frame*, and she admired the picture.

"I visited the gallery, to see the jewel-room I have neglected till now.

"'No more, oh, never more!' what sadness in the words! I was wretched to think I should never be again before these glorious things. Madame de Staël says—

'Voyager est le plus triste de tous les plaisirs'—
and, though I do not fully accord with her reasons, yet the grief of parting, so often to be repeated, makes it so indeed.

"I believe I have never looked with such fondness, such intense and melancholy enthusiasm, upon the glories of the gallery as to-day. I lingered over the round and flesh-like limbs of the Venus, the fearful curiosity of the Slave, the sweetness of Correggio, as friends I would not leave, but was forced from. As I moved up the gallery, the care-worn brow of Cæsar, full of painful study, occupied my attention. Then came the great Pompey; the beautiful child, Germanicus; the fat, round face of the baby Nero—no trace of vice yet in those infantile features. I stood before the odious Messalina; she has a mouth sunk and dimpled, and her head behind is, according to phrenology, licentious. It was with pleasure, on the other side, to turn to the amiable Trajan—one can not look into his face without loving him—to the stern Severus, and the sharp, Wellington features of Nerva. There is more excitement in running over a gallery of Roman busts than can be got in any other way. It is history in marble. They are full of truth, and one reads the satire of Tacitus and the judgment of Gibbon in every head.

"After dinner, a last visit from Pacciani, dressed *come un orso*, and bearing the marks of intelligence and dissipation both in his eyes and features. He has 'narrowly escaped being a great man,' as the Irishman said. He was an intimate friend of Shelley, and gave me the full story of Shelley's shipwreck.

"*January 31st, Friday.*—This morning, at half-past eight, with a brilliant sun to encourage us against Friday proverbs, we took leave of Florence. Our carriage is light and commodious, and, when heaped with all our traveling apparatus, looks indeed like a long journey. Portmanteaux and sacks upon top; Mary's hoop slung on in front, behind Gaetano and Pauline. The interior, besides ourselves, is full of

books, and a *canestra* of all the little wants gastronomic of an Italian journey. Our big-footed *vetturino*
cracks his whip over the backs of four fat, round
horses, with their tails tied in trig knots, like one who
girds himself for serious battle.

" My parting with my landladies was dolorous.
Tears were plentiful, and I only gave them consola-
tion by promising to send remembrances by Percival."

Finding his friends the Curtises in Florence was
one of the happy chances always befalling Mr. Appleton through life. Mr. T. B. Curtis, his lovely wife,
and little daughter, were old Boston friends ; they
were upon the packet Philadelphia, whose voyage had
given to Thomas his first delightful impression of
ocean travel ; and now he came across them, after
six months of Europe, unexpectedly. They met with
great satisfaction in Florence, " told each other," Mrs.
Curtis wrote in her journal, "all the news we had
from home in letters, all talking at once ; and the
next day the same items passed for news again."

CHAPTER XI

1834.

Now began a charming journey through romantic
scenes full of classical associations.   The big carriage,
besides Mr. and Mrs. Curtis and Miss Mary, held Mr.
Appleton and his friend Mr. Percival ; so that a congenial and sympathetic party was formed, of which
the members shared the novelty of the scenes through
which they were passing—not hackneyed, it must be
remembered, and made commonplace at that time, by
countless guide-books and notes of travel.   Virgil and
Byron were their forerunners, furnishing them with quo-
tations apt, and indicating to them where to dilate with
the right emotion.   They drove up the Val d' Arno at
its loveliest ; through cultivated country, where old,
brown, castellated towns peered out from masses of
pale olive-trees—the soul of Etrurian scenery.   The
fruit was just being gathered by men in the trees, and
girls with baskets below.   They drove through an-

cient towns—Arezzo, Castiglione, Cortona—delighted all day by the charm of the scenery; amused at night, rather than discouraged, by the discomfort of the inns. At the Papal frontier they stopped to have trunks examined, and the gentlemen walked on to scan the view of the Thrasymenian plain.

"Everything about here," says the journal, "has an air profoundly old; the very ground is hillocked and worn as by the plows of eternity. Every foot of it is kneaded with the dust of a hero; the trees gnarled and crooked, the peasants brown and rusty; the very buildings seem to grow from the soil and be of equal antiquity.

"This battle-field is one of the most interesting in history, and it is perfectly comprehensible. I could see the low and shaggy hills on which Hannibal had his horse and troops hidden; and the narrow, foggy plain, sweeping in an amphitheatre to the shores of the lake. The ground is gullied by rains, and broken into rugged and irregular tumuli, where the affrighted Romans were slaughtered without being able to see their foes or to form their ranks. It is, indeed, '*locus insidiis aptus*,' and all remains now as then, except that a peaceful fertility has sprung from that day's carnage. A brown peasant-girl, driving an obstinate flock of black pigs over the rough ground, was a sort of caricature of the flight of the luckless Romans. I could fancy the shallow current of the streamlet crimson with Roman blood, and the shores of the lake heaped with Roman shields ; but now, as the Childe sings—

> ' Far other scene is Thrasymene—
> Her lake a sheet of silver, and her plain
> Rent by no ravage but the gentle plow.'

"PERUGIA, *February 1st.*—I think we shall scarcely find any older people than this. The shops bear such names as Cæsar and Pompey, and the cart of the peasant is almost exactly the old Roman car, with low, heavy wheels and triangular body. In a chapel are two pictures—the first by Raphael, the other by Pietro Perugino. The church of San Pietro is perfectly covered with pictures ; several admirable ones of Pietro. One by his master was curious, as showing that he has made as great advances from the stiff and colorless mannerism of this old master, as his illustrious pupil, Raphael, from his own.

". . . On descending the hill from Perugia, as we crossed a bridge, a boy cried out, '*Eccolo, il Tivere !*' It was an interesting moment, and I was glad to find it was not the pitiful stream I had feared. It was not '*flavum Tiberim,*' but of a pretty green, and as large as the Arno. Some miles farther on we came to the banks of the sacred Clitumnus, a brook of sunniest

waters, and now, as in Virgil's time, with its banks of
a living green, and white oxen :

> ' Hinc albi, Clitumne greges et maxima taurus
> Victima, saepe tuo perfusi flumine sacra.'

"*February 3d.*—We drove to the falls of Terni,
from the old town, through a twisted grove of '*fron-
dentes olivæ*'; walked through orange-groves until we
came to a most romantic wood of ilexes. The scenery
about was majestic, with mountains soaring to heaven,
and piled up in all variety of shade and outline; the
green and glancing river rushing below, through rocks
worn and hollowed. We gathered many flowers, and
ran over the hills till we reached the grand point where,
as the guide said, all painters sketch the fall.

"Beggars are rife on these hills, and have all ways
of earning their money. One spreads olive-branches
to make a seat, another sweeps the platform, a third
presents a bit of petrified earth, and all unite in their
clamor and tenacity.

"I sat on the bank and read aloud Byron's description to my companions. It is beautifully true,
only giving rather too savage a tone to this charming
scenery. I see not how Addison could find anything
here to warrant him in calling it the passage to the infernal regions. The height of the *chute*, we were told,
is as many feet as there are days in the year. The

river suddenly tumbles from the mountain's head into a chasm where boils up an unceasing shower of spray

'That is an eternal April to the ground,'

giving to the grass a luxuriant emerald tint. It then slides over the rocks in two other falls of silver, whose grace and lines, constantly vacillating, form a beautiful contrast to the thunder and lightning of the first. On every side the scene is glorious. We climbed to the top, not equal to the lower view, but with a rich, Claude-like picture of the plain and town.

"*February 4th.*—Though the road was very heavy, Percival and I walked on, rewarded by a magnificent view on descending to the plain, through which in graceful windings meanders a lovely river. I asked an old peasant-woman what name it bore. '*Se chiama il fiume*' was the only answer I could get from her. Soon we met a man, who said it was the Tiber! To think that a peasant-slave should live on the borders of this mother of streams, and not know it as other than 'the river'!

"*February 5th.*—A date never to be forgotten, for last night I slept in Rome! Walking as usual beyond the carriage, Percival and I advanced amid the morning fogs, having started thus early to be at Rome betimes. It was imprudent getting beyond the carriage just here, as there is special danger, for a straggling oak-wood, full of low brush, near, is a famous haunt for banditti, and Gasparo regaled us with stories of persons variously ill-treated therein. Only last week, on the Siena road, a courier, with two Englishmen, was stopped. We were more fortunate. We noted every mile-stone that brought us nearer the city, and fancied that many were the old Roman ones. Our excitement was constantly on the increase, and we rushed on at last to gain the view which we were sure of having from the hill-top. This summit was Soracte. My eye caught instantly, far in the blue distance, amid the sparkle of its palaces, that illustrious dome which Buonarotti hung in air ; at the same moment flashed upon me the long, white line of the Mediterranean. I cried out to Percival as he came running up—

'The Niobe of nations, there she stands !'

We chose a flowery seat and gave way to the intensity of our feelings. For a long, silent hour we were indulging in the excitement of the situation, calling up all those bright things that make Rome the most interesting city on earth. It is not sentiment, it is not an artfully stimulated ebullition of romance, but awe and sublime joy which every student must feel when looking his first upon the 'lone mother of dead empires.'"

In this enthusiastic spirit the party entered Rome

at a fortunate moment, near the close of the Carnival, just as the *Corso di cavalli* was beginning ; the whole square of the Popolo was crammed with carriages and people, every balcony was full. The scene was far more gay than the languid merry-making of the Florentine Carnival ; there was every possible drollery of costume, and the air was buzzing with the flight of *dolces* and the chattering of the masks. The war was carried on with great spirit.

"*February 7th.*—Without wishing any guide, we wandered down the Corso. Shattered columns and mutilated statues, the façade of a temple protruding from some stall or shop, served to link us with the idea we wished to realize ; wandering on, we passed the magnificent column of Antoninus, now 'purified' by the Pope, and surmounted by a bronze of Saint Paul. More than half-way down the street, we turned to the left and came upon the Forum of Trajan, its massy granite columns lying scattered or broken round the area, with at one end the famed column. I need only glance at the antiquities we fell upon, for beyond all was the prince of ruins—the Coliseum. I have no time to express the emotions I felt at first standing within that terrific area where the blood of slaves and martyrs has so often run at the feet of thousands."

After much difficulty, Mr. Appleton succeeded in finding excellent rooms in the Via Tritone for himself and Mr. Percival, up three long flights of stairs. He says :

" My old woman seems honest and kind, and we trust that our ox-eyed boot-black will not steal anything. My landlady *says* I may leave all my things unlocked ; but I am too old for that."

On the last day of the Carnival, to give it a *coup de grace*, the whole party determined to go to the masked ball of the evening.

"We supplied ourselves with dresses from the shops, and put them on in Mr. Curtis's parlor. Our toilets furnished us with much laughter before we stood complete. I was a sailor in blue stripes, with Percival's Tyrolese belt round my waist, and a straw hat on my head ; Mr. Curtis was very droll without a mask, as the veritable Madame Starke" (the writer of the only guide-book for Italy then in use), "with Mary's cottage-bonnet on the back of his head, Pauline's gear for his female-ship, our lunch-basket on his arm, containing a mirror and the latest edition of madame's valuable work. Percival dressed as a dowager of the last century. At the ball we chanced to meet with no acquaintances, but had a deal of fun with the masks. Percival waltzed *à l'antique*, Mr.

Curtis told folks the price of washing, and I halloed my brother ship-mates. It was very crowded and hot, though brilliant. Mr. Curtis was half afraid of meeting the other Dromio, Starke the veritable. A man came up to him, felt his pulse seriously, and said, ' *Siete uomo !* ' "

Lent now began, and Mr. Appleton, without distractions of society and the theatre, could apply himself to the wonders of Rome, which are fully described, as he visited them from day to day, in the journal, as well as the studios of artists and firesides of friends.

" *February* 13*th.*—This morning we visited Thorwaldsen's studio, and spent much time there. He has many rooms, all full of unfinished works. An immense *basso-rilievo*, and the twelve apostles, for the King of Denmark, fill several rooms. We saw a fine statue of Byron, much admired a full-length likeness of a Russian princess, pensively touching her finger to her cheek, and with a figure of Innocence. There were some miniatures of the Lion of Lucerne. Thorwaldsen is very like the busts of him ; the image of a patriarch, with a strong expression of amiability in his features. He wore a hairy Danish cap, quite droll—his silvery hair escaped from it upon his neck."

At St. Peter's, on a first visit, he says :
17

"We had no time to study out the Titanic groups on the ceiling of the 'Last Judgment,' but merely felt the usual emotion of disappointment. There is much wanting to this performance—held to be the highest effort of human genius. It has little to which humanity can attach itself; and it is with a feeling of doubt, and a suspicion that the artist was not of the first cast of mind, that one examines the details of the great fresco.

"Jackson talks much of Shelley. He knew him well; says that he was a perfect child in his habits. He remembers Shelley telling him how fine a death he thought it would be to be shipwrecked in the bay of Spezzia. Poor lad! He learned to know too well.

". . . While we were visiting the Palatine to-day, we made the alarming discovery that Mr. Curtis had lost our inseparable Starke. We were in distress; but on driving back to the Farnese Garden were fortunate enough to find her enjoying a *tête-à-tête* with my volume of Byron.

"*February 24th.*—Two nights since I visited the Coliseum by moonlight. It was one night only before full moon, and darkness seemed to have been annihilated; long before the sun set, the effulgence of the moon seemed to rival it, and the garish, rosy hues of day changed, without death, into the broad silver glow of an Italian night. The night skies here are very peculiar; they have no share of the obscurity of other lands, but their deep azure has a transparency and life that are inexpressibly beautiful. Byron knew what this was when he wrote the line—

'Hues that have words and speak to us of heaven.'

"We drove to the amphitheatre, and found, to our surprise, nearly a dozen carriages drawn up before the entrance. I thought the number of visitors would kill the solitude, but they only enforced the vastness and grandeur of the pile. Their voices were at times heard as from a far mountain, and their torches, as they burst from under some gap, poured a shower of light upon the old, haggard arches, their red play forming picturesque effects of *chiaro scuro*, that contrasted with the coldness of the moonlight. The effect from the moon was that all was light or all shadow; the ribs of the seats running down to the arena seemed restored, the seats were in shadow, and the simplicity and force of the contrasts accorded with the sublimity of the structure. The contrast of the present and the past was full of poetry, thus to be contemplating, under a melancholy moon, in mournful silence, the arena which once rang to the applause of thousands peopling its stately walls. We joined a party also furnished with lanterns, and rambled everywhere. Every moment the effect was new and delightful. The vivid light broke through the darkness of the circular corridors in white patches upon the pavement; on every side rose arches upon arches. The stars 'twinkled through the loops of time.' Jupiter, especially, shone with fine brilliancy through an arch upon the northern side.

"Rome is now a city of artists; they have a delightful society of their own, and are held in high esteem. The name *artist* is the best passport to favor and kindness here. They have not the jealousy and ill-blood that mar other professions, but assist one another with the greatest good-will and *esprit de corps*. One can not take a walk without seeing some fellow seated on a ruined column, with his colors beside him, sketching some temple or group, unmolested and abstracted. The galleries are full of them copying, and weeks may be spent visiting their studios. There is, too, a race of beings called models, a profession that exists by the artists. One man has a fine head of hair, this other a well-turned arm; such a girl has a noble head, and such a one a good body. Each lives upon some natural beauty. A man who is slovenly and miserable in all other respects, keeps his beard long and unsullied; it is his stock in trade.

"*February 26th.*—To-day, again, we visited the artists; refreshed ourselves with the sweet things of

Wyatt and Gibson. While we were at Gibson's, a boy came in with two snow-white pigeon-wings, to be modeled for Cupid!"

The party left Rome for an excursion of a few days to Tivoli, Adrian's Villa, and other objects of interest in the vicinity of Rome. When they returned they found, to their regret, that during their absence an application for audience with the Pope had been answered, and the day before fixed for the ceremony. They had lost the chance, by being away. They wrote for another audience; but the answer was, "Too late."

"*March 6th.*—Yesterday we ascended St. Peter's. The day was fine. The ascent is of brick, and without steps—an inclined plane as far as the roof of the body of the church. The apostles, on nearer acquaintance, we found to be rough giants, and the leads a perfect town, covered with sheds and corners without end. When standing within the railing of the dome, it was terrific to look below. Men were mice, and the marbles of the floor, at that distance, seemed a calico pattern. Above it was as if 'heaven were mining in.' All the dome is mosaic; the bits are nearly half an inch square. It looks rough when seen close at hand, but very delicate at a distance. The ladies held fast to the railing, swimming with giddiness.

"From the lantern the view is very extensive, and we saw distinctly the sunny Mediterranean.

"The rest of the day I gave to the Vatican, no longer a maze to me. I spent some hours in the Sistine Chapel. As I expected, I have completely changed my first ideas about this. I fully believe in the pre-eminence of Buonarotti, and almost own it superhuman for any man to execute the ceiling in nineteen months. The colors are much faded, but seem to have been worthy the drawing. In fact, after coming from these grand forms, I almost condemn Raphael for careless and trivial drawing. The 'Last Judgment' is so very startling, one with difficulty gets over his first ideas of it ; but the more I study it, the more I am reconciled to the figure and attitude of the Saviour. He is full of an anger which is foreign to .him, but is justly excited by the wickedness of the condemned ; it enforces a more salutary and impressive moral than the sedate meekness with which he is usually invested.

"The 'Stanze' of Raphael I can not too much admire. The 'Incendio del Borgo,' the 'Chase of the Wicked from the Temple,' and the 'Miracle of Bolsena,' are among the finest works of this wonderful youth. What wonder he died at thirty-seven, consumed and exhausted by the ardent visions that every day grew more vivid to his fancy! The sword destroyed the scabbard too soon for the delight of our race, if not too soon for the full illustration of how near to angelic genius the creature may ascend.

"I was joined in the galleries by a priest, who was a droll character, and not a little crazy. He made the strangest remarks upon the pictures, and constantly bothered me with polemic subtilties. He wished much to know what was my idea of the particular nature of the fruit with which Eve tempted Adam. . . .

"To-day we visited Pinelli. I have had a desire to make his acquaintance, as he is an original. We found him modeling some of his famous terra-cotta groups, and it was delightful to watch the stroke of his stick. He is a perfect master of Roman character, and every dash he made was happy, bringing out some new expression. His manner is artificially brusque but his genius is marked.

"From him we visited Severn, the young artist who attended Keats in his last moments. In the parlor was a picture of his from the 'Ancient Mariner,' poetically treated. Standing upon the ribs of the specter-ship, Life in Death holds up the die and exclaims, 'I've won! I've won!' Severn's pictures have a rich manner of coloring, though he appears as yet young in art. There was a portrait of Keats which represented him less thin, though pale, than I had imagined him, and three likenesses of Trelawney. He has a fine head; but no one would imagine him an Englishman; his locks and mustache are black as ink, and his hue and expression are Greek. I spent several hours with Severn in most agreeable conversation. He told me a thousand things about Keats, and regaled me with choice Falernian, very like claret, a present from a friend of Keats. We talked of Allston, Leslie, and poor Newton, and a thousand things, and parted with mutual wishes that we had sooner met.

" *March 8th.*—Already the fever of departure has begun. I look upon all the old familiar columns and ruins as if to rivet them in my memory, since so soon they will be seen by me no more. In some places we have been taking up dropped stitches, revisiting the Vatican. We warmed ourselves before the Apollo, the Niobe, the Aldobrandini Marriage, the Minerva, etc. We roamed again over St. Peter's, and gained permission to descend into the old church built by Constantine. There we saw, among others, the tomb of Hadrian IV, the only English Pope, and the tombs of the Pretender and his brother Henry.

" *March 9th, Sunday.*—The last day ! We none of us had seen the Pope ; and as to go to Rome and not see the Pope has become a proverb to prove a fool, we determined to-day to be at the Sistine Chapel. We walked up the magnificent entrance to the Vatican through ranged files of the antique and many-colored Swiss Guard. Their costume is most gaudy, and unbecoming a Pope's attendants. They carry halberds, and their red-plumed caps, slashed breeches, and ruffled necks, make them look like relics of the fourteenth century, as in fact they are. . . .

"We were well tired when the rites were over, but my time was not lost, for I was studying all the while the wonders of the ceiling overhead.

"I have paid for all my mosaics and cameos. Our imperial seems made *aposta* for our prints, of which we have bought a large supply.

"*March 10th.*—We drove silently down the Corso, looking our last at the columns, and when we swept under the Coliseum it was with sad feelings. We traversed the desolate part of Rome on the southern side, where the finest churches seem planted in a desert.

Mr. Percival left the party at the end of their visit in Rome, remaining there while they went on. His place in the carriage was taken by Mr. Barnard, who had been found by his friends very ill on their first arrival in Rome. He was now well enough to be removed, although almost too weak for the journey.

They were now on the way to Naples. The first night was spent at Velletri; then they crossed the Pontine Marshes; and beyond Terracina they came suddenly upon the sea.

"Our feelings were tumultuous. We rushed down to the soft, sandy shore, and almost kissed for joy the ripples that broke upon the beach. We listened to the old familiar music of the waves as to the welcome of an ancient friend. We sat upon the rocks, and fancied ourselves at Nahant. The rocks were redder, and the sea was bluer, and the far headlands wore a different, soft, sunny clearness, but the dashing of the billows was the same, and it seemed as if they must be the ones that had so often broken at my feet. Vessels skimmed along .the horizon, and I watched them as if they were messengers from home. I had touched upon a sudden spring of warm home-feelings and old memories.

"*March 12th.*—To-day we left St. Peter's estate and entered the kingdom of Naples. Our passports were examined, and we lost half an hour, but nothing further. Passing on, the scenery became deliciously Italian. We have seemed to note the increased tropicalness at every post. Now we have reached a clime where a serene and languishing air steeps everything in sunny indolence, where the far sea wears the look of *lapis lazuli*, and over the senses is wafted a blended perfume by every breeze. We went through a perfect orange and lemon grove, these fairy fruits gilding the deep green. A variety of flowers I knew not were under foot. In short, we had entered the garden of the earth, or, as the natives say, '*un pezzetto di cielo caduto in terra.*'

"As we drove up a hill once celebrated for banditti, we remarked two fine caverns where doubtless these gentry stowed their spoils. Gasparo says he once was robbed in this very place, and soundly bastinadoed—although he is a stout fellow! We stopped at Mola, most gloriously situated on the Mediterranean. Upon the terrace of our hotel the view was strikingly beautiful. Under and around us was all the glory of the Mediterranean. A number of Claude-like islands hung upon the horizon. One of the farthest, dimly seen through a cloud of sharp-sailed feluccas, snowy as sea-fowl upon the waters, was Capri; on the left was Procida, and above it, still farther coastward, Vesuvius reared its bifurcate head, its faint white smoke at times perceptible to the eye. On our right, far into the sea, stretched the bold town of Gaeta. Behind it rises a gentle hill. Surrounding our terrace a grove of oranges invited us to pluck, and the waves in long, silver ridges broke at our feet. All that my eye embraced, as the scene of the last book of the 'Æneid,' has been immortalized by Virgil."

With as little delay as possible, to spare fatigue to Mr. Barnard, the travelers went on to the city of Naples, which they reached on the 14th of March. They established themselves with the caution and experience of old travelers, and devoted nearly three weeks to the city and its environs, although the weather was dull, the summit of Vesuvius veiled in mist, and beggars were rampant. But weather was of no importance when once they were within the walls of the Museo Borbonico, where there was enough to occupy the mind and delight the eye for any length of time. To their vexation, a *fête*-day closed the doors of the museum on their second attempt.

"All the public buildings and many shops are shut. We made instead several visits. Called on the Jacksons, and found them melancholy as cats, on account of the weather."

The next day they returned to the inspection of the Museo.

"*March 21st.*—To-day it is my fate to describe the most *blasé* excursion in the world, one that is quite threadbare even to myself: we went to *Baiæ*."

Another day was devoted to shops; lava and coral ornaments tempted them not in vain, and the Etruscan vases of Giustiniani. The weather continued stormy and the sea roared beneath their windows "like uncaged lions."

He says of Cumæ : " The Cave of the Sibyl is no great affair. It seems to have been the city residence of her ladyship, whence she went to bathe at the Tartarean Lake."

" EASTER - SUNDAY, *March* 31*st.* — To-day is my birthday, and the anniversary of my departure from New York. Certainly one year has taken off not a little of the edge of youthful adventure, not a little of the *vivida vis* of life. I got a letter from Percival to-day. He is pleased with Holy Week in Rome, and will join me here for Sicily."

On the first of April, the Curtises and Mr. Barnard left Naples in the Francesco Primo for Leghorn; but the rough sea prevented much progress, and the steamer, having received an injury to her piston, was obliged to put back. Mr. Appleton, on his return from Pæstum, an expedition of two days, found them still at Naples; he also found his friend Percival, and was ready to depart.

" *April* 5*th.*—In the greatest hurry, got my passport completed, took leave again of the Curtises, and all my other friends, and, leaving all my baggage but a *sac de nuit* and my haversack, went on board the Real Ferdinando with Percival. The paddles flew round, and we extricated ourselves from the forest of masts, with a fine wind on our quarter, which, as both our sails
18

were spread, aided us much. We had about seventy on board, most of them English. The notable Madame Starke was of the party ; I was very attentive to her, for which she expressed much gratitude, and invited me to her house at Sorrento. She is a very different body from what I had imagined She can not be far from seventy-five, stout, and with a face good-humoredly ugly, seamed and burned with much travel. She did not seem very intelligent, though pretty learned, and quite feeble with age. She was surrounded by toadies older and uglier than herself. She had made a capital mistake in bringing the body of her carriage to sleep in ! It was of no use,' and it caused her much trouble to send it back from Messina.''

They passed between Scylla and Charybdis, without experiencing any of the dangers which have made these names famous, and the lovely Messina was reached. The steamer stopped, and they were surrounded with boats pouring forth Sicilian cries to attract attention. Mr. Percival and Mr. Appleton were rowed ashore, and found themselves upon the soil of the garden of Proserpine.

This voyage was a round trip ; the steamer touched at the various ports of Sicily, allowing, at the least, an interval long enough for the passengers to inspect each place. Catania and Syracuse were thus briefly visited ; they then crossed to Malta in a heavy sea, which caused many of the passengers to take to their beds. At Malta they found English carpets and English hospitality, called for a bottle of English ale, and felt quite at home.

On the return they stopped at Girgenti, and passed several days in Palermo, of which the bay, in Mr. Appleton's estimation, is more beautiful than that of Naples.

"On the morning of the 29th," he writes, "we were skimming between the romantic heights of Amalfi and Capri, with the huge bay just in front. We came cracking up the gulf, old black Vesuvius looking a little ill, and not discharging his smoke so stoutly as before. Fresh from Palermo, I could venture an opinion, and boldly now assert, that bay to excel this of Naples. This glaring white town, the unrelieved brown of the hills, are inferior to the Sicilian beauties of Panormus. I began at once to prepare for departure next day. I visited Mr. John Lowell, and listened to his tales of travel. He has an artist with him on purpose to sketch for him, and intended going through the East with a cavalcade of twelve horses.

"*April 30th.*—At ten, all things in order, I found

myself on board the Francesco Primo, a little French steamer of sixty tons.   It may be imagined I had had enough of steaming, but the comfort of quiet sketching and reading makes me ever enjoy it.   Our party, too, was good.   Folks in a packet begin by staring, and end by shaking hands.   Mrs. Gower, the clever wife of a Leghorn merchant, I had a legal title to be attentive to, and a blonde, blue-eyed German girl, and a newly married English lady, did not take my knightly devoirs in dudgeon.   We jounced out of the bay and waved our adieus to bella Napoli.   The proverb, ' Vedi Napoli e poi mori,' I felt not inclined to follow ; I can not say I left it with regret.   Our sail was delightful, and unwillingly we retired to our couches.   I had come so late as to be forced to take a berth in the second cabin, eating and sitting with the first-cabin passengers.   When I descended the narrow stairway at midnight, I was reminded of the Campo Santo at Naples.   In the dim lantern's light lay two or three gaping servant-maids, children were sprinkled over them, and around, sailors, waiters, and unfortunates like myself, all in their clothes, assumed various awkward attitudes.   At the sides, more lucky ones were laid in berths, like the dead in the catacombs of Syracuse, with as much space, and as silent.

" Despite the prospect, next morning I had to thank the Virgin for a quiet and unbitten night."

The steamer stopped at Civita Vecchia, where all went ashore; but at noon they were off again. Mr. Appleton read the "Pilgrims of the Rhine," while Mrs. Gower embroidered, and the doctor sketched her. Before night they had glimpses of Elba and Corsica—"the propinquent cradle and cage," and, at seven the next morning, were riding in the open road-stead of Leghorn, amid *feluccas* and men-of-war.

"The Baron de Poilly and I had combined, and we now took rooms in common. The baron is a Frenchman of the best sort, witty and full of good-humor—in short, a charming companion."

A rapid excursion to Pisa, in a *calèche*, gave Mr. Appleton a chance to see the famous leaning tower, the Campo Santo, and the palaces of the city. He came back in time to see somewhat of Leghorn; called upon Mrs. Gower, now at home in tasteful apartments. "She showed me the table of Byron, a round, neat one, on which he wrote 'Don Juan.' I envied madame this relic. It was left by Byron to Mr. Gower's partner, who received his last letter from Greece."

One more night on board the steamer brought him to Genoa.

"Here the baron surprised me with an early visit,

and an offer quite pressing that I would join him in his phaeton, and drive to Marseilles along the Cornice, that we might enjoy it together, while his servant Edouard should take my place in the steamer. I consented, and we arranged matters. I had only time to see some of the interesting objects in Genoa—a Madonna by Paget, and a relief of Michael Angelo."

This excursion proved delightful, as many other travelers have found it, the road hanging constantly upon cliffs over the Mediterranean. In the midst of a description of it, the journal stops abruptly, and, after a few . . . , is resumed in Paris on the 22d of May :

" Alas for my neglected diary ! Paris and Parisians, bewildering, have quite driven its existence from my memory. I find it impossible to retrace my impressions of fair Nice, industrious Toulon, and revolutionary Lyons, and must resume my tale in the very heart of the Frog nation."

CHAPTER XII.

1834.

Dramatis Personæ:

The BARON DE POILLY.
His daughter CÉCILE.
Her husband CHARLES.
DUCHESS OF FITZ-JAMES, the mother of Charles.
LUCILE, younger daughter of the Baron.
HENRI, younger son of the Baron.
Governess.

MR. APPLETON has described in later years the beginning of his acquaintance with the Baron de Poilly, which grew into one of the pleasantest relations of his lifetime. " Gliding along," he says, " under a Mediterranean sun, I was making, with the dreamy activity of the traveler, a sketch of a picturesque person in the steamer which was carrying me from Civita Vecchia to Marseilles. My subject was an alert, active Frenchman, with a flat traveling-casquette, and a ribbon at his button-hole, which somchow seemed to have been worn in imperial days, and on the field of battle. Such proved afterward to be the case. After a fashion, a tolerable likeness was accomplished. This led to that easy acquaintance and fellowship so natural to unoccupied minds, when congenial. . . . We disembarked at Genoa, and went forward by land accordingly. The lovely coast, where our post-horses ran on a narrow ledge, smooth as a floor, with precipices and summits towering above us, scalloped into little indenting bays, each with its village as a center, made every moment a surprise.

"We dashed across France ; trying in Burgundy, as the accomplished baron insisted, the cheap *crus* of the country, to test his statement that this native wine has a flavor of the soil, and a homely merit of its own. We went twenty miles out of our way to Mélun, to try its famous eels. Finally, Paris was reached.

"Then, for the first time, I really heard French. The grace and charm of it, as spoken by the family into which I was introduced, I had previously no idea of. And the pretty, old-fashioned, friendly, family ways were delightful. Games, in the evening, whose childishness would have repelled a Briton ; dances, in which old and young shared, their only *raison d'être* being the seeming cheerfulness by which they were moved ; amusing talk with the duke—for there was a duke in the center of the circle, who, in the house of peers, led the Carlist chivalry of France. These were all novelties to me, freshly delightful, and justly seeming the fair spoil of travel. At that time Lafayette died. With a dignified wave of his hand, my duke permitted me, as an American, to join the funeral *cortége*.

"'The most dangerous man in France,' he said; 'and he is well laid away in his family vault in the Picpus graveyard. With him lies buried the republic; and in America, even, you will soon be of our opinion, and desire the dignity and comfort of a monarchy.'"

Mr. Appleton enjoyed the society of these charming friends as long as they remained in Paris; a fortnight after their departure, he followed them, by cordial invitation, to Picardy, where his journal is resumed:

"FOLEMBRAY, *June 5th.*—Two days ago, at eight in the morning, I was glad to leave the steamy air and stunning streets of Paris, in the diligence for Compiègne. The features of our drive were those universal to a French highway—a huge, wide road with a raised, rumbling *pavé* in the middle, flanked as far as the weary eye can reach with files of elm, or that nuisance of France, the poplar. Villages numberless we went through, of equal beauty—or want of

it, as you please; in one of them we met a bridal-
party, all with big bouquets in their hands.

"Passed the night at Compiègne, and went on the
next day to Chauny, a town of about five thousand
inhabitants, full of glass-factories. There I borrowed
a chamber at a *café*, and made my toilet, while I
hired a lad to hire a vehicle to carry me to Folembray, which is off the diligence-route, about two
leagues away.

"After passing through a lovely country, I turned
a corner, and saw the house of my friends afar at the
end of a long forest of magnificent trees. I jumped
out of the gig in my ardor, and hurried forward. On
ascending a swell, the whole estate burst upon me in
its loveliness; at my feet was spread a little lake, and
on its farther side, behind a quaint old dove-cote and
various out-buildings, rose the elegant house of the
Baron de Poilly. It is large and square, with a terrace supported by columns in front. The moment
I had mounted the slope, I was seen, and hats and
handkerchiefs were waved to me from the windows.
I rushed forward to embrace friends as kind as I
ever had, and ones of whom I am proud, as their
acquaintance is all of my own making. They all
met me in the court-yard, and Dash and Love leaped
upon me with affection. Edouard, too, the valet,
welcomed me with his civilities. I was instantly

carried into the house and installed in a room next the baron.   They all took me over the house, which is furnished in a style of simple elegance.   The baron's apartment is decorated with boars' tusks, stag-horns, and the like.

"Instantly a thousand plans were projected for my amusement.   After a bottle of cider, they all accompanied me over the grounds.

"We passed over a lovely lawn to a white bridge spanning the little lake.   By winding paths and tufted groves of various trees, we wound up the side of the hill behind the house, and visited a neat and pretty garden, and, passing through *berceaux* cut in the forest, we gained the height whence an enchanting prospect burst upon me.   At our feet was the little village of Folembray, of which the baron is the lord and patron ; it has only nine hundred inhabitants.   The valley before us was full of round and verdant forests, and bits of water running off into the far blue ; while on the left, from the crest of a bold rock, rose the fine ruins of the château Coucy, completing an unrivaled picture.

"We returned, and horses were ordered.   In a trice the groom brought four to the door, and madame appeared, lovely in full riding-dress.   She tells me the family are called *Minotaurs*, on account of their fondness for riding.   We mounted and rode through a

rich plain till we reached the Coucy cliff, up whose
green side we wound, the baron nodding on all sides
to the passers.

"The castle is the finest ruin I have seen in
France. The Coucys were the tyrants of this prov-
ince, and waged constant war with the suzerains of
the environs. There is a horrible legend of Raoul
de Coucy, who made his wife eat the heart of an
enemy! Nothing can be imagined stronger than this
workmanship of the thirteenth century. It has suffered severely from an earthquake, but is still full of
interest. Everywhere are little niches in rich Gothic,
giving an idea of what the whole must have been. In
the small town on the right hand is an *oubliette*. This
tower retains its frescoes.

"We returned by a circuitous route through a
charming country. Suddenly a thunder-shower passed
over and broke upon our heads. We were almost
pelted from our saddles, and, spurring on, pushed like
the wind for home-shelter. Madame bore herself most
gallantly. Every one laughed at us as we dashed
through the villages. At last we gained the *basse-
cour*, and hurried in to change our habiliments. Soon
we were laughing it over in the parlor. Delicious is
the view from this room, and most comfortable it is,
with flowers and prints, and drawings of the baron's
favorite dogs. We dined capitally, at half-past five,

vegetables, in honor of my English notions, being served with every course. Afterward, we smoked on the terrace, while Madame Cécile made a cap for her baby. The evening was spent, without candles, chatting. The *gouvernante* told me she felt perfectly acquainted with me at once, principally because I had been educated after the Fellenberg manner !

" To finish the evening, after a game of billiards, they got out the rare books of the library. We all retired early—about ten, and so ends one of the pleasantest days of my life.

"*June 6th.*—By accident, I was dressed to-day before the baron, entered his room and found him reading. At eight I joined Charles and Cécile, who went to the lake to fish for carp and *brochet*, of which the lake is full. While they fished, I took the boat and rowed out into the lake to sketch the house and this group of fishers. They had no great good fortune except bites, and Cécile returned to the house in de·spair. Charles soon after was rewarded by jerking into the air an enormous carp, which, however, escaped him. We occupied ourselves as each saw fit till breakfast—sewing, walking, reading, sketching. They had sent me coffee at eight, therefore I was quite equal to awaiting lunch ; I sketched the wood-scene from the bridge, with the swans.

" Lunch was, as in England, copious and almost

a dinner, but here it is a breakfast. Capital potatoes, the first I had seen in France. After this meal, a gentleman was descried descending the hill, and all ran to meet him, as he is the chief friend of the family. He ate bread and milk in the arbor for his breakfast. The baron then took me to visit his glass-factories, which are just behind the house, and the smoke of which made me at first fear it was a fire. This establishment he inherited, but has much enlarged it.

" The dinner-bell rang at six, and all having completed our toilets we descended. It is usual to dress completely twice a day. In the morning a free undress for fishing, driving, etc., but for dinner full dress is requisite. We had a *brochet*, taken in the lake, a noble fish resembling a pike. The dinner was excellent, and the cream for our strawberries thick as oil and yellow as gold. After dinner we smoked, and in the *buio* had a conversation upon literature, in which the *gouvernante* denounced the generality of modern French novels as of the worst influence upon the young, whether it be the 'horrible' school of Victor Hugo, or the amorous tales of other writers.

"*June 7th.*—Edouard brought me my coffee early, after which I sauntered forth to sketch. I met a gentleman (whom I afterward ascertained to be somewhat light-headed), who accompanied me to the spot I had in mind. This poor gentleman believes that we

Americans eat young children, and it was my cue to astound him with Munchausen stories. Once when I sprang up to look for my India-rubber which had escaped me, he fled in terror, crying out, '*Il a eu un accès!*' At breakfast we amused ourselves with him, and I continued to be a sort of wild animal in his eyes.

"The baron proposed a visit to Saint-Gobin, a famous manufactory of mirrors, and we went on horseback, I riding the 'Cossack.' This establishment is the largest of the sort in France.

"*June 8th.*—To-day we were to hunt the *chevreuil*, and departed early with a *garde de chasse* and the Comtesse, a dog of an indigenous breed, excellent for hunting wild-boars and the roebuck. We trailed across the woods for a league, until we reached the hunting-ground, and loaded with about a duck-charge, though our pieces were short wood-guns. We were stationed along an *allée* in the wood, down or across which we knew the beast would make when started by Comtesse, the guard beating round with the dog higher up. After only a short interval, for the forest abounds in game, we heard the deep, earnest baying of the dog moving from left to right and advancing upon us. Presently, through the thicket, I saw the roebuck dancing along with Comtesse at its heels, tossing her nose in the air, and giving tongue most sonorously. I thought the *varmint* would take a stand in a sort of *berceau* in front, and therefore I advanced upon it, which was wrong, as the beast saw me and fled incontinently. However, soon he crossed the alley lower down than where we were, and descended the hill into the bosom of the forest. We followed hotly, when suddenly we roused another old fellow with longish horns ; having put the dog on this new-comer, we again took our stations, and seemed likely to get a shot, but the buck made off, and, after waiting some time, we went home without a shot.

"*June 9th.*—To-day was proposed a visit to the Duchesse de C——, and a cruise round the country. To-morrow Charles goes to town, but he accompanied us a part of the way. The morning was perfection, and our path was as usual across the woods. The long, green branches filliped our noses as we rode through them, and the birds sprang away screaming when we invaded their remote bowers.

"When we emerged, long, sweeping hills, thickly wooded and crowned with waving wind-mills ; valleys shining with villages and a sheet of cultivation, were the features of the scenery. We cut across orchards, stealing cherries from the trees. After about two hours we came in sight of the château of the duchess. It is a great modern affair, with little wings and a large body, like a show-turkey. In front is a sward, with a little *étang* and a white bridge, like the baron's, but not so pretty. We found the duchess had 'gone to vespers,' though it was noon; and there was no servant to help us in stabling our horses, except a big-armed wench of Picardy. We made ourselves at home, however—walking, sketching, and gathering flowers. At last, however, the duchess returned with her husband. She is a short little thing, amiable, and so *forte à l'esprit* that we never heed her lack of beauty. Her husband seemed very good-natured. They were both very hospitable and kind. The duchess got out curious books for me. They insisted upon our staying to dinner. The duchess is a *savante*, has read Mrs. Trollope and the Prince Puckler, and is full of a short, repartee wit. She spent the evening picking out colors for embroidery, while we laughed over her excellent caricatures.

"We were to have departed at seven; but Saint-Médard, whose day it is, and who, being a neighbor, is especially attentive to all hereabout, brought up a banging rain over our heads, which obliged the duke to order beds for us. I slept well; and, in the morning, after coffee in my room, the duke appeared in his dressing-gown, to see us off. It still rained, and, leaving our horses behind us, we took the diligence for Laon.

"I can not think that this easy hospitality would

be shown to a stranger in England; every day con-
vinces me of the untruth of the statement that there
is no home comfort in France, or never beyond Paris.
We reached Laon in two hours, and dried our clothes
before mine host's fire, at the Hure or Boar's Head.

"There we found Monsieur de L——, and with
him sought the house of a friend of the baron, who
gave us a glorious breakfast, with artichokes cooked in
the incomparable way I find hereabout.   The rain
moderating, we sallied out to visit the cathedral. . . .

"We drove home in the baron's tilbury, which was
sent after us, leaving Édouard to pick up the horses;
and returned to a late dinner, while the family, who
had done, sat round us for the sake of chat.

"*June 11th.*—At half-past six in the morning the
baron sent to inquire which of four plans for amusement I should prefer.   I decided to accompany him
to breakfast with a family about two leagues off, known
in the neighborhood for their excessive pride of birth.
When once there was some prospect of one of their
family becoming a cardinal, they are reported to have
said, '*Le bon Dieu veut pour la réligion quelqu'un de notre
sang.*'   Afterward, when this scion of their stock was
not appointed, our witty duchess remarked that the
bon Dieu seemed to have had enough of that blood.

"Unfortunately, the two ladies, who are genuine
characters, did not appear—one was ill, and their

sympathy is such that, when that is the case, the other goes to bed too. The château, with its grounds, which are very English, is pretty, and justified their good opinion of it.

"At Chauny, on our way, the baron stopped to visit an old woman, whom he esteems much for her conduct when the Cossacks were here. Her two sons were shot dead at her door for firing on the Russians, and left there three days, as an example to the town. During this time the poor mother could not leave her house without passing the corpses of her sons.

"I spent several hours among the ruins of Coucy, examining the enormous tower, sketching, and dreaming among the shrubbery of the days of past glory of the house. The frescoes still remain, and the circular chambers must have been very grand.

"We spent the evening merrily, with many a lively tale. My mis-attempts to pronounce the French *queue* amused the family much.

"*June 13th.*—Saint-Médard yesterday and to-day has continued to sustain his reputation ; we have scarcely dared venture beyond the garden, so frequent and so sudden are the showers. I have been reading Dumas's 'Impressions de Voyage,' and find it very clever—particularly interesting to me, as he had the same guide I did (Payot) through the environs of Chamouni, and he made many of the same remarks to me that he did to

Dumas. The important event yesterday was the arrival of a rich *cousine* of the family, an original character. She is quite rich and entirely independent. She prefers to live in a little, plain house, all alone, without ostentation. She does much good, sending cows, flannels, and all things needful to the sick and suffering peasants in her neighborhood. She gave Henri one day a present of several thousand francs, all in hard cash, which she found and took out of all sorts of curious corners, tobacco-jars, preserve-pots, etc. !

"To-day arrived a still more important character, the Duchess, *la belle mère*, who appeared in a pouring shower. Cécile and the baron had gone forth to meet her, and returned with her. She came in her flowered *calèche ;* much time was consumed in unpacking the vehicle, and others that came afterward containing her effects. At dinner I saw her fairly. She is an old lady, with one of those comfortable, unmarked faces that one can not remember a long time. She was dressed very simply, and her manners are as plain as possible. She has not the wit of the Duchesse de C——, but quite as much good-nature. She spent the evening at her embroidery. Cécile, the young mother, made a *froc* for her baby ; Lucile threaded a bit of stuff with silver; and the baron turned over some views in Switzerland. As usual, all retired by half-past ten. Now Charles is gone, M. Q—— is my

opponent at billiards, and I find him a hard cus-
tomer.

"*June 14th.*—During the intervals when the sun
shines and the birds sing, we take the duchess round
the grounds. She is delighted with the charming
views and umbrageous alleys.

"We were very lucky in a drive we took to Coucy.
A blue sky relieved the sun-struck towers, and the
gray shadows falling sharply at the angles and softened round the old tower like the deepening tints
of a flower, made the place wear its finest charms.
Around the tower flit numbers of rooks, the only
ones I have seen in France. They give an admireable
effect.

" The duchess proves a most amiable person, and
as we sat *vis-à-vis* in the carriage, we had an agreeable
conversation upon Cooper's novels, on which she surprised me by the justice of her criticisms. In con-
versing with the French nobility, no idea of rank
comes into one's head, they are so natural and modest
in their manners. Perhaps one springs a *little* quicker
to pick up the fan of a duchess than another, especially if she be agreeable ; but that is the only difference.

"Cécile, the charming daughter of the house,
whom I sometimes call *mademoiselle*, she is so young
and girlish, is a most amiable wife and mother. She

awaits with impatience the return of her husband, who writes her every day. She has copied for me her brother-in-law's 'Lines written in Prison,' and she has also presented me with an Egyptian idol! This evening was passed as usual, except that the duchess and Cécile joined us and played billiards. They play with cues, like all French ladies, and Cécile was in fine play. She beat all the gentlemen.

"*June 15th.*—Birds and sunshine to-day have got the better of Saint-Médard, and after breakfast we all took a promenade up to the hill-top behind the house. *La vieille cousine* was dragged along, much against her will, and contrary, I fancy, to her habits, as she seized every opportunity to rest upon the benches we met.

"The others could not wait till I had finished my sketch; so they left me basking upon the turf, and penciling the humble roofs of Folembray, the proud towers that crest the distance, and the forest waving between.

"Cécile has been all day in a flutter, for Charles was to return; and that he might be welcomed with due honors, after dinner, at the hour he should come, we formed a *cortége* to meet him. Henri, in a droll surtout, and looking like an English huntsman, and his father, were on horseback. The duchess and the rest of us were in the *calèche*, driven by Monsieur Q——; the servants in livery, as usual. Love, in his excitement, nearly leaped out of the carriage, till Lucile restrained him with her handkerchief. Cécile was near imitating the dog in her impatience for her husband, and she was the first to cry, 'I see him!' afar down the avenue, in his carriage. After the shower of welcomes was over, Cécile got into his carriage, and we all drove home, so soon that there was no need of the stock of cloaks with which we had been provided.

"Charles returned laden with the results of his commissions — ornaments for the baby, my watch, which he had taken to be mended, and, best of all, a box of excellent cigars, which we forthwith proceeded to essay on the steps.

"*June* 15*th.*—All things have an end; and, after a fortnight, I must close my visit. I am pressed to stay, and, I doubt not, with genuine sincerity.

"I sent to Chauny to order a vehicle for nine tomorrow—the same in which I came; but how different will be my sensations from those with which I mounted before its crazy steps!

"Before bedtime, Edouard had packed all my things skillfully. I took farewell of the duchess, as she rises late, and I shall not see her again.

"Saint-Quentin, *June* 16*th.*—Last night was troubled; thunder pealed and the winds howled as if to share my distress at departure. I took my solitary bowl of milk, garnishing it with three eggs, against grief and the journey, and then visited the baron's chamber, where I found Charles and Henri, all in morning-dress. We smoked until my *voiture* was announced. All the family, the duchess excepted, were on the steps to see me off. I lingered as long as possible, fixing and refixing my various little packages. The baron has my address, and we have promised to write. On saying that ugly word 'adieu,' I kissed warmly the cheeks of all the gentlemen, and the fair hands of all the ladies, and did not find the custom either affected or ridiculous. Then, jumping into my gig, I was driven from the door, amid the waving of handkerchiefs and the bows of the servants. As I jolted down the avenue, I took a *last* look—I have faith that Heaven will not make the word literal—at the white mansion and the sparkling lake.

"I was too sad to speak, and the commonplace efforts of my driver to be agreeable but added to my gloom.

"As a traveler I have acquired a philosophy for the severing of pleasant ties generally, but I confess that here it fails me.

"I arrived at Chauny in an hour, and just in time for the diligence for La Fère. I was in the *coupé* and alone—it was well."

Mr. Appleton resumed his solitary travels, and drove through Belgium to Brussels, where he stopped a few days, then passing on to Antwerp. There was some difficulty about crossing into Holland, as Belgium was not then in accord with the Prince of Orange, and Mr. Appleton was obliged to pass a dismal night on the frontier, awaiting permission to leave.

" We were allowed to proceed some small distance on the Dutch side without molestation. The Belgians had amused themselves by scribbling on my passport, and all seemed in a prosperous way. But we were hailed at a guard-house, and ordered to stand."

In a small, ten-foot cabin, with other travelers who had arrived before, he was obliged to wait indefinitely for "further orders."

" I was the last the house would hold, and engaged to sleep in a low, musty room, with a courier. I say to sleep—the future was not then unveiled to me. My companions were artists, who had been waiting eight days, carrying on a long correspondence with the Prince of Orange. Their crime is being Belgians, and they despondingly said they saw no end to the matter; but stay they must, as they

20

have not money to make the *détour* of the longer
route.

"To cheer me, when the landlady discovered my
nationality, she said there was another American who
waited twelve days ere he passed, awhile since. All
this frightened me, but I buried my sorrows in my
dinner, which consisted of a certain black, grainy material the landlady hesitated not to pronounce beef-
steak.

"My afternoon was spent in cogitating the advantages of passports, wars, and frontiers, and in pok-
ing the peat-fire with my stick. I took a walk and
sketched a cow ; the association reminded me of my
supper, so I returned and ate a bowl of bread and
milk. We smoked, we chatted, took down the old
draught-board from the wall and played.

"At ten all were in bed but myself. I seem to
have had a sort of presentiment. At length I threw
myself on the pallet beside the snoring courier, and
actually fancied I was going to sleep. Vain hope!
Hungry and innumerable hordes of such warriors as
do infest lowly couches campaigned on my wincing
limbs. I rolled and rolled again, and, horrid thought,
I feared I should never sleep! I sprang from my
enemies, and, not knowing why or how I dressed, I
darted forth into the street, rushed up and down
the solitary road, and, getting weary, crept into a

silent farm-yard, and stretched myself upon a cold, hard cart in the middle of it. I was nearly asleep, when rheumatic chills reminded me of the exposure of the damp boards. I burst again into the house, and, throwing myself into a chair before the extinguished fire, in an instant was asleep. Unconscious that a moment had passed, I found it broad day as a man in the dress of a postilion touched me on the shoulder. 'Here it is,' said he; 'I have ridden long and late, not to detain the gentleman.'

"'Here is what?' I seized the paper; it was the permission—the dear never-to-be-too-much-welcomed permission to cross the frontier, and in a few moments, waving triumphantly the paper in my hand, I started in a crazy chaise, with a soldier and a *garçon de poste.*

"The artists looked wistfully after me.

"'You have no permissions?' I asked.

"'No, but we are resolved to steal across the frontier to-night.'

"'*Bon voyage,* and *au revoir* in America, where there are, thank Heaven, no passports and no frontiers!'"

Here the journal ends in a burst of gratitude for the royal permission of the Prince of Orange, at Breda, on the 19th of June, 1834.

CHAPTER XIII.

WANDERING YEARS.

I.—1835–1844.

THE curtain falls abruptly, and shuts out the scene which has shown so vividly the events of Mr. Appleton's life. Suddenly, the picture which appeared so close to us that every detail of it might belong to yesterday is withdrawn, and a gap of fifty years renders everything dim and distant. For the motive of actions we are left to conjecture; only bundles of old letters, yellow with time, connect the chain of events, besides the friendly reminiscences of the few remaining companions who are still here. Mr. Appleton from this time dropped the good but difficult habit of keeping a regular journal; there are one or two exceptions, but in general he trusted to his letters, especially those to his father, to give an account of himself.

His little sketch-books, however, of which there was always one in his pocket in the early days of his travels, carry on the story for a time. A small, yellow, marble-covered duodecimo, much worn at the corners, shows that he spent the summer of 1834 in England and Scotland. Nothing escaped his quick eye and ready pencil.

The study-window of Geoffrey de Monmouth, the cone-like outline of Malvern Hills, a little sketch of Grisi taken at Cheltenham, the interior of Shakespeare's room at Avon, a specimen dowager at Leamington with a cap terrific in frills and feathers—Warwick and Manchester—are followed by a series of Scotch subjects, in one of which Ellen, the fair Lady of the Lake, awaits Fitz-James in her boat, beneath the overhanging branches of Loch Katrine.

The last sketch in the little book is of stewards on shipboard, from which we may gather that his face was turned homeward. After eighteen months of wandering in Europe, in fact, Mr. Appleton sailed for New York, October 1, 1834, in the packet North America, arriving November 6th. His pleasant traveling companions, Mr. and Mrs. T. B. Curtis, with their little daughter Mary, were again fellow-passengers. There were thirty in all, but, like most return voyages, this one seems to have lacked the sparkle of the first. Mrs. Curtis, not long after this return home, wrote to a mutual friend in Florence :

" Our friend Appleton is one of the lions of society, having a great variety of Parisian and Highland vests, an English white top-coat, and fancy studs from all parts of the world, exhibiting all the ruins of Rome in mosaic, and Berlin-iron in every shape. In fact, he is voted a fop ; but he and I laugh at the report, it is but a whim of the day."

The delight of his return, and the great happiness of joining again his father, whom he so revered and loved, and of sharing with his dear sisters and brother the repose and comforts of home, were disturbed before very long by the anxiety of the family on account of Charles's health. He was ill during the summer, under the care of Dr. Warren in October, 1835, and died before the end of the month. On the 16th of November following, Mr. Nathan Appleton, with his remaining children, Thomas, Mary, and Fanny, sailed for Europe, accompanied by William Appleton, a second-cousin of the young people, and another cousin, J. Appleton Jewett, who afterward published his impressions of Europe. Apparently there was a dog in the party also ; Mr. Jewett writes from the cabin, to Mrs. Samuel Appleton :

"PACKET-SHIP FRANCIS DEPAU, *November* 16, 1835.

" Here we lie, still moored at the very point where we took leave of you this morning. The wind has been so unfavorable that the pilot would not venture to weigh anchor. . . . When you had vanished from our eyes, we gave way for a time to some melancholy emotions, and then addressed ourselves to business. All things were set in order for the voyage, and then we promenaded, and chatted, and laughed, and inquired out the company. Miss Fanny took a very pretty sketch of the surrounding scene, and Miss Mary went with me into a little, hot kitchen. Uncle Nathan ingratiated himself with the captain, and Tom made merry with his dog, and declared that 'his tail would soon put forth leaves'; Mr. William looked, as Miss Maria might say, 'angelic.' . . ."

T. G. A. adds a postscript to the letter :

"I am almost sorry I did not go ashore yesterday, if only to get the kiss I missed when we parted. I inclose two warm ones in this sheet, freighted with my last American ideas, hopes, and fears. We have for a day been rehearsing the voyage ; lying still—an excellent plan, as it gives the timid time to recover. I give you one wild farewell, and a sketch of our party (in pen and ink on the margin) in their present attitudes, looking their last upon the land of liberty.

"Yours affectionately,   T. G. A.

"P. S.—Alas ! we have no buckwheats on board."

Mr. William Appleton, who went abroad in search of health, died the following summer at Schaffhausen, deeply regretted by a wide circle of friends. He was a young man of great promise and charm of character.

Two years were pleasantly passed in traveling on the Continent, passing over ground where Thomas was well able to act as guide, visiting scenes new as well to him as to the others. The family traveled in Switzerland in their own carriage, and he sometimes left them, to walk from one place to another, rejoining the carriage at points agreed upon beforehand. It was on one of these occasions that he found, on meeting the family, his place occupied by a young American gentleman, whom they had lately met—Mr. H. W. Longfellow, of Portland.

A tedious interruption of their travels was caused at Mayence, where both the young ladies were attacked by a sort of gastric fever, by which the father and brother were detained with them, in a dull German town, for several weeks. It may be guessed that Mr. Appleton, in this later experience, had enough of Germany, for in all his subsequent travels abroad he avoided that country, in favor of England and sunnier climes, and he never had much sympathy for German traits, or proficiency in the language.

Mr. Nathan Appleton and his son endured their enforced stay at Mayence with wonderful patience. Thomas writes to a near relative at home :

"MAYENCE, *October* 10, 1836.

"I do not think it is fair, after all your kindness, to allow a post to escape uncommissioned by our party, and as the ladies fair are *hors de combat*, I champion myself to say something in their place. You may like to know that the foul fiend that just now so annoys us is gastric fever, a sort of infliction of these regions for the vile compounds of their kitchen, bred of grease, lard, and all the abominations of the German sausage. The doctor, one Herr Grosé, a vast, rotund, cane-sustained stranger, most attentively pock-marked, dares not confess this, but shakes his head and says eternally, '*Ayez de la patience.*' What with him and the fever, the girls have dragged through a most unsentimental month. The prominent feature of the malady, its slowness, is just now, within jump of Paris, the ugliest that any disorder could wear. But I am happy to say that all goes on well, and soon we shall be cracking our whips over the *chaussée* to Paris, where we shall make up for lost time. Father and I lounge an hour at the Casino over the 'Charivari,' and another at the Favorite, a delicious promenade along the Rhine, and then hurry home to drown our sorrows, amid red-legged partridges, with the tender exhilaration of Mr. Kaiser's very best Grafenberger. So you perceive our days are much like days in Boston—meaning to pay them no very extensive compliment on the score of variety.

"We have actually taken to window-gazing, and I recount to Mary, as Rebecca to Ivanhoe, the marvels I espy abroad. We are just on the river's brink, and opposite the only bridge; so we have a famous selection among barrels and tarry Dutchmen on week-days, and trim and well-laced officers on Sundays. Out of this it is no difficult matter for do-nothings to weave long romances; we have also ferreted out a nest of overgrown rats, at the corner of our hotel, said to be of the same family who, of old, ate up the wicked Bishop of Mayence, and 'nibbled his very miter,' as says the ballad. I have often seen them, of a shiny morning, waddling about with a most diabolical leer in the shadow of our neighbor's house; I see the inherited stain of blood in the very timidity of their mincing steps. So you perceive we are as full of news and bustle as a ship or a prison-yard.

"Father seems to take it all quite patiently. Quiet is in his way more than in mine. We have a theatre, but there he is shy of going; he is almost as hard to drag out of an evening as at home. He consented, however, to see with me 'Hamlet' in German. We were both much edified, and the tears came into our Appleton eyes as naturally as if we really understood what was going on."

All dullness was forgotten in the rapid journey

from Mayence to Paris. Every mile that brought them nearer to the great capital was a gain. They passed through in their traveling-carriage much of the territory which became in 1870 the battle-ground between France and Germany, little dreaming as they did so that the insignificant towns where they "baited" were to become historical, like those already famous as battle-fields in the wars of Louis XIV.

In 1837 the Appletons returned to America, and to the pleasant home in Beacon Street, where the three young people entered with zest into society. Boston was a different place from the Boston of to-day. Small it was, and provincial, perhaps; but the intimacy of the leading families, the ease and simplicity of social gatherings, accompanied as these were by the cultivation and intelligence for which the town was then gaining its reputation, made it a charming place to live in. And, though Mr. Appleton early described his native city as " a good place to go away from," none more thoroughly than he enjoyed the friendly luxury of its life.

Two winters were passed in Boston; the summer home of the family was at Pittsfield, the native place of Mrs. Nathan Appleton, in the old mansion belonging to her people.

During his father's absence, Thomas keeps him informed of the family welfare :

"Boston, *May* 2, 1838.

"Dear Father : I will not insult your memory of the past by hinting that there can be news. We are hopefully torpid as ever, painfully waiting the rolling off of this wet blanket of a storm, to believe that May it is. Some of the schools yesterday had planned an old-fashioned Maying. What came of it I don't know, through the mud and pother. Fancy the poor things dabbling in pools for buttercups, their India-rubbers ankle-deep in mud !

"The Allston Gallery draws famously when the sun peeps out, and every day some new hand cracks off a puff at it. Holmes has a loud one to-day in the 'Transcript.' Did you see Miss Fuller's in the 'Daily'? It is thought very well of.

"At home it is very pleasant, nor are we much annoyed even by the racket of cleaning, except as we descend stairs and behold the frippery mass of boxes, chairs, and statues that appears in every corner of the entries. Cook and his broth-spoiling minions we found had taken down the busts, and disparted the pedestals. However, with all care I have made them replace them, and have seen nothing broken yet, though of course there will be basketfuls of fragments."

The year 1839 brought many changes. Mr. Nathan Appleton was married for the second time ; in

1840 Mary Appleton was married to Mr. Mackintosh, and went soon after to live in England, where her brother and sister visited her at—

" St. Catharine's, *May* 18, 1841.

" Dear Father : . . . I have just returned from a delightful walk through the Zoölogical Gardens, almost the first rural walk I have had as yet in England. Nothing can be lovelier than they are just now, such a profusion of blossoming bushes and trees ! Our house is more like an angle in one of the Oxford colleges than anything else, with a Gothic fountain in the court, an embayed window overhanging the turfy square, and ivy creeping up to the sill; over the way the umber turrets of the modern-antique dwelling of the head of St. Catharine's. Altogether our position is one of the pleasantest in London.

" Tell Mr. Prescott that we were in charming rooms, quiet and sunny, with laburnums waving at the window, in fifteen days after quitting East Boston, without anxiety or fatigue, and do make him feel that he ought to have come, as we wanted him to.

" . . . The more I see of the play of the English machine, the more I see the imperfection of our boasted one—public opinion. I find nothing here resembling the 'it is thought' of America. Individual morality and harmonious complexity of interests make the reins draw evenly. Everything here is *under*-stated ; every man colors the fact by his personality, and none but the *lions* fall into that extravagance which, with us, is the effort to state still stronger what is already stated too strongly.

". . . There has been a sale of pictures, first-rates, the Lucca Gallery ; I came near bringing you in a bill for one, they were so sacrificed. If I had bought a dozen, I could have sold them at home for double the money. Think of a half-length Titian for seventeen pounds, an exquisite Murillo for thirty pounds ! "

It was at this sale that Mr. Appleton saw the "Virgin of the Candelabra" knocked off at a low price—the picture which, lately on exhibition at the museum in New York, was offered at a much larger sum.

Mr. Appleton could not resist a visit to Paris.

"RUE DE LA PAIX, *June* 18, 1841.

"Though most of the fashionables have left town, it is cool and pleasant, and the evening stroll along the Boulevards, after all, is prettier than any of the street-scenes in winter. Last night we were at the first representation of a new ballet, which is as pretty as even the 'Sylphide'; and, now that the *haut ton* has left the town, it is amusing to witness the noisy enthusiasm of the second class.

"Tivoli is no more; we drove there the other evening, and paid a franc, only to see what a scene of desolation it has become. 'On va percer des rues, mon cher monsieur,' told the story of the monster Improvement devouring these pretty suburbs.

"We have tried the Versailles Railroad. One goes in a half-hour, and every half-hour. All the engines are Scotch-built, with French names. We went on Sunday, and the train was full. Nothing can be more splendid nor more tiresome than the miles of gallery at Versailles."

" PARIS, *July* 1, 1841.

". . . I have been about seeing old acquaintances. De Poilly is away, but his servant was very glad to see me, and assured me that *Boston*, my dog, is now the hope of the kennel, for Dash and Love are dead or lost, and mine reigns supreme. He is related as wonderful for sagacity and beauty; draws a boat full of people after him by a rope, etc."

This was the dog which embarked with the family in 1835.

"*July* 15, 1841.

". . . My friend the baron is gone with all his grandchildren to Dieppe, but I saw him plentifully before he went. We dined at the Café de Paris, and talked over old times. . . . Healy is an excellent fellow, and, if he perseveres, will come back to us some day with the best reputation for portraits of any American of his time."

"LONG'S HOTEL, LONDON, *July* 30, 1841.

"DEAR FATHER: I am going immediately to the city to take our places for the 1st of October. I saw Macready last night in 'Money,' which you liked so much. I cried a good deal; but still, how inferior it all was to an inferior French play with trashy virtuous sentiments and conventional French gestures!"

"TUNBRIDGE WELLS, *August* 15, 1841.

"We are all comfortably housed in a rural yet elegant town, once a sort of rival of Bath—Tunbridge Wells. The town is high, and the air blows over woods and healthy downs, until it is full of sweetness and freshness. We found the place so much to our liking, while trying it for a day or two, at the Mount Ephraim Hotel, that we descended the hill, and took lodgings for a week in a snug half-house, half-cottage, that rejoices to be called No. 2 Clarence Terrace. We sally forth with our sketch-books, about eleven, and find cottages in abundance to adorn our sheets; we have had the luck to discover two walks composed of woods and brooks, and heights of land overlooking a broken and most generous country.

"All Kent, that we have seen, is lovely, fertile, and most beautifully undulating, giving at times startling overlookings of the richest fields. I have taken out an armful of books from the library, and among others we have read Miss Burney's 'Camilla,' which young lady met once many old-fashioned adventures in these very streets that now look so provokingly unadventuresome. If you wish to get a notion of the place, turn to the last volume of that novel.

"We know nobody, and, if we should stay till we occupied the pretty grave-yard, probably should know no one. I brought no dress-coat, aware that the Wells had had their day, and that now no spangled Camilla sighed and loved in the semicircular lobbies of the Parade. We all drink the water, for form. It is not bad, and probably also not good—a very weak Saratoga species. Aged widows and harmless old women of both sexes seem to be the natural inhabitants of the place."

Mr. Appleton, with his sister Fanny, returned home in October, 1841 ; but he was soon again upon the other side of the Atlantic, where he was always multiplying the number of his friends. The residence in England of Mrs. Mackintosh was a strong attraction, and other ties drew him thither, although, when he was away, the attraction of home was equally powerful, so that his absences were seldom long. He was a good sailor, and the voyage was nothing to him—indeed a pleasure, even in the days of long packet-passages. He could extract something from all characters—interest from the agreeable, amusement from the dull; with sketch-book and blotting-book he was always busy—the great secret of comfort at sea.

Mr. Appleton went into lodgings in London, and it was not until after the season that he crossed to the Continent. He writes from Bordeaux:

"*August* 24, 1843.

"Dear Father: . . . I have not written you before in France. Spain is too restless for comfortable traveling, but I thought I would just take a look at the Pyrénées, and walk a bit on the hills. I found nobody in Paris; was only a week there. I brought over the Sedgwicks. It is wonderful what a deal of history Mrs. Theodore knows. She has more to say of Philip Augustus than of Louis Philippe, and the Fronde is about as low down as she goes with interest. The Baron de Poilly was in town, and very glad to see me. He is desirous that I should visit him on my return from the south, as the duchess and a pleasant party are at Folembray.

"I went from Havre to Nantes all the way by steam, which shows how considerable, even in France, the changes are in travel. A brother of the Vendéean hero, M. La Rochejaquelin, owns a line of steamers on the Loire, one of which I came in. They are all of iron, the size of a canal-boat, and are waggishly called *les Inexplosibles.* On the safety-pipe is written, in large white letters, *système de l'inexplosibilité.* We constantly scraped over the river's sandy bed, and twice stuck fast; had to all leave the boat and wait till she was jostled out of the sand. . . . At Tours I saw Plessis-les-Tours, the den of Louis XI, so capitally described in ' Quentin Durward.' It is nearly destroyed, but what remains is very interesting, showing how gangrened the clever king was, mind and body, to live in such a way. He kept his friends round him, boxed up in dungeons, ready for use, I suppose. I saw where Cardinal Baluc languished for years in a cage. It was Louis who invented them, unless it were Bajazet."

Many years later Mr. Appleton saw this "den of Louis XI," and the monarch himself, reproduced by Irving, with great enjoyment. In October, 1843, Mr. Appleton established himself in Rue Richelieu, at Paris. He writes :

" I am snug and comfortable here. My nearest neighbor, in the Hôtel de Paris, whose deity is the mercurial Miss Michel, the adored of her guests under twenty, and smiling only upon some twelve spaniels ' of each degree of littleness and tendency to bark.' I

find I began above about a neighbor, seeking in vain
for a verb. She is Lady Staples, of Marion Square,
Dublin.   Her suite consists of Sir T. Staples, Dr.
Banks, and a hairy King Charles, the torture and envy
of Miss Michel, its toes being fringed at least an inch
and a half beyond its nails. We dine together at the
table d'hôte; she comes in to see my sketches, and I
hold *Fanny*, the dog, in my lap and hear Lady S. play
the concertina, a new instrument, like an organ, while
Sir Thomas draws gut across an enormous violoncello.
My friend *par éminence* is a youth of nineteen, who
asks me daily, ' Dites-moi, m'aimez-vous beaucoup ? '
He is a Hungarian count, officer in the Austrian service, who bought, for I don't know how many thousand
coins, the duplicate of the Correggio ' Magdalen,' at
Dresden.   He is fiery and Teutonic, talks English like
a vague approach to hog-Latin, and takes me for a
mentor. . . . But I have not mentioned my noblest
acquaintances ;—Mrs. Erskine, whose dewy eye speaks
pity and pardon for all human ills and vices, whose
very smile is an absolution ' un vrai ange,' as Leduc
calls her, and the compact-browed Miss Stirling, whose
keen mind looks Mystery in the face. They have with
them a refugee Sardinian to complete the group—
Gratitude waiting upon Aspiration and Faith. One
day they put me in their carriage and bade me preach
Soul, as taught by magnetism. I never enjoyed so

much unlocking as then. I talked two hours, finding full sympathy, the strong Lady E. weeping when I told her of the material proofs of re-existence, from the pure individual being, of powers undeveloped here."

It was at this time that Mr. Appleton made a visit of inspection to the haunts of robbers, which he was fond of telling about in after-years. He described it, in a letter to his father, just after it had happened :

" PARIS, *December* 30, 1843.

" . . . There is a strange book you must have heard of, called 'Les Mystères de Paris.' Wishing to judge if its fearful pictures of crime were true, with Bruce (the son of Lady Elgin) and Ledru, I visited, protected by two valiant guides, all the worst haunts of the robbers, the other night. We were armed ; and in one huge hot cabaret were three hundred of the worst villains of Paris drinking and howling. We were halloed at, insulted, and, but for much coolness, might have been roughly used. Our guides said they would make nothing of falling upon us and stabbing us. The police, every quarter of an hour or so, descend into this hell and carry off a victim. We were thought to be policemen in disguise till two robbers recognized Ledru, who is called, in the prisons, ' Le Petit Mirabeau.' I never shall forget the faces we saw there. We then visited the day-time haunt of the thieves, where they lie *perdus* from the police. It was then nearly empty. We went to all the vile places our guides knew of, and I had the satisfaction of drinking with some vagabonds and passing off for one of them, calling myself a *commis-voyageur*, with a long story, which seemed to pass perfectly. All that you will read in the 'Mystères de Paris' I can vouch to be under the truth. The spectacle was the most eloquent moral lesson. It gives one matter for thought for a lifetime. I saw it but for one night, and it seemed to me a revelation from the devil; what must it be to the poor creatures not quite hardened, to whom it is all they see every day, and the same! No wonder that at length their faces gain an expression which, to call beastly, is to insult the brutes."

Fanny Appleton was married to Mr. Longfellow in 1843. The pleasure the new connection brought to her brother is shown in a letter addressed to Mr. Nathan Appleton in Washington, in May, 1844:

"DEAR FATHER: Here I am at last, safe and sound, though I find some fears have been had for our safety, and with reason, for we were besieged during a day and night with floating ice, and hung after that in a fog, at the mouth of the harbor of Halifax, for as long.

"I am, half in your house in Boston, and half with

Longfellow in Cambridge, amply repaid for coming home, by finding dear Fanny so poetically and happily situated. Their house is charming, and I really lose my way in the many turnings. They both give me the sacred welcome of friend and brother, so dear in this world of strangers. . . .

"I tried to hear the Whigs last night, at Faneuil Hall, but could not get in for the crowd. We had a dance at the Inglises, where many friends shook warm hands with me. I really think people like one better for going away. To-day I dine at the Ticknor's, and take your place (how poorly !) at your club."

CHAPTER XIV.

II.—1845.

MR. APPLETON was now thirty-two years old. He
was fully able to understand his own nature and its
capacities. The indulgence of his taste for travel,
during ten years and more, instead of satisfying him,
had proved, to himself at least, that he was not fitted
for the sedentary, monotonous life of a profession
at home. The pursuit of the law, which he had accepted at first in accordance with the wishes of his
father, he learned to find as unsuited to him as he was
to it. Proud and sensitive, he carried the conviction
to an exaggerated length, that he had nothing of the
kind of talent then needful in America for what was
there called success. He felt, as he expressed it,
"humbled and despicable before men who could build
towns, pour whole villages into factories, and under-
mine the everlasting hills." Deeply and sincerely as
he admired his father's qualities of character, he had
no pretensions to become, like him, a leader of public

opinion, nor did he find within himself the dogged perseverance required for a life-long devotion to some practical business. "And yet," he writes at this time to his father, "I can not see that a man, improving his character and mind, living modestly on a moderate income, is wholly despicable. If he tries to do good and to find the truth and speak it, I can not see that he is inferior to a man who merely toils, nobly to be sure, but still without leaving himself time for much of these. . . . My ambition is my own, and it is as strong as any man's, but it has not triumphs which the world can appreciate or behold. It may not be a lofty or very useful one, but it is to the best of my abilities."

Such a life as he was thus imagining for himself was little understood, in 1844, in Boston. He was conscious that he was regarded as a mere idler; and that his enthusiasms, poetical and artistic, were wholly unappreciated. Most of all, he feared to forfeit the good opinion of his father, whom he intensely loved. These thoughts and tendencies, pulling in opposite directions, had made his early manhood full of unrest. It was now that he came to a full understanding, not only with himself, but with that kind, generous father, who, although doubtless he was disappointed that his son did not accept a career of usefulness and distinction, in some direction allied to his

22

own, never wavered in the affection and indulgence he had always borne for him.

Thus relinquishing definitely all pretense of office or even studies at home, Thomas sprang away to his friends in Europe, among whom he found or fancied himself free from the painful sense of being misunderstood, which oppressed him at home.

Yet it should be remembered that, from the first, Mr. Appleton had a strong affection for Boston, and that after short absences he returned to it always with pleasure. As he grew older, and his thirst for travel abated, he was content to settle down in his native place. The last twenty years of his life, with few exceptions, were passed in sight of the gilded dome of the State-House.

He writes to his father, then in Pittsfield, from—

"BOSTON, *July* 18, 1844.

"I am off to-morrow. There is every appearance that we shall not have many passengers. I am very sad at leaving Fanny, and all my friends, but that is an inevitable feeling when one quits those one so much loves. You shall know, as soon as I have made definite my plans, what these are. At all events, I am determined to be as happy as a poor mortal can who is not in active business. . . . Receive my embraces, and never cease to love the economical prodigal,

"Your affectionate son, T. G. A."

This jesting fashion of speaking only covered a deeper and more earnest state of feeling, which found expression in a later letter. He writes :

"If an ardent wish to do good and be of some use indicates anything, I feel that some day I shall be better understood and loved for other reasons than at present. . . . I do not suppose I should, or shall, ever do much very American; it is too late to achieve strict habits of business and method; but I shall be able to handle my talents so as to satisfy a little the natural demands of society upon me."

With some friends, Mr. Appleton passed a part of the summer in Derbyshire, in a charming little cottage, "looking," he writes, "from some points not larger than one of our Nahant cottages. The Howes (Dr. S. G. and Mrs. Julia Ward Howe) and the Sidney Brookses all are here, and the rest of our party are very agreeable people — among others, Hallam, the historian, Lady Sitwell, and Mr. Smith Wright, neighbors of the Nightingales'. We breakfast at half-past nine, with, among other things, some Derbyshire cakes, tough and gritty; lunch at two, in a very moderate way; and dine at half-past six. It is a quiet but very charming life we lead, with fine mountain-walks, and horses for those who like them. The Nightingales are as delightful as ever. Miss Florence and Mrs. Brooks are very excellent friends,

chattering like sparrows together, while Partley and
Lady Sitwell are dabbling over their water-color
drawings.   The country hereabout is very like our
Berkshire—the same woody amphitheatres, the rushing water, and the dry roads."

He adds, referring to a standing joke : "I do not
feel so sure of marrying an Englishwoman as I did,
though they are delightful ; at least, I have asked none
yet."

"August 31, 1844.

"Since I wrote, I have been a week with Lady
Sitwell and her husband, Mr. Smith Wright, not far
from here.   The house is a model of taste.   Lady S.
is famous for her flowers.   Her conservatory is superb,
and her white yuccas unrivaled.   Yesterday she drove
me to Sir George Beaumont's, the nephew of the
famous art-patron.   He received us at his superb
porch, and took us over the fine house, a miracle of
taste, as was everything of his uncle's ; and at length
into a conservatory-like gallery he had built to hold
the over-abounding pictures.   Here were all the first
good things of Wilkie, Leslie, etc., which Sir George
bought to encourage these young artists ; but his own
sketches were as interesting as any, and as good.
Allston's picture is in a lovely gray stone church close
to the house, a sort of guardian angel to the place.   It
is the one he often spoke to me about.   An angel in

white, with sky-blue scarf fluttering, points, while standing on the steps, to the prison-door, with a radiant hand, while Peter lifts a majestic face, heavy with sleep, upon the angel, from between his bent and drowsy guards. There is a huge patine of moonlight breaking through the grates of the prison above. We thought the angel a trifle too robust for air; but who can fitly imagine these dear brothers of ours? The figures are life-size, and the picture one of Allston's fine ones, though not equal to the 'Jeremiah,' 'Miriam,' or 'Belshazzar.'"

This picture, "The Angel releasing Saint Peter from Prison," was painted by Allston for Sir George Beaumont, and placed by him in the church at Ashby de la Zouche, here mentioned. Mr. Appleton's admiration for the picture had for a result its coming to this country; for Dr. R. W. Hooper was led, by his friend's praise of it, to buy it in 1859, from the nephew of Sir George. It was exhibited at the Boston Athenæum, and afterward at the Museum of Fine Arts, and a few years ago was presented by Dr. Hooper to the new State Lunatic Hospital at Worcester, where it now hangs, in the great hall, in an excellent light, and gives great satisfaction to the patients.

The autumn and winter were passed in Rome, which Mr. Appleton found to have lost none of its

charms since his visit ten years before.   His friends
the Perkinses made his stay especially pleasant.   Their
Christmas dinner is described with great enthusiasm.
The days were passed in drawing from the life, painting la Grazia, a model then much in demand, and in
visiting the studios.   In the spring of 1845, in company with William M. Hunt, his mother, sister, and
brother, Mr. Appleton went to Greece and Constantinople.   The party was delightfully congenial.   William
Hunt was, about that time, a pupil of Pradier, and
"in a fair way," as Mr. Appleton expresses it, "to become a sculptor."

They sailed from Ancona early in April, had a few
hours at Corfu, and a day at Corinth, on their way to
Athens ; there they spent several days visiting all there
was to be seen of interest, going to the Piræus and to
Marathon.   There is a sketch-book amply filled with
rapid water-color impressions of these places.

On their way to Constantinople, they had a day at
Smyrna, and a few hours at Gallipoli ; they stayed
some time in the Eastern Capital, and then returned
to England by the way of Trieste, etc.

"ROMA, *March* 28, 1845.

"MY DEAR FATHER: At length I am off for
Greece—a rather rapid visit, as I dread the hot
weather—and a run to Constantinople.   Thence I am

not very decided; perhaps up the Danube, perhaps back by steam to Marseilles and the west of Spain, and then home. I shall thus have exhausted all there is of the wild Indian in me, and shall stay at home like a good boy.

"I have lingered and lingered in Rome, deferring my Eastern trip, snared by the charms of this old artistic town, and the graces of my friends the Clevelands, etc. My winter has been monotonous, but studious. I shall have the company of a pleasant family from Ancona to Corfu, if not farther—the Hunts, of Brattleboro, whom you know."

A long letter to his sister calls upon her for the sympathy he is sure of.

" ATHENA, April 17, 1845.

"MY DEAR FANNY: It will be a satisfaction to you to get a letter from me dated Athens, and I assure you it is the greatest satisfaction to me to find myself here. It is only for a few days, for it is getting warm, and on the 20th I shall steam for Constantinople. The Hunt party have decided to go too, so I shall not want for acquaintances on the way.

"I left Ancona in the Austrian steamer of the 4th, and came hither, touching at Corfu, and getting a hurried visit to Corinth. We have now been here about a week, which has been one of the most memorable of my life. It is such a strange and perpetual

pleasure to have the names of Theseus, the Academy,
Phidias, and the rest daily in our mouths, and whenever we doubt if all be not a summer dream, to see
from every point the Parthenon flaming like a vast
altar above our heads. What a morning I passed
there yesterday! One gets up here by sunrise, and
the pure, elastic air is something to intoxicate one,
if the Parthenon were not enough alone. We all
sketched; I in the lovely little Temple of Victory,
without wings—a figure of a victory binding its san-
dals, very likely from the chisel of Phidias; what a
delight to find myself sketching that there! Then I
drew in water-colors an interesting monument on
the hill opposite. At ten we descended and lunched,
and at eleven all set off, some in one of the wild-driv-
ing carriages of the place, and the rest on horses, for
Eleusis, a pretty drive of two hours. We passed the
Academy and the plain beyond, and when we drove
beside the sparkling sea, blue as the eyes of Minerva,
we were wild with delight. At Daphne we rambled
over a quaint ruined convent, with a head of our
Saviour in mosaic, in Byzantine fashion, so quaint and
fierce as to seem almost a robber. At length we
reached Eleusis, where we found a party of English
officers pottering over an incomprehensible monument, once a sort of huge medallion, with a head in
alto-rilievo, but now destroyed; we rambled about,

looking at the few remains of that famous and mysterious city, sketching many little girls in their pretty costume. Here each damsel carries her dowry in solid coin on her head, and feels the weight of riches from her earliest years. We saw a girl of eleven, very pretty, on the point of being married, with plenty of gold mingled with the silver coins. This coiffure looks precisely like an old helmet, having a band of coins to hold it on, passing under the chin like the band of the helmet. The evening I spent at Mr. Hill's.

" This little sketch of a day gives you an idea how we spend our time. The weather is delicious, and the sunsets—bathing all the town in gold, even making the palace of Otho endurable, while behind Hymettus is the glow of violet—are the finest in the world. Dr. Howe and others gave me letters, and I have more friends here than time to see them in. To-morrow I dine with Sir Edmund Lyons, and breakfast with the Hills, who are the best people in the world. There is no one in Athens more respected than he, and no one who does more good. They are both friendly and merry, enjoying life as very few missionaries do, and every day more and more beloved of all. Every one sings their praises, and indeed when one witnesses the things they have done at their school, the five hundred children so orderly, so obedient, and so clever, it is with pride that they are of our country that one sees it all. The school is on the Lancastrian plan, and the quick demonstrations of the scholars, by gesture and voice, altogether show the most perfect training. I went to hear Mr. Hill preach on Sunday in an ugly little Gothic church, like one of our dreadful efforts at home ; but it is pretty within, and some of the scholars who sing have exquisite voices.

"But what shall I tell you of the ruins here ? Nothing, for one can say nothing ! They must be felt, and that is all that can be done. We have been to Marathon, over the glorious mountain-passes, and over the worst roads, where my horse, and the guide's, pitched us headlong without harming us. I have wandered in the Academy, and recalled the Plato we read in the cave at Newport. I have been on the Bema where Demosthenes tamed the 'fierce democratie,' and which is as fresh as then ; on Lycabettus, to see beyond the town Ægina, and the gulf leaping to the sun ; every step we take is over the memory of some great man. To-day I go to Pentelicus, far less interesting than before the barbarians came as gunpowder-blasts to destroy the neat excavations of the days of Phidias. We shall return home by a young moon, which here is indeed lovely.

"Dr. Howe is everywhere here remembered. I have shaken hands with friends of his, whose eyes sparkled when they spoke of him."

"Stamboul, Pera, *April* 27, 1845.

"My dear Father: Fanny was, indeed, right when she said, in one of her late letters, 'Fail not to pass that Golden Horn, which shall unlock more enchantment than ever did Orlando's.' Tell her the old enchantment still lingers about these shores, that fairyland begins with the blue entrance to the Dardanelles —but let me not rave in general.

"Two days have I been here, two days of Arabian Nights' entertainments. Even Pera, dirty Pera, favors us, for the season is so dry we walk without filth to the scenes of the various tales of Scheherezade. Our good French captain halted his boat through the night, before we arrived, that we might have a sunrise impression for the first. Good fellow! he is an artist, and sympathizes with those who love the beautiful. We were all up bright and early, you may be sure ; and, shining afar off, with wavering lights glancing here and there over the mighty sweep of shores, slowly rose Stamboul.

"We came so slowly, we drank in every slight change of this unrivaled panorama. A writer for the London 'Times,' who was with us, told me, though often here, he never saw the city show so fine. We swept by the seven towers, Galata opening over our bow, with fringes of dark red from the Judas-tree relieving the young green of the other foliage. Like candlesticks of some heavenly Jerusalem, burned in the early air the minarets, while the white domes of the mosques, suspended among the trees, reminded me of Aladdin's famous roc's egg, which none but a magician could furnish. Seraglio Point we lingeringly rounded, wondering at the latticed kiosks, the delicate trees fresh with their earliest green, the cypressed-walks of the garden, where we fancied sultanas, lights of the harem, were culling flowers, with night's diamonds still upon them. The Golden Horn then, like a cornucopia, poured its treasures at our feet, and, amid ships and steamers, and thousands of caïques, we dropped our anchor.

"We were soon, after no bother of passports, or nonsense about baggage, snug in Madame Giuseppina's lodging-house at the top of Pera, looking down into a Turkish burial-ground, with tombstones like petrified Turks—scarce stiller or more sedate than the living ones.

"We are in great luck. We at once took caïques for a tour down the Bosporus, to see the Sultan go to mosque. No sooner had we arrived than, amid prancing Arabs and lines of Europeanized soldiery, the Sultan stumbled along, almost supported by two officers, to his phaeton, rather gay with gold, and, after taking one long, sleepy look at us, he drove off with a grand chatter of attendants.

"We there saw, also, the famous Riza Pasha, the real head of the government, whose portrait Mr. Kellogg, a clever American artist, is now taking. We ascended the tower of the Genoese, to get a map-view of the town. While taking a pipe and coffee in that airy *café* we looked over sea and town, lingering at every window, and lapped in a true Turkish Elysium. After this we visited the Armenian and Greek churches near us. It was their Good-Friday, and we witnessed very curious ceremonies, and saw gorgeous church-costumes. It is our luck, after having it at Rome, to find Easter everywhere. Reckoning by the old style, the Greeks gave it to us, and now the good people of Constantinople—like strawberries following one as one goes north in spring.

"But our crowning treat was yesterday. As luck would have it, yesterday was the betrothal of the last sister of the Sultan to Mahomet Ali Pasha, and, with all the world, we went to see the presents carried by. During a long detention, our time was spent (besides long chats with excellent Mr. Carr, our minister, and Brown, his dragoman) in trying all the sweetmeats, lemonade, etc., and peeping into all the droll *arabas*, where, with faces hid in their *yashmaks*, were all the wives of the various pashas, as well as those of the *bourgeoisie.* Little Mussulmen trotted about on ponies with running servants at their side, and in the gayest

23

dresses. Every wall and balcony glowed like a tulip-bed. Such colors and such silence ! Black eyes alone spoke through their narrow door in the *yashmak*. We perched ourselves on a pile of boards, where we were long examined by the Sultan himself, from the artillery magazine near by ; soon his *cawass* came and told us to go down lower—we were, probably, cutting too much of a figure.

"Not till after two o'clock did the procession come, to the clang of Turkish music. After servants to clear the way, supported on the shoulders of men in double file, came boxes of jewels, dresses, etc., and of sweetmeats, a hundred or more trays, covered and bound up in cone-like shapes, with vari-colored gauzes. Behind came the rest of the paraphernalia, splendid, but not so rich, they say, as when the other sister was married.

"I shall, probably, send home a parcel through Smyrna, as no one can resist the thousand pretty things here. Our room is a litter of Damascus blades, silk, embroidery, etc., etc., all dear but divine. I may return by way of Trieste, or to England direct, by steam, so avoiding quarantine."

Mr. Appleton writes from England on July 2, 1845:

"DEAR FATHER : This is the last letter I shall send you from this side of the water, if I succeed in getting off, as I hope, by the middle of the month. You sent me an invitation to spend August with you in Pittsfield a long time ago; I have been acting on it ever since; I have come night and day to Paris, and should by this time have been in America, but for the plans of others. I shall soon be there."

This promise was fulfilled, and August found him in America, with his father. He passed a part of the autumn at Newport, of which he writes: "I find Newport as pleasant as in the olden time, though widely different. It swarms now with fashionable people, and the study of my fair countrywomen has been to me a very pleasing occupation since my arrival here. If you have not been to Newport since we were in the Lawrence House, you would be amazed to find so many huge caravansaries, so many new cottages, and so much new company."

The original manuscript remains of this poem, written on the steamer:

ALBANIA.

Beneath Chimari's peaks of snow
   We sweep with flying keel,
The murmuring wave rolls blue below,
   Above the rare clouds steal;
With faces turned toward the land,
   We watch the strengthening lines,
Where o'er our tossing bow expand
   Albania's far confines.

No tree, no shrub, relieves the dark
   And barren precipice ;
No perfume greets our hurrying bark,
   From mountain-peaks of ice.
To Fancy's eye, only, the goat
   May tread those fierce defiles,
The circling eagle's shadow float
   Along those splintered piles.

No streamlet from the fissured rock
   Drops with its murmuring sheet
Of dew, to nurse the fading flock
   Of wild flowers at its feet.
Stern cliffs, all thirsty for the rain,
   ·Implore the passing cloud,
Which droops with heavy fringe in rain,
   While thunders mock aloud.

Oh ! well in those tremendous vales
   Must echoing thunders speak,
With antique cries awake the gales,
   And man the mountain-peak.
With grisly shapes, which throng to hear
   Those martial sounds again,
Gleams fast and far the Dorian spear,
   The dead desert the plain !

The men of old, the immortal dead,
   Are now again alive ;
The phalanx musters overhead,
   Where airy armies strive ;
The watch-word, and again the sweet
   Call of the Spartan flute
Above in grand confusion meet,
   Where late all heaven was mute.

Better such dream, than where the shore
   Swarms with its living dead ;
Men on whose sordid souls no more
   Fame's fiery light is shed.
We listen where, 'mid thunder rolls,
   Old Freedom's echoed cry,
Nor turn to look where meaner souls
   Pollute that holy sky.

CHAPTER XV.

III.—1846–1854.

IT would be difficult to follow Mr. Appleton at this period, in his shuttlecóck passages across the Atlantic. Space forbids more than slight gleanings from the sheaf of letters at hand, written with a full heart, and overflowing with matter, to his father, commenting freely upon men and nature.

In 1846 he spent some time at Malvern, whence he writes :

"I board in a genial old house with some Cheltenham friends. It is called the Abbey, and is hundreds of years old, with corridors, carved panels, diamond lattices, and old matters. The guests consist of frouzy old matrons, pursy East-Indians, etc. The landlady is as old and as odd as her house, and the servants are all originals.

"At tea, each of us has a separate tray, and makes his or her own tea. It is very droll, and looks like

four-and-twenty housekeepers all in a row. I mean to
hold on to the Abbey, and get all the oddities of the
place."

The winter of 1847–'48 was passed in Paris ; and
again, after a summer at home, a journey to Niagara
and Montreal, with an English friend, Mrs. Wedgwood,
Mr. Appleton found himself in Europe. The spring
of 1848, in Paris, was an exciting time. After the fall
of Louis Philippe, the provisional government found
itself beset by immense difficulties. The moderate
members, Lamartine, Garnier-Pagès, and others, were
opposed by the party of Ledru - Rollin and Louis
Blanc, who held extravagant socialist or communist
opinions. The Assembly met on the 5th of May,
pretty evenly balanced between the two antagonistic
parties. Mr. Appleton arrived in Paris just in time to
see the opening of the Assembly. A few days afterward he was present at a stormy meeting in the new
Chamber of Deputies, when its halls were invaded by
a mob. The excitement of that occasion was quelled
for the time. It was not until June that the struggle
took place in which the Archbishop of Paris lost his
life, when General Cavaignac, nominated as dictator,
restored order after six days of anarchy. On the
10th of December, 1848, Louis Napoleon was elected
President.

On the 10th of May, 1848, Mr. Appleton writes :

"I was yesterday at Lady Elgin's, where there was no talk but of the state of affairs. Some predicted utter ruin, some had hope; all told stories of the wreck of their friends' fortunes. The servant announced *Monsieur* Rochefoucault. The young man came in laughing, saying that two months ago he was a duke! Like every Frenchman, he has no imprecations against the government, but hopes for the best. Poor Madame Baudraud, who is half ruined (her husband educated the Count of Paris), received me sadly but with pleasure. I find Paris too sad a place to be in very long; it wears upon one, and, though I hope to see it somewhat brighter, it may darken."

In the autumn of 1848 Mr. Appleton was at home. He made a brief trip to the West Indies, to escort Mrs. Mackintosh, who had been visiting her New England friends, back to St. Kitt's, where her husband was at that time governor. Much as Thomas was charmed with the beauty of the islands, "the mosquitoes and lizards, and the perpetual sauce which the sun serves up," were too much for him; he was in New York, and off to London, before the end of the year.

"England," he writes, "is staggering along under her many difficulties, trying to keep up heart, and yet feeling that in all probability she has seen her best days. There is in the air a something not full of confidence for the future. The fact is, she is frost-struck at the root, at the top, and in her branches, at once. The people will run down into an Irish condition before many years ; the nobility are made to feel poor by the corn-laws, and the colonies are restive. All this changes the tone of feeling very much from what it was two years since. But, if possible, Englishmen are finer fellows than ever. Never was there so much goodness, so active virtues—tolerance, patience, charity—in men and women as now ; never before such restlessness to hunt up ways and means of relief— such sacrifices of time and money. It does one good to see such things. . . . I spent evening before last with Carlyle, who was very pleasant. Emerson had sent him Indian corn, ground and unground, and Carlyle was preaching it with apostolic fervor. The English millstones, he says, are too soft for it ; it comes back full of sand. Mrs. Carlyle produced some half-Indian bread of her making, which had a home flavor. Carlyle has been in Ireland, but brings back no plan of cure ; it seems beyond his grasp, or any man's. They say in the spring whole counties will take ship. Can we stand this indefinitely ? I wish they all could be dumped among the Mormons at once ; they might bump their Celtic cocoanuts against the Rocky Mountains, and so gain a spark or two. . . . There is a new life of Swedenborg ; he says people are not well in the other world ! That is rather hard, and yet one can't imagine the identity of a confirmed invalid and a robust angel ! "

"*January* 3, 1850.

"Cobden is passing over the land like a prairie-fire. The mechanic is become master of England. He will gain more and more boldness, draw from America his doctrines, and before twenty years England will be a republic in all but the name. . . . I shall try to write Jewett a 'screed of my mind,' as Carlyle says, whom I made roar by telling him Prudhon's last saying, '*Je déteste un Dieu qui ne s'explique pas.*' "

The whole winter of 1849 and 1850 he passed in London with Mrs. Mackintosh, whose husband was still away at St. Kitt's. He greatly enjoyed her children, and was prime favorite with them, teaching them how to make molasses-candy, "which was a failure," he says ; "Mrs. Lawrence thinks we boiled it too long," and telling them wonderful stories. The other children across the Atlantic began to be powerful attractions toward home, for every letter contains messages, and many report boxes of toys exported for the benefit of the new brood of half-brothers and sisters who were coming upon the field, and for Mrs. Longfellow's little ones. " Uncle Tom " was a wonderful and exciting relative ; now here, now there, always turning up with his hands full, and then disappearing without warning.

" PARIS, *March* 6, 1850.

" Never was Paris gayer. I hear on all sides that the profusion, the luxury, the living *au jour le jour*, have been something remarkable. This haste to enjoy was one of the features of the first French Revolution. I hear the upper classes reproached for a lack of real fusion with the lower, for no real effort to meet the present feeling, no interweaving of common rights and common ideas which might bridge the gulf which, to the socialist, divides as between heaven and hell. I doubt not it is true. The French, sunk so low in their own esteem as to have been caught in this republican trap of 1848, accept a lower position, and have not manhood enough to overcome difficulties they did not seek. They have no fear for the present, but all talk of some possible bad bloody future. The Reds are kept at bay, but they stand firm on the grand ground of pillage ; no reason, no argument, reaches them. It is the finest dramatic exhibition of Satan and the Spirit of Good, in dialogue, which, I suppose, the world has seen for ages. It gives me a wholesome belief in the reality of the devil; and a disbelief in him, and such as he, I have ever considered as quite absurd. The spirit surely is of evil as of good, and why, in the spiritual world, there should be any barrier to prevent the development of spiritual evil, I never could see. After all, goodness is only a force ; so is evil; one exists as well as the other. . . .

" I was agreeably struck by the President. He is reckoned as ugly, and said to resemble me : but his phrenology I liked, and his mowed hair unveiled his organs—fine courage, good firmness, small self-esteem, fair frontal width, and reasoning powers, with large observing organs, and an eye strong, concentrated, and thoughtful. These things are well, and people till lately have not done him justice. I saw him at a splendid show. The aunt of the President, the Grand Duchess of Baden, had that day arrived, and the diplomats and officers were in *grande tenue.* Many a fair shoulder was plowed with those small wings of the army-cherubim—epaulets. . . .

' My poor Baron de Poilly is dead, of cholera, after typhus, last summer. He seemed to me as much a part of Paris as the Pont Neuf."

The next year was passed in America. Mr. Nathan Appleton, whose health was failing, went abroad to try the benefit of a change of air for a troublesome cough, and Thomas remained at home as the head of the family.

He writes his father from Boston, in November, 1850 :

"The parties rattle round our ears like the leaves of autumn. It seems November is our party-month; certainly the fever is on. Mrs. Paige's great ball comes off to-night, and will, no doubt, be splendid. . . . We have a capital show of two Aztec nobles, half the size of Tom Thumb, and infinitely diverting. Theorists of a gloomy turn of mind predict from these the fate of the Beacon Street nobility. They seem very happy and lively, though pygmies, and certainly have a very distinguished physiognomy, very like the heads on Catherwood's monuments. . . . There is nothing I more envy you than seeing Mary's children. A year's romping with them has made me very fond of them. I have no fear that they should forget Uncle Tom."

The summer was passed at Pittsfield and New-port; at the latter he found "the same scheming mammas and polking daughters, the same roaring *table d'hôte*, the same Bloomer bathing. Newport is indeed unique, very amusing and instructive, abounding in fine studies of human nature and panoramas of mankind."

24

"Newport, *August* 5, 1852.

"Yesterday the sea wrote in heroic measure. It had been composing a poem all night, and we went to the Spouting Horn to the hearing after breakfast. It was Shakespearean, and of the finest. · A sustained march of noble rhymes, with every now and then a sounding Alexandrine tossed to our feet. Never have I seen the scene there so fine. It was like one of Napoleon's great battles, whole parks of artillery blazing away at every reef. Sometimes the spray would stand for a second in. the air, one lovely tree of silver with all its shining leaves, and then melt as a frost-tree does on a window. At times the angles of the rocks would send off rockets of foam clear over our heads, and the big-backed waves growled afar on the beach. I think it the finest sight in nature, such power, such variety, such beauty. Our party went to the verge of the rock, and were remarking on the playfulness as well as the terror of the ocean, when the jolly sea shook a whole wave over us. We were drenched to the skin. Delicious ! "

Mr. Nathan Appleton returned in September, much improved in health. In November, Thomas established himself in Paris for the winter. He was in fine bodily condition and great spirits, and the time passed delightfully, with American and French friends. He was in comfortable *garçon* quarters at the corner of the Rue de la Paix and the Boulevard. "Would you ever have thought," he writes, "that the ugly clump of buildings crowding the court of the Tuileries at the farther end would come down? Well, down they are, and our clever Emperor has now to contrive to make the two ends meet, which he can never do without an angle, and it will be an ugly one. We have just done voting for emperor, as you for president. Both have swept the country, both talk of peace, and I hope both will keep it. Already a solemn print of Louis in imperial robes is in the shop-windows. It looks fearfully old-fashioned and impossible, and seems powerfully to criticise the situation. *Nous verrons. . . .*

"Last night I was at the Vaudeville to see the "Dames aux Camelias," the most renowned of the plays now going, by Dumas *fils*. It is wonderfully clever; as a piece of acting, far beyond anything we can do—a play full of that sickly interest the French like so well. Great red faces were streaming with tears at the pathos, and, when each act was done, a flourish of nasal trumpets proclaimed the clearing of the shower. There were belts of these happy, mobile Celts, their faces discharged of care, and devouring every word and feature. Rows of little children in the highest tier fluttered with their oranges and barley-candy, and their obeliskal *bonnes* nodded in

Norman caps at their sides. No one could feel the heart of that audience without believing in the difference of races. No Anglo-Saxon actor, by any chance, could have performed the meanest of the characters, and no American or English audience could furnish that brooding and intelligent content with which the play was received.

"The Hunts are near me. I went to-day to see packed a very admirable picture by William, bought by young Brooks, a 'Fortune-Teller'; you will do well to see it when it arrives in Boston. Hunt is doing uncommonly well."

"December 22, 1852.

". . . Yes, I am pretty comfortable. I dine out very often, sleep well, paint in pastels, talk a good deal, and enjoy life.

"It seems to me that the sort of thing people would like, and that they find they miss, called *happiness*, is not quite that, but will turn out, when we get it, to be something with a nobler edge than that has. Happiness is a feather-bed ; the sort of thing intended for us may be a wing, something on which we can either lie hushed in dreamy calm, or cut through the keenest and most bracing air. The body loves effort and repose, the spirit loves struggle and calm ; our happy destination may be a wonderful alliance of all these. . . . I do not know why I have written to you in such a strain. It is this smooth quill which does it, so different from the harsh, unloving edge of a steel pretender. How admirably our improvements are typed in that pen! The charm taken, and the use left—a business utensil indeed. I do not believe I ever wrote three words of sentiment, affection, or feeling with any of them, and who ever did? If Lamb had lived in the day of steel pens, he never could have got beyond his ledger. . . . I send by the America a box from the good city of Paris, containing Christmas-gifts, but nothing for you, dear papa, who give me everything—but what to send you? I could think of nothing; Cordelia-like, I hope. I would send you, if possible, the whole Palais Royal if it would give you pleasure. You do not want a French carriage, some porcelain, some Carcel-lamps, some bronze statuettes, some French wines, boots, toys, dogs, cats, do you? I . think a good Angora cat *would* be the thing. They are immense, very strong, very long hair, very scratchy. I saw one at Madame Mohl's, who went through my trousers as if they were paper. I do not think they could stand our climate. Madame Mohl is as usual wonderful: hair, a mare's nest; dress, a pen-wiper; wit, exuberant; oddity, immense. She lent me books, good ones. Perhaps you will be glad to know that Lucrezia Borgia had the fairest of golden locks. . . .

"I dined last night at Lady Elgin's. She is won-

derfully alive to our knockings and spiritings, and had
two philosophers to meet me. I propounded my
strongest statements, and they all swallowed them.
In return, I was told of one Mr. Forster's new system
of reading hieroglyphics. He conceives the pictured
lion to express the letter L, and not the animal—
spells away, and finds he makes old Arabic words.
There are gullies in Mount Sinai he reads off in the
same way, and finds they are the same Mosaic account
of the Israelites we have in the Old Testament. But
this is all new, and against Champollion, so he rather
gets laughed at by the *savants*. . . . I dined a few days
ago with Ary Scheffer—very pleasant, delightful anecdotes about Béranger. Once a poor fellow, at whose
bedside he was, unable to speak, could only turn his
eyes from his old wife's face to Béranger's till he died.
So Béranger toddles across the room, tells the old
woman he has great need of coarse sewing, etc., and
carries her off home with him, obeying the silent
look of the dying man. I have bought a little Diaz—
the French Rubens—Spanish blood and Murillo stealing constantly into his pictures. The Louvre has a
tribune now—the great square room. It aches with
immortal pictures—the focus of human genius."

This Diaz now belongs to the collection of the
Boston Museum of Fine Arts.

"The Emperor lives snugly in his palace, but rides and drives out in very simple and confiding style. Every one here agrees as to his abilities. To have fatigued and used up all the clever *entourage* he had showed remarkable independence. He gradually numbed them all, and then, with one torpedo-touch, sent them under. He lives in an austere solitude of will. No one can divine the future, no one knows his secret intentions, his future wishes. The peace of Europe, the happiness of France, depends upon one life, his single brain. It is ghastly to look into this blank, unknown to-morrow ; luckily, the French never do care to look ahead. For us it would be intolerable. Every man would make it a matter of conscience, thereat to be miserable, but here they cry, '*Vogue la galère !*' and snap their fingers. . . . I met at dinner the other day Mérimée, a good writer, whom I have long wished to know.

"He was very pleasant, indeed; gave puns and conundrums, and spicy historical anecdotes, of that rare sort that do not get into the books ; anecdotes of Hoche, Napoleon, Josephine, and others ; he was de-lightful, and kept my carriage waiting two hours, so that I lost another party I was to go to.

"I dined also, a few days ago, with Bristed, who has taken a funny little hotel in the St. Germain quarter. The grand *salon* is like a private chapel, with a gallery all round, plafond painted to imitate fresco, and rich Italian furniture. Altogether, I was much amused; our gay party of Yankees, drinking their champagne in all this splendor, was like Sam Slick musing in the ruins of Carthage.

"I received, yesterday, from Longfellow's London publisher, a new edition of his poems. Prefixed to it is a woodcut portrait, which, of course, resembles not at all. It is as fine a flight of fancy as any in the book. I will send this to Jasmin. Mérimée says Jasmin does not understand one word of English, but will be delighted with the present, and will get somebody to translate all there is about himself."

There is an account of this Provençal poet in Mr. Appleton's "Sheaf of Papers."

"*May* 4, 1853.

"I have had a new, very agreeable pleasure. You know how often I have bored you with stories of the delightful new forces in table-moving, and such like, which found no favor among the sagacious people of Boston. A few days ago I was importuned to show something of it here, and did so with full success, not a person witnessing but found it genuine. Peter Parley, at whose house it came off, gave immediately a grand *séance*. I happened to be dining with the Mohls, where we had Mignet the historian, Lady

Elgin, and others. I carried them all off to see the fun. We had over fifty people assembled — many *savants* and remarkable men, the young people of Arago, he being too infirm to come. In a quarter of an hour we were under way. M. Coste (the Government agent for the new pisciculture) made the table move by his unspoken will, while Arago's nephews were seen hugging a little table, which trotted under their hands. So I was content. No one has called me odd or crazy, but I get satisfaction on every side."

"*June* 9, 1853.

". . . *Je rêve un* cottage at Newport, and look forward to a snug house, and a snug wife, and a snug leg of mutton. . . .

"Thank Henry for his joke. I return him one of mine. A play by Ponsard, 'L'honneur et l'Argent,' is playing here ; the heroine is called Laure : so I say of the lover, 'Quoi qu'il méprise l'argent, il adore Laure (l'or).'

"So he has taken leave of Hawthorne. We shall see how such a ghost-seer will manage as consul at Liverpool."

When the weather grew too hot for Paris, Mr. Appleton broke up his establishment and went to Dieppe, where he took much pleasure and good from sea-bathing. He received news there of the death of his uncle, Samuel Appleton, which was a great grief to him.   He returned to England and joined Mrs. Mackintosh, who had been in America, at Tenby, in Wales.

" *October* 5, 1853.

"DEAR FATHER: I have been now some three or four days at this Welsh watering-place, certainly one of the prettiest I ever saw anywhere. I look from the window upon a semicircular little harbor, filled with shining brown-sparred fishing-boats, driven in by these equinoctial gusts, as, for instance, day before yesterday, when the whole sea was starred with little, straight-down hits of wind, and many a sea-sick craft crawled round our corner. The coast beyond is wonderfully like our cliff-house view at Newport—the same ledge running out, overhung by cliffs, and green and sloping shores beyond. This is softer and bigger; that is richer and brighter.

". . . I wish to heaven God would make people well and keep them so, and at last knock them off their perch in a comfortable and manly manner! I can bear seeing a man or woman suffer, but I loathe a morbid disposition. I have been looking over the life of poor Henry Ware. Capital fellow, good as gold, but all sickly, and made wretched by a want of reasonable physical life, such as every animal has, and most savages. It may be one of the advantages of the next world, and of not being encumbered with bodies, that we shall not trail these hindrances and checks.

"The children are nicely and charming, so well behaved and very companionable. I drove them, yesterday, to see an old castle of Lord Mitford's, a noble ruin, very fine Norman style, said to be of the days of Rufus. Coming back we stopped at Lydstep to see some extraordinary rocks. You would have enjoyed the sight; I never saw anything finer. The strata are perpendicular, honey-combed beautifully by wind and wave, and with three lofty and picturesque caverns, growing on a soft, smooth little beach. One would be the *beau-idéal* of an opera pirate, far beyond any Saddlers' Wells smugglers. I should have well liked to hear Grisi in it. All along this shore the Old Red is in great force, lying in ridges and sidewise. The shells and algæ are also very fine here. We go to-day and get an early dinner with the Misses Allen, two good old ladies, quite the model of the olden time, like Miss Hannah More, Mrs. Barbauld, and Mrs. Trimmer—I always fancied her name most as a teacher for the young. They live in a pretty cottage with such a lovable view, headland and isle and plunging beach, broad seas, and the bright flowers of a very tidy garden to give value to all these neutral tints. In the second place is the Burrows, a favorite spot with the children, whither they led me, and we ran

up and down the grass-tufted sand-hills and peeped
into the holes to see the rabbits; but all the Welsh
rabbits I have seen are in our supper-plates at home.
. . . The children have brought in their letters, and I
must finish. Soon this will be leaping on the bright
billows and tumbling into your hand. I am much
tempted to take a trip to your side, and see you all
before you lie shut in with snow, like plums in a
wedding-cake. I should so like a crack with you over
the mahogany, this goose-quill substitute is so poor
—no eye meeting eye, no voice echoing to voice ; but
one writes away into the void, like a man talking
against the wind, though haply believing the voice is
heard, and not lost on its way. Good-by.

"Ever your loving son   Tom."

As it happened, not long after, Mr. Appleton
returned to America, and really settled down for a
longer time than ever before. His sister, Mrs. Longfellow, who was happily living in Cambridge, persuaded him to take a house near her ; and finding one
in Phillips Place which suited him, he there established his household gods, and for the first time set
up housekeeping for himself. The wandering years
were at an end ; he began to taste the comforts and
delights of a home; indeed, his *rêve* of snugness was
realized, with the omission of one of its three items.

In his Cambridge house he had a good cook, and gave delightful dinners. He soon surrounded himself with a pleasant circle of friends, and it was easy to supplement guests and viands from Boston when the nearer supply gave out. He had a favorite story of an occasion when the ice-cream ordered from Mrs. Mayer's did not arrive in time. The anxiety of the host, the despair of the cook, the ill-concealed *malaise* of the guests were reaching the tragic point, when the longed-for wagon rattled up to the door, and all was well. .

Mrs. Longfellow's children, as those of Mrs. Mackintosh had been, became a source of interest and enjoyment to their uncle ; his strong affection for their mother, and their own development, were binding them closely to him. With Mr. Longfellow, Mr. Appleton took a cottage at Nahant, which to the time of his death was his favorite home. Close to the rocky edge, its piazza overlooks the water and the bay, with a-view of distant Boston, commanding the sunset view behind the town. Yachts, steamers, catboats, come and go directly in sight, and in later years, at her moorings, within easy hailing distance, swung his own yacht, the beloved Alice, always ready for a sail.

Nahant had always been a favorite resort for all the Appletons, and Thomas had passed many gay days

25

at the old hotel there.   In 1855 Mr. Nathan Appleton
bought a place on Ocean Street, in Lynn, within easy
driving distance of the cottage at Nahant, where was
to be found the happy family circle of half-brothers
and sister, fast becoming favorites with the oldest son
of the house.

CHAPTER XVI.

1855.

It was not to be expected that a planet with so erratic an orbit should at once become a star absolutely fixed. Frequent runs to New York, where, as in the large European cities, Mr. Appleton found always hosts of friends, interrupted the even tenor of life at Cambridge. In New York he was at home in the studios of artists, a race of beings with whom he had close affinities. Church, Darley, Kensett, were among his intimate friends. The tie with the latter was peculiarly strong, and lasted until the death of the artist.

In the summer of 1855 Mr. Appleton was busy with the *début* of Elise Hensler upon the stage in opera, and went to New York in order to interest his friends there in the prima donna, and the occasion. He writes from the Everett House:

"*June* 16, 1855.

"I am very well entertained here, and not a little busy, trying to give Miss Elise a good start. To-night is the eventful occasion. I have interested my friends here, who gladly lend themselves to a pretty girl's *début*. So we are to take a box, encourage the *débutante*, and hit her with bouquets." He adds: "Yesterday I took a run up the river, by slow train, saw better than ever the lovely features of this river prince, and dined at Cozzens's at West Point ; saw son and father. The old- man reminded me of twenty years ago, and I heard him complaining of a barrel of eggs broken, which had been brought from New York so that country visitors might have them fresh. The serious faces of several Boston people caught my eye under the spacious verandas. I took a drive down the banks for an hour ; saw landscapes beyond expression lovely, and painted at hand from them a dozen big pictures ; when back I was just in time to ferry over the river, and whirl to town for Elise's serenade and supper, both of which failed, however !"

That summer was spent at Newport with the Longfellows, and two or three friends ; among them Kensett and George William Curtis. "We find," he says, "our plan of a mixed household as pleasant as ever. Never were Curtis and Kensett more agreeable or sunny. Mrs. Perry is as strong and willing a body as can be, and her daughter, next door, is Newport's best washerwoman. We had Mr. Boker, the dramatic author, to dine with us yesterday. We called on his wife at Bateman's, where we saw swarms of children, dogs, swings, and black-fish. We do have a good time. The weather is rather helpless, lazy, and good-for-nothing, but we become sociable in proportion. North, South, East, and West fuse very well, and ought to be even better friends than they are. . . . Mr. Everett is at the Bancrofts', charming the young people with his affluent mind. For long I have not seen him so happy, even gay; I do not recognize the austere president of City Library Trustees. . . . We, that is, Kensett, I, and the boys (Charles and Ernest Longfellow), were out fishing for four hours yesterday in the foggy, soft morning, and yet got pretty well burned. Mine nose feels rather loose to-day, and looks like a lobster's claw. We caught, that is, Charley did, who beat us all, one big tautog, eight or ten sculpin, and four or five flounders, besides one blue-fish I got, which proved very good to-day for breakfast. So as yet Kensett and I have not painted. He chooses sites and takes it easy. It is full hot to work in the sun as yet. I am trying to get up concerts for Elise Hensler here. Newport needs something to fill up the time, and I may amuse the public and put money in her pocket."

"*August* 9, 1855.

"We are all charmed with Tennyson's new poem, of which Fields has sent us the proof-sheets. We even took it out to Lawton's Valley, and read it to Mrs. Howe, to the tune of her leaping brook, and, when we were done, went and took tea under the trees very merrily, looked at with wonder by the good people going by. We hope soon to share your content with the Sydney Smith Life. He was wise and witty, which is a much happier alliteration than witty and wicked, which Heine, whose book I have just read, seems to have been."

This poem of Tennyson's was "Maud," which appeared in the spring of that year.

"Mrs. Anthony's, Church Street, *September* —, 1855.

"Dear Father: I suppose by this time the Longfellows are with you, to our great loss, who will at the Saturday dinner tell you all the latest summer news. Here now, luckily, we have none. Long, balmy, placid days, untormented by the restless male and female dandy, glide over our heads. Nature, with a sad sweetness in her fading smile, says, 'Come quick and paint me, ere my last leaf is ravished, my last colors pale.' And we go and paint her, poorly, meanly, with the soul, the sunshine, the heart of her left out. But in our defeat some of the tender meaning, the grace, the glory, gets into us—let us hope for good. My dear Kensett, that sweet child sitting at the feet of Nature, is gone to wrestle with the mountains, to put down from their haughty scalps something of their ethereal crown and nobleness. He is gone, to my great regret ; but the Storys have come, old friends of mine—he, the ready, quick-witted artist ; she, the full-hearted, unpinched woman ; and here in our new house, with Curtis, we live the heavenly autumn hours. To-day is to be turned to special account. With the Shaws we are to spend the day at the Glen ; we take our wine and chicken, and by the gentle sea, and near a picturesque mill, we shall use well this latter sunshine.

Pleasant as was this experiment of Newport life, the next July found the inveterate wanderer on the Atlantic, writing as usual from the steamer, " This is *certainly* one of the pleasantest passages I have made." The ship's company were especially agreeable ; his friends the Storys went on that voyage, and Mr. Richard Dana (then *junior*, the writer of " Two Years before the Mast "), and there were a number of less intimate acquaintances who proved amusing ; one of them a Mormon elder on a proselyting tour, whose nasal twang, as he described the interview between Joseph Smith and the higher powers concerning the authenticity of the Mormon tablets, Mr. Appleton used to imitate to his last days, "which being shown to the ăngel, proved to be abso*lewt*ly caorrect." Mr. Barry, of the Boston Theatre, and Miss Biddles, the pretty actress, were on board ; the gay party found the paddle-box a nice place to sit, in the morning, where they told stories, recited poems, and talked of writing a book, to be called "Spray from the Paddle-box."

With these friends, Mr. William W. Story and his family, Mr. Appleton took a house for three months, at Walton-on-Thames, in Surrey, not far from London, just by the country-place, at that time, of Mr. Russell Sturgis, Mount Felix. He describes it thus :

"OATLANDS PARK, *August* 15, 1856.

"DEAR FATHER : Once upon a time there was a rich Englishman whose name was Hughes Ball (reverse it, and you have a poor American sculptor). Now this man was a prodigal, and spent his substance, and his estate is called Oatlands Park, and has been brought to the hammer. It is to be sold in ten days, and won't bring more than four thousand pounds ; and if I could only transport the whole to our side, I should consider it a bargain. It is most tastefully and comfortably fitted up, the drawing and dining rooms are exquisite, and it has a conservatory full of promising grapes and flowers, a capital stable, a large garden full of fruit ; the grounds are well laid out and picturesque. We have the silver Thames just by, and a large lake of our own, full of carp, mullet, and jack. I have my painting-materials, and yesterday painted a distance, tender wheat-fields, the heavy sheaves looking from afar like a yellow mass-meeting, a few farm-houses, and a square church-tower in light, sentineled by black and burly elms against the faint gray hills beyond. That is one view ; and I shall do many more ; there are river-views full of beauty, and we have in our park large places wild as Wisconsin, with trees freshly planted. It is ridiculously like America for a place so near London. . . . Thackeray is gone to the Continent with his two daughters ; he is not well, and is to begin there a new book, which he says he means to make good. I hear that Lady Byron wishes to talk spirits, etc.; she is a neighbor of ours, so I may drive over and see her. It feels unelectrical here ; I should be surprised if the ghosts could keep dry enough to rap in these mists. They drop down now, like mercy, in an unstrained shower, making the roses hang their heads, waving before the distant farms in lawny veils."

" OATLANDS PARK, *September* 3, 1856.

" DEAR FATHER : The Saturdays fly in so thick, I almost forgot that a letter will not be to you unacceptable ; of late we have been particularly busy. Our friends Lothrop Motley and family have just left for your side, and you must *fête* this lucky author, who has so well explained how the Dutch came to take Holland. He has made us very lively, and to him our lovely river-brink after Germany was an Armida's garden.

" Besides dinners and lunches, which between our two houses were daily varied, we boated down to Hampton Court, and though somewhat bored by its ill-cared-for gallery, were more than delighted with the Raffaelles and the grand grape-vine hanging full of nearly ripe bunches. It is a wonder, a miracle; I saw not a spot or blight on a single leaf.

" The shooting is in full play, as the frequent bang near me reminds me. I do not make as many pictures as I wish, as lunches, visits, dinners, eat into the time. But the *idlesse* of this rural life is the greater reason. One reads the ' Times,' with the wide shadows falling across the sheet, in a garden-chair, and music all around from the shrubbery, and one gets to protract the reading and enjoy the sunny garden-side. Sometimes, upon our lake, I watch my quill and float, but never get a bite. I have not, as yet, tried in the river ; but last night, as we rowed up through rocks and osiers, and fringed banks, we passed many a punt holding a whole family, the papa whipping the stream while the daughters read or sewed, sung under their umbrella-hats ; and though the fish might be small, the fun evidently was great. I saw one rather majestic barbet taken, which reminded me of Izaak Walton. There are perch and trout, and many more fish, in the river. We have an old church and quaint churchyard, and we have a pew. It is rural and pleasant, albeit so near London, though certainly the clergyman is no wonder. I went to-day through the village, and was wonderfully reminded of all the novels I have lately read of English life. The same style of men in the same tap-rooms, and the village oddity and snob, seem here well imitated from the books.

" Love to all the chicks, and to the Nahant cottage."

The house at Oatlands Park was taken for three months, and Mr. Appleton stayed there till the middle of November ; his gay party gathered around them a succession of guests, with whom, and their neighbors at Mount Felix, there were nightly frolicking, charades, music, tableaux. Mr. Hurlbut was a frequent and welcome visitor ; Mr. Charles Norton came ; in fact, the capacities of the house being overstrained, the lodge was fitted up as quarters for bachelor guests, and at the same time as a studio ; it had a lattice-window, oak benches and chairs, and clematis flourished over the porch.

Mr. Appleton writes on the presidential prospect of 1856 to his father: "If Buchanan comes in, and goes on, if ever so little, in the Pierce fashion, we shall have to pull down our pretensions to liberty in Europe. I dare say we may yet turn out a strong, rich, clever, tyranny-loving people. There still will be a few nations worse than we shall be, but nowhere are the free energies of a people like New England's so adroitly and constitutionally enslaved as the North will then be by the South. It will be hard to bear, but may do us good, make us more humble, and more willing to look after our sins. . . . I am now awaiting the arrival of Mrs. Rich and the Wedgwoods and Farrars, who are coming from London to lunch with us, if not deterred by this fog ; to-day is better, but yesterday was a day of Acheron ; as Mrs. Story cleverly said, it was like biting into a raw potato. We have asked Lady Augusta Bruce, and she promises to drive over with the duchess's carriage. If they all come, we shall have the merriest of meetings, such good and friendly people."

This pleasant episode, which Mr. Appleton used to refer to in later years with great satisfaction, came to an end. The party broke up ; the Storys went to Rome, and Mr. Appleton to Paris, for the winter. This time he took an apartment in the Rue de Luxembourg.

"I went last night to the Piccolomini's *début*—a dear little woman, singing with feeling and heart, and some voice, in that sad and nasty opera 'La Traviata.' It was a full house, all artistic and literary Paris there —Scribe, Gautier, and other clever Parisians. No Emperor, however; but after a short waiting for him we began—amid what eagerness and interest! Before the trashy opera was over how much were they cooled! There seems here a general want of first-rate talent— on the stage, in opera, in the cabinet—I suppose, the old complaint of all time. Last night I was at a very agreeable house, that of M. de Tourgénieff, a Russian, who has forfeited his life at home for trying to free his serfs, and has to live here; a noble fellow, with a charming wife speaking perfect English, and a daughter. I met there Mrs. Stowe, who was very pleasant; so I asked her to dinner for next Thursday, to meet Madame Mohl, etc. I shall start my cook and valet, and hope they won't blunder and bother. . . .

"Yesterday I went to the famous doll-shop (imagine how it was overrun, anticipating the *jour de l'an*), and found such a cunning box of doll, three dresses, hat, cloak, etc.; I bargained for it for little Alice, and it will go in the box with the cast of the Venus de Milo."

26

"I do not know if you understand the Crédit Mo-
bilier, but if you do you are among the happy few.   It
has its offices, in an imposing way, in the stately Place
Vendôme.   The very look of them has a humbugging
air ; and that they should be in that famous place
built, you may remember, by the Scotchman Law, is
ominous.   So violent is speculation here, that many
pieces on the stage satirize it.   To show the temper of
the times, I give you the saying of a witty St. Germain
dowager the other day—that to marry a girl, nowadays, she must have her fortune *en rentes*, and her
parents *en terre*.   The Emperor holds good ; I hope
you read his opening speech, one of his best, full of
good sense and character.   He extorts a sort of admiration even from his enemies.   Our medium-friend,
Hume, is capsizing all Paris.   The Emperor sends for
him very often, and he and the Empress shake hands
with the other world and see marvels, to which the old-
time imperial writing upon the wall was but a phos-
phoric trick.

"Miss Hensler first touched here on her way.   She
is much admired, singing at private concerts, and soon
will get a good engagement."

Thus passed the winter ; in May, 1857, Mr. Appleton left Paris ; as it happened, this was his last stay
there for any length of time.

"DEAR FATHER: To-morrow I am off for England, and I think for home, and that speedily. I never make up my plans till the last moment, which gives them great freshness and vigor. My heart yearns toward you, and I must see you. I shall find you at Lynn, listening to the rustling billows, and will take a good swim with Master Will. I have some coins for him. I am giving away my pictures, and leaving sundry half-finished *toiles* to the dogs. . . . Well, I come home on the 13th, in the Persia, once again with Judkins; it will be pleasant."

CHAPTER XVII.

HOME WANDERINGS.

1856–1863.

AMONG the artists whom Mr. Appleton met at Kensett's studio, on his frequent New York excursions, was Mr. F. O. C. Darley; in the summer of 1859 Mr. Darley was visiting him at Cambridge, when a visit to Moosehead Lake was proposed, and put into execution with that suddenness which characterized all his excursions. His admiration of the wildness and beauty of the scenery of Maine was unbounded. He was particularly struck with the cry of the loon; its strange, wild voice, with the fiend-like, mocking laugh at the end of it, inspired then and there these lines:

THE LOON.

When swinging in his silent boat,
  The sportsman sees the happy lake
Repeat the heavens which o'er him float,
  A quiet which no whispers break—
     Then, ah! that cry
     Drops from the sky,
In mournful tones of agony.

The spirit of the lonely woods,
  Of wastes unseen and soundless shores,
The genius of the solitude
  In that complaint appealing pours—
      One voice of grief,
      Appealing, brief,
  As hopeless ever of relief.

When evening breathes with perfumed air,
  Delicious sadness, longings high,
A pensive joy, untouched by care,
  Then hark, a laugh falls from the sky—
      A mocking jeer
      Floats o'er the mere,
  And Eve-born sorrows disappear.

'Tis thus, when Nature overbears
  Our human needs of joy and woe
Too much, these link it to our tears,
  And shame us in their overflow :
      That laugh, that cry,
      To us come nigh,
  And solitude's society.

There is a fragment of a journal begun but never finished on this trip, called, "The Sporting Tour of Messieurs Romeo and Chunks." It begins thus :

"*July* 6, 1859.—We left Boston by the Boston and Maine Railroad, at 7.30 A. M. We were mentally busy counting the various sundries which constitute the total of sporting-people's outfit, sure that some if not more items were forgotten, but after the tenth time of counting we wiped the slate of memory and organized ourselves as cheerful. We decided to keep our eyes buttoned open, not to miss one startling or picturesque fact of our tour; and so sharp were we, that we almost squeezed something to note out of the heavy basketful of chips which always constitutes the contents of a Yankee car. One stalwart man, with suppressed neck, and staff longer than an umbrella-case should be, I already spotted as a fellow of the craft; need I add that he has dogged us ever since? A sort of committee of Maine men, all in the national red-shirt (which goes to show that, if the Indians are gone, there are a few red-men left), burst into the car; they had the tan of a hundred noons on their merry faces, their straw hats had a touch of the smuggler and the peasant, broad and serviceable, with flowers and tap of ribbon. Later we made their acquaintance, and talked of their adventures, and their high spirits raised ours. They had been driving logs in Canada. Here are some of their mugs, sketched by Romeo (Mr. Darley), *vide* sketches.

"We reached Newport, where we left the rail, about 5 P. M. Our stout friend and his rod-case got out with us and scrambled up on the only coach, while we walked up the hill to the inn, had a jolly supper with our lumbermen, whose child-like fun began to be a little embellished with liquor. They drove off in a big wagon, screeching and laughing like wild Indians. We chartered another wagon to fetch us on. We had a capital fellow for driver, an egg-merchant, who keeps eggs six months and sells thirteen thousand dollars' worth of them to the Boston markets. He told us wonderful stories of his mare and his frolics. We rattled along for two hours under a pleasant moon to Dexter, where we found our stout friend and rod in profound thought in the front parlor. We took a copious tea, and retired to rest to the music of a brook behind the house.

"*July 7th.*—The scenery grew and grew into no-ble mountains, sparkling lakes, and wild, fascinating country. The day was hot, the valleys plunged into *musquitory* stillness, and the elevations showing the sailing cloud-shadows and many hills.

"We lunched at Abbot; nothing but an inn. Wild-strawberries, brought in by the boarders, saved a fearful meal. We are in the heart of the famous *cuisine* of New England—doughnuts, as if a hail-storm had dropped over us, huge cake, scalped and painted like a sachem, and meat which gave us for its origin the choice of quadruped or old shoes. After lunch a grim woman, in heavy glasses, burst into the parlor, and gave us a shower-bath of all her family events: how her husband was gone to Californy, and did not mean to return for five years (looking at her, I thought this exile might be wise); how she lived in a level country, and the first day she got here she thought she must go back right away, the *meauntins* looked so *duberous*, she could not get used to them no ways.

"By 5 P. M. we were at Greenville; the splendid lake washing the town, and the hotel agreeable. We walked through a clearing to see a young moose caught last winter. We pitied him, tethered and bleeding from the cuts of cord, dancing about his tree with untamed haughtiness. . . . The evening was perfect; the moon came out, and the broad lake, the many isles, all with perfect black shadows thrown into the tumbling opal of the water, made the scene like a first-rate one of the Grand Opéra. An old unpainted tow-boat partook of the picturesqueness that all things gain from ruin. What broad, tender tints washed the mountains! How reluctantly they parted with their beauty and color! . . .

"*July 8th.* — At breakfast we found our trout, though the ruddiest ever seen, not so wonderful, treated by the imbecile cook; these fine gentlemen, disguised in the vulgar dress of a Greenville kitchen, were changelings. By eight o'clock we were off in our yacht Katahdin. Delicious was the sail; from little to little, we fell into dreamy calms, monotonous but charming; yet we crept along, enjoying scenery and cigars, saw all the wonders of the lake, admired and trolled and bathed, and so spent the day. Mr. Romeo sketched, and Mr. Chunks confided his feelings to verse.

THE YACHT KATAHDIN.

Like cherubs nestled in a cloud,
We float along the mighty lake,
    Our shade Katahdin's sail—
We float along, and see our wake
    Of frosted silver pale.

Louis, the brother of the moose,
Whose step recalls the springing trout,
    Watches our tinkling prow;
We lie, like gods, and gaze about,
    And feel contented now.

At first, so sweetly earth and heaven
Agreed, each seemed the other's twin—
    Earth an inverted sky;
Now some dark, heavenly hand has driven
The brightness, stamping, soft and dim,
    Each isle and mountain high.

The ranks of pine are twined with mist,
On Lily Bay the smile expires,
    Her brow in sorrow veiled;
On the far reach die out the fires
    Where late the sun prevailed.

But fair our lake at crimsoned eve,
Or wavering in the moonlight wild;
    At morn a cup of pearl:
Though wild, her face still glances mild—
    A sweet New England girl.

" After this serious effort he felt better, unscrewed his comforter, and blew a cloud, which Romeo immortalized on paper—'The Helmsman.' Later, Chunks got off in another strain, as the dejection of calm came over him :

DECEPTIONS.

Our thought is on the monstrous moose,
  Our thought is on the trout ;
We long to see the first run loose,
  To pull the other out.

Two guides took us to see the moose,
  We fired up our tobaccos ;
We found him haltered in a noose,
  And looking like a jackass.

Beside him was a little pool.
  " Trout there ! " the guides said ; so
We looked down through the shadows cool,
  And saw a minnow go.

We thought the bottom of the lake
  Was trout all laid in stacks ;
We thought a walk we could not take,
  For fear of rifle-cracks.

I guess the bottom's fallen out,
  The shooting but report;
We've bagged three horse-flies—that's about
  The total of our sport.

" The calm increased. Louis, silent, sculled the heavy boat. Our only music was the squeak of his oar. Chunks, fallen into deeper gloom, came to this :

CALM.

It's getting calm, and I am not;
   It really is provoking,
To help ourselves to hot and hot,
   With baked puns for our joking.
Our Romeo sits, as Memnon did,
   As silent and as sunny;
And Chunks towers up a pyramid,
   And just about as funny.
Mount Kineo's off full fifteen mile—
   We'll reach it when we get there;
Before we do, our dinner'll spoil,
   There'll be another *het* there.
We've drawed the hills, we've writ the varse,
   Each one in his gray jacket,
And just saw that old steamer pass
   With most insulting racket.
Oh, dear! the Bourbon's nearly out,
   Our lunch is stuck at Dexter;
We see no likelihood of trout—
   We're vexéder and vexed-er.
The landscape's going from our sight,
   We're both of us lugubrious,
And think the Abbot woman right—
   We called the mountains "*duberous*."

". . . My bath in the lake was delightful, but not
long, for the boat, drawing ahead, would have deserted me; so Louis drew me in, and I reposed, like
a gigantic frog, upon the sunny deck. It was the
heaviest fish he had ever got in. Suddenly, whisk!
came a shower, and such a one! From one or two

big drops, the field of the lake became a huge chess-board, where pawns, jet black and white, were moving and taking each other, and then were put away in some invisible box. It was we who were the stake of this diabolic game.

"Then, from tumult, we fell again to calm ; but we were under Squaw Mountain, and Kineo was in sight."

Soon after this the journal ends abruptly—either never finished, or missing.

———

Mr. Appleton was very fond of the out-door delights belonging to camp-life. One of the best beloved of his reminiscences was of an excursion to the Adirondacks in the autumn of 1859, with an exceptionally agreeable party of friends. For a person who loved his ease, and was singularly well versed in the methods which conduce to ease, Mr. Appleton was wonderfully able to dispense with it. He endured the discomforts of camp-life with cheerful heroism, and rose in the early morning from a bed of boughs, fresh and refreshed, as from the best of mattresses.

The travelers left Boston in a driving easterly rain-storm, such as we have sometimes in September, on the journey that was to be such "a joy forever" to all of them in memory. The rain ceased by the time they got fairly into the wilderness, and when they reached Bartlett, on the upper Saranac Lake, the clouds lifted, and they had delightful weather all the rest of the time.

"You may well imagine," writes Mrs. Lawrence, who was one of the party, "what it must have been to travel through those lovely regions in company with Mr. Appleton. The gorgeous tints of the autumn, the mellow sunshine, the open-air life, and the peace and stillness of all around us seemed to sink into his very soul, and to develop all the poetic elements of his nature. Wonderful talks we had while gliding down Rackett River, or seated beneath the shadow of the pines, or couched among the pale mosses and scarlet whortleberry-bushes of the fairy-like islands."

This Adirondack trip inspired many an *impromptu* poem; among them the following:

> When autumn leaves were fading fast
>   In the keen October weather,
> Two fair ones from the city passed
>   Out to the woods together.
> The sunshine which the day denied
>   Lived in their eyes entrancing,
> And, as they stepped, their mutual stride
>   Was as a brooklet's dancing.
>
> Through mist and rain and cloud they faced
>   With sunshine in their faces,
> So bright, no melancholy dared
>   Live in the dreariest places.

27

The Saranac stood robed in mist,
  Struck through with gold and cherry,
And all its hemlocks would have kissed
  Those cheeks so round and merry.
In keeping with the dying year,
  Their Balmorals repeated
The tints on every mountain sere,
  And crimson crimson greeted.

. . . Thus guarded, they confiding roam
  Through all the forest mazes;
Each cavern is their happy home,
  And safe the wildest places.
. . . His war-horn no mosquito dare
  Sound as they float between the islands,
No midget bite, no spider scare
  Where all is perfume, dream, and silence.

The pine-tree, like a Persian chief,
  Bearded and dark above them towers,
His carpet rich with many a leaf
  And wine-red moss and scarlet flowers.
Beside him, like a daughter fair,
  The birch leans trembling modestly,
The golden sequins in her hair,
  Which, caught by zephyrs, fall and fly,
Flooring with gold the amber sheet
Which spreads in beauty round their feet.

An undated letter from Trenton Falls, N. Y., to his father, expresses his appreciation of the beautiful nature of his own country:

"I shall never more wonder at your enthusiasm about this place. I hold it to be the noblest cascade I have ever seen. When I arrived, the waters of three days had swollen it to wildness. It has not one mean or paltry accessory to all its mile of wonderful beauty. How unique is that magical walk, close to the whirling water, and the rich trees, with sweeping and grooved rocks below ! Nothing can be finer.

"I find here my friend Church and his new bride. I have lent her my Claude mirror to see the falls in ; but she has or ought to have a mirror within for everything now which Claude never dreamed of. She is lovely, like a marble by Palmer, whose studio, by-the-way, we had time to visit in Albany, and saw lovely things, though he was away."

The memory of his early camping experiences was bright enough to induce him, in the autumn of 1881, when he was nearly seventy years old, to yield to the persuasions of Mr. and Mrs. Church, and go with them and a little party they formed, to Mr. Church's camp on Lake Millinoket in Maine.

The weather was exceptionally warm and summerlike when the little fleet of canoes was launched to ascend the Penobscot. Mr. Appleton bravely stepped into the one prepared for him, a mighty craft of birch, exceptionally large and strong, with a wise and experienced guide at each end to pole it up the rapids.

All day the canoes glided over the water, sometimes
through placid places where pond-lilies were seen
floating on the surface, more often picking their way
along the stony, turbulent bed of the swollen stream.
Two nights were passed in tents before the destination of the party was reached. They slept well on
couches of pine-boughs, to the music of the mosquito
and kindred melodies. No one in the morning was
more gay, or with a better appetite for delicious fried
salt pork, than Mr. Appleton ; he was the first ready
for the walk through the woods across the " carry."

Mr. Church's luxurious log-camp is on the edge
of a lovely lake, confronting Mount Katahdin, which
rises in all its majesty directly opposite. Little waves
plash upon a beach of yellow sand ; a tiny rivulet of
ice-cold water trickles through the thick forest to the
shore. A huge fire of logs, in the open air, blazed
before the camp, and, when evening came, glowed
afar. The band of guides made a most efficient staff,
anticipating every want of the party, and cooking the
ample meals demanded by out-door appetites.

Mr. Appleton enjoyed everything—the bath in the
lake, for which the weather was mild enough, the ex-
peditions in canoes to beautiful points, the wondrous
effects of sunset upon the mountain, and even the little
hardships inevitable to the smoothest sort of " rough-
ing it." With his cigar he reclined upon the sand,

under a fragrant pine, and listened to a novel, read aloud by one of the party, interrupted, perhaps, by the sound of a gun from an absent member, shooting ducks upon the lake, or by the melancholy cry of the loon.

When a telegram, announcing illness in the family of Mr. Church, summoned the happy little party suddenly home, Mr. Appleton bore the enforced haste of the return with his usual cheerfulness and gayety.

This reminiscence of the last camping excursion is anticipated, in order that it may find its place with the other out-door episodes of Mr. Appleton's varied life.

CHAPTER XVIII.

1864–1874.

WITH the death of Mr. Nathan Appleton, in 1861, the letters come to an end which have hitherto served as the best journal of his son's life. From that time until his own death, the sources of information to be relied on are but the ever-fresh recollections of his surviving friends.

Thomas took a lively interest in the enlargement of Boston by the addition of the Back Bay lands. Everything, indeed, which tended to the adornment and improvement of his native town was sure to find his ready sympathy. He had already been active in the project, successfully carried through, of erecting the statue to Benjamin Franklin, in School Street. He was, from the first, a trustee of the Public Library, as he had been, from its early beginning in Pearl Street, one of the Boston Athenæum.

He watched with delight the rapid growth of streets on the " New Land," and, when Commonwealth

Avenue was laid out, he was among the first to make sure of possessing a house-lot while he could select the best situation. He chose one on the north side, with sun at the back, near the Public Garden, next his friend Mr. Erastus Bigelow. Then followed the absorbing interest of building, under the advice of an experienced architect.

The result was a delightful library, with a house built round it. In a long, large room in the middle of the lower floor were arranged low book-cases on all sides, where his collection of books, accumulating for years, might now expand and "suffer themselves to be admired." The room was lighted from above by means of a well, running up through the house. Soft light, through a ground-glass ceiling, fell upon the pictures gathered together from his frequent travels in Europe. His favorite pictures hung always in this room, where he loved to spend the greater part of his time; but they overflowed into the drawing-room, which occupied the front part of the house, and into the sunny dining-room behind; they climbed the stairs, ornamenting the halls, and invaded the large bedrooms, penetrating to the very top, where the billiard-room occupied the front of the upper story. Mr. Appleton used to say that he never bought a picture unless he liked it. His taste, cultivated by the long study of the best, was admirable, while at the same time it was always indulgent. He was never afraid to buy a picture that he liked, and his kind sympathy for talent and genius wherever he found it, above all, in his fellow-countrymen, led him to encourage many a struggling artist, not only with words of praise and just criticism, but by the more solid test of a purchase. His own pictures also added their charm to the series, helping to tell the tale of his wanderings. His copy of the " Madonna della Seggiola," taken, in his first enthusiasm, from the original in the Pitti Palace, at Florence, hung for many years on the wall of the dining-room, by most of the guests in that hospitable place little suspected to be the work of their host.

So full did the large house become with all the pictures, books, bibelots, curios of all sorts, it seems hard to understand how its owner could have previously lived in closer quarters; the numbers have gone on in rapid increase, until now, at the sad breaking-up of this home, it is a difficult task to imagine what will become of them all. Mr. Appleton in his later years was an insatiable reader, and books poured into the house—not only books, but magazines, reviews, weeklies, daily newspapers. A pile of the latest foreign literature from Schönhoff found its place in a corner of the library, until, in a short time, it had been thoroughly read; then it disappeared to the binder, to be replaced by a new set ; the bound books, in due time returning in their pretty coats of calf and paper, were relegated to closets and shelves above-stairs, until every crack and corner were filled, and then the cry was, "Bridget, what shall be done with these books ?"

Unlike many book-collectors, Mr. Appleton was always ready and willing to lend ; but even this habit of his did not perceptibly diminish the amount.

The death of Mrs. Longfellow, in 1861, closely followed as it was by that of Mr. Nathan Appleton, came as a double blow and terrible shock to the brother and son. The affection and reverence he held for his father was the underlying sentiment of his life from early childhood; as has been seen in his letters, the closest confidence existed between them, and, in his ripening manhood, the intimacy between them was more like a friendship of young men than the usual ties between son and father. Next to this feeling, his affection for his sisters held its place in his heart. Since the marriage of Mrs. Longfellow, to watch her happiness, and the growth of her young family, had been among his chiefest satisfactions. He became deeply attached to Mr. Longfellow, and upon all these dear ones, including the absent sister in London and her children, he concentrated the warmth of an affectionate nature. Two of the circle were now gone—suddenly taken away, and at the same time. The blow to the current of his life was a sharp and severe one.

A marked characteristic of Mr. Appleton's mind was his vivid perception of the other world. At all times his sense of the nearness of those who have left us was active; his faith in the unseen ran, like a bright thread, through all his currents of thought. It was this tendency that made him ready to investigate and even accept the wonders of "spiritualism," so called, growing out of the phenomena of magnetism and table-tipping; seeking, as he always did, the highest manifestations of spirit through matter. It would be a mistake to suppose that he derived his belief in another world, in the presence around us of spirits, and his firm conviction of the reality of future existence, from the idle feats of the medium and the tipping-table; on the contrary, he grew weary, in his latest years, of such manifestations, because they took on methods too coarse and material to match in any measure the delicacy of his own perceptions. It was his theory—not taught him by Hume, or any mercenary medium, but his own—that the spirit-world is ever close to the world of matter; and that, with the advance of time, the slight barrier between them may be broken down. Such a conviction, underlying as it did his whole being, and not merely taken up from time to time as a matter for speculation, made the memory and presence of his lost friends ever near to him, though it might not do away with the pain of losing their daily intercourse.

The wandering years were over. Mr. Appleton was now prepared to reap the benefit, in tranquil and wise living, of the years of intellectual training that had gone before. Ripe in years and judgment, he was fitted to give to his town and to his time an example of the results of the highest culture upon a generous nature.

His ideal of twenty years before, " of improving his character and mind, and living modestly on a moderate income," had indeed been fulfilled, but at the same time he had been, consciously or unconsciously, educating himself for the position of a man of means. The inheritance left him by his father, by judicious management, went on increasing until his death ; in the wise dispensing of his ample fortune, the liberal sharing of his possessions with the less fortunate, revealed him as a man accomplished in the difficult art of generous living. It has been said, especially of America, that there are plenty of men who can make money, but few who know how to spend it. Mr. Appleton understood and practiced the knowledge. He spent money for the enjoyment not only of himself, but of others, and was not happy unless the luxuries and amusements with which his intelligence, even more than his wealth, surrounded him, were amply shared by others.

His health was admirable ; for he had outgrown, it would seem, the hurt which affected so seriously his earlier years. His disposition and habits were of great activity ; his luxurious idleness was not indolence, for his active brain and mind were always on the alert.

When the war came, in 1861, Mr. Appleton's patriotism was aflame. Like many others of his contemporaries, he had never been what was called a " free-soiler," nor an abolitionist, although a personal friend of Charles Sumner, and admiring his heroism for a cause which won his sympathy, while he shared the opinions of his father and the older men of Boston, in favor of moderation and compromise in dealing with the question of slavery. But when the crisis came, there was no faltering ; his feelings were intensely Northern, his speech strong and sharp against the rebels, and his purse open to furnish to the Northern army the sinews of war. Much as he loved England, where he had so many friends, his wrath knew no bounds for the English tendency to sympathize with the South ; his brilliant, witty tongue lashed those miscreants unsparingly who dared to be on the wrong side. He was especially interested in the colored regiments ; he was a personal friend of Governor

Andrew, and a useful one, with a hand that knew how to sign a check. Private and public subscriptions of all kinds found their way easily to the house in Commonwealth Avenue. Mr. Appleton's correspondence for the last twenty years of his life, in great measure, consists of letters acknowledging sums greater or smaller, for all sorts of enterprises, from those of large patriotic weight, philanthropic importance, or æsthetic attraction, to private gifts lifting loads from the humblest homes.

The winters of this period were passed in Boston, the summers sometimes at Newport, but oftener at Nahant, in the cottage shared with Mr. Longfellow. In these summers Mr. Appleton sketched and painted most industriously, his quick eye for the beauty of Nature selecting with great judgment the right "bits" for landscape, which his favorite way of noticing was by transferring to large pebbles, painted in oils with admirable taste. In the winter, too, he painted, but not so much. In 1868 he discovered for the first time the amusement to be derived from writing to dictation; and after that he composed a number of essays prepared in this way for the press. Never before had he published anything, with the exception of a few fugitive poems; after his early journals had come to an end, his pen ceased to be so active as before. It is much to be regretted that his delightful

letters too had grown "small by degrees."   He found
dictating was more like talking than writing down in
silence and solitude words for an unknown audience.
Nothing that he has dictated can compare in brilliancy with his talk ; but the essays thus written have
preserved reminiscences and speculations that would
otherwise be wholly lost.

In this full, active life of philanthropy and intellectual enjoyment the years slipped by, the old rov-
ing instinct lessened but not wholly lost.   In 1866,
to satisfy his own fondness for sailing, and to indulge
the same taste in his nephews and nieces, Mr. Appleton gave orders for the building of a yacht.   He
has described this, and the first voyage of the Alice
(named for his niece, Alice Longfellow), in " A Sheaf
of Papers," published in 1874.   He says he "felt
himself bitten by the gad-fly of construction," and determined "to encourage native talent and build within
our own borders."

When the Alice was finished, the young people,
whose pleasure it was built to serve, were seized with
a desire to cross the Atlantic in it.   Mr. Appleton was
still young enough to sympathize with this longing,
and his consent was soon obtained.

" Parents and relatives were weak before the ardor
of youth, and, to the astonishment of many and the

terror of some, the little creature was actually soon found to be taking in stores, and then quietly facing the breadth of the ocean, as if she were an India-man or a Cunarder. Amid many hands upheld in warning, many solemn words of discouragement, with three stalwart, confident seamen, with a youthful captain, who has seen his flag fly in every quarter of the world, and a quaint Chinese steward, whose face suggested remoter foreign parts than it was proposed to visit, away went the Alice."

The captain was Arthur Clark, and the other young men were Charles Longfellow and his friend Harry Stanfield. Mr. Appleton published his recollections of the voyage in the " Sheaf of Papers."

While the yacht was triumphantly making its way through the waters, its owner crossed in a steamer, and joined his young friends at Cowes on their arrival. The little vessel was received with wonder in England, and her officers with courtesy, who passed the summer in sharing the honors of their craft. They returned home in the autumn, leaving the yacht to winter at Cowes. She was brought back the next spring, and, for many a happy summer, was the point around which centered the pleasures of the young people, and of their indulgent uncle as well. Year after year, from the piazza of the house at Nahant, the Alice was to be seen all through the summer, at her moorings within easy whistling-distance. At the summons of a note, or the waving of a handkerchief, the skipper comes on shore to receive his orders. For a few moments all is bustle in the house, running up-stairs for wraps, searching for parasols; the morning newspaper and the novel must not be forgotten, nor the cigar. The gay party hastens to the rocks just below the house, where a "bright" boat, manned by dapper, saluting sailors, lies waiting to row them to the yacht. The broad sail is up, the anchor-chain is wound; Mr. Longfellow from the piazza waves a genial farewell, and the graceful Alice glides from her moorings and sweeps away, freighted with happy spirits—none more gay, none so important to the pleasure of the day, as the master of the yacht.

One of the pleasantest of his European tours was made by Mr. Appleton in 1868–'69, when he went with Mr. Longfellow and his daughters abroad. To revisit old, familiar scenes in company with such dear friends is the best form of traveling. A part of the winter was passed in Rome, going over the old ground, now enhanced by the presence of many acquaintances.

The following years were spent at home — the winters in Commonwealth Avenue, the summers at Nahant.

Although Mr. Appleton at this time lived alone, his hospitality was such that he was seldom left to himself; a small circle of intimate friends was always about him, many of them artists. Among these may be mentioned Mr. Petersen, whose marine - pictures, and his thorough knowledge of everything belonging to ships and boats, were very attractive to Mr. Appleton; and especially Mr. William Allan Gay, between whom and Mr. Appleton there was a warm and lasting friendship. At that time Mr. Gay was very important to Mr. Appleton, as an ardent enthusiast for art, and an appreciative listener. The closeness of their intimacy, never broken, was interrupted only by Mr. Gay's departure for Japan. His fine picture of a wood-interior hung always in the library, where Mr. Appleton could see it, when enjoying his cigar upon his favorite sofa. He had the happy faculty of enjoying his own possessions, and especially his pictures, and not losing sight of them through familiarity, as sometimes happens. He often spoke of the lasting charm of this subject and its treatment.

From all his European travels the Nile and Syria had hitherto been omitted, and, as he advanced in life, Mr. Appleton had it on his mind that this Eastern tour was yet to be accomplished. In the autumn of 1874, after various false starts, he found himself in Florence, on his way to Egypt, without as yet having secured for himself any party or congenial companion.

One day, in a gallery in Venice, he entered into

conversation with an artist who was copying before
one of the masterpieces of the collection. After some
easy, agreeable talk on matters of art, this gentleman,
turning round, said :

"Although I have never seen him, I should guess
you were Mr. Tom Appleton."

"What ! are you so good a Yankee as that ?   You
have guessed right."

"I have heard my friend Kensett describe you and
your 'talk' so often, that it was impossible not to recognize you," replied the artist, who then introduced
himself as Mr. Eugene Benson.

In less than five minutes, according to Mr. Appleton's way of telling the story, he had invited Benson
to join him and go up the Nile. It had been the
dream of the artist's life, hitherto unattainable. On
learning that his new friend, less "unattached" than
himself, was married, Mr. Appleton at once extended
the invitation to his wife and her daughter, Miss
Fletcher, and thus a party was rapidly formed of just
the right size, and, as it proved, of admirable elements ;
the proposal proved one of those lucky hits which Mr.
Appleton always loved, which insured in advance their
own success, by the pride he felt in his "flair," as he
used to call it.

They all repaired to Alexandria and Cairo ; a *da-
habich* was procured, with all the accompanying para-

phernalia of dragoman, cook, sailors, provisions, etc. The winter was passed upon the Nile in high enjoyment; sketching, shooting, writing, filled up the time, with ever-flowing congenial conversation.

Miss Fletcher's pen was ready to put on paper the journal dictated by Mr. Appleton, and this account of the trip was published in London and Boston, on the return. In the spring Mr. Appleton went into Syria, with the same companions, and then returned as far as England, where he visited Mrs. Mackintosh.

That summer, with his niece, Eva Mackintosh, and a friend, Mrs. Erskine, he made a trip into Scotland, and the habit of dictation then being strong upon him, they kept a journal, which begins thus :

"OBAN, *August* 22, 1875.

"That double Sabbath of Scotland, of seriousness as well as rain, constrains us Lowlanders, kirkless and confined, to attempt our long-contemplated journal. We have hours behind us too faint and far for memory, though here and there some peculiar gleam of brightness holds the past unforgotten.

"A jolly triad of us—an oldish gentleman, doubled by two young women, make our party. Two of us feel the pull of Scottish blood in our veins, and the other, at least, is so saturated with Scott and Burns as not to be behind them in interest."

They went by rail to Glasgow, up the Clyde in a little steamer, running upon Loch Gyle, to its head, the scene of Campbell's poem, "Lord Ullin's Daughter."

"What we saw was no dark and stormy water, but imagination could see the black and boiling loch into which the conflict of marital and parental love drove that fated pair. Evidently the chief of Ulva's Isle was a man of small possessions, and that silver pound may have been his last penny, in which case he may have been well out of the scrape altogether."

At Inverness he writes :

"The Assizes have begun, and Lord Muir has opened the court. I was just in time the first day to see his lordship return to the Caledonian Hotel. Justice was not without its pomp and circumstance. His lordship's carriage was drawn by four horses, with two postilions ; he was escorted by a file of Highland soldiers in kilt and sporran, the pipers playing away at their head, followed by a silent band. His lordship was attired in white satin, with scarlet crosses upon it, a hood of scarlet ; above all a wig towered, divided into little curls, and over all something flat, like a buckwheat-cake. It was high-jinks with the barefooted *gamins* of both sexes; they followed the band with a tenacity which I emulated, and we all marched to the playing of the pipers down Church Street and over the bridge to the barracks, where all but the band were dismissed, but I stuck to them, with only three other *gamins*, till we reached the bridge near the cathedral; there they disappeared, and I came home musing upon the advantage it would be to us in America if justice there had these august surroundings. Yet Justice Gray persists in towering upon the bench in the simple dignity of his white cravat."

Thus, in alternate travel and repose in picturesque places, the month of September was passed. The journal closes on the first of October, with an account of the wedding, at the cathedral, of the Lord of the Isles :

"The bridegroom drove up in coach-and-four, with postilions in scarlet jackets. Later came the fair array of bridesmaids, and last of all, in a fly, the bride and her father. She was very handsome, and her dress perfection. Many of the party came in full Highland dress, and never have I seen such a display of beautiful stockings; they looked like a procession of those plaid boxes which Edinburgh offers to the traveler."

Not long after Mr. Appleton returned to America. This was really his last voyage across the Atlantic. Spain was still unvisited, and Norway; plans for journeys to these countries often occupied him, but were never realized. The attractions of home, the magnet in his sofa and fireside, became too powerful even for his hitherto insatiable thirst for travel, and he was content to "fight his battles o'er again," for delighted listeners, and occasionally to dictate reminiscences of the past for the pleasure of the public.

CHAPTER XIX.

YEARS OF REPOSE.

1875–1883.

NEARLY all of the last ten years of his life were passed by Mr. Appleton in the tranquil enjoyment of the comforts and luxuries by which he was surrounded, and the active use of his faculties and talents for the benefit of others. After the maturity of manhood, it may be said that a man's life from day to day is but the printing off of impressions from the types of character which have been set in earlier years. In such impressions may be read the lessons learned, the experiences stored up in those previous hours, and by them may be judged the value of the course of life which set these types and no others.

Mr. Appleton's friends, now that he is gone, love to remember the home he made for his last years, comfortable without parade, luxurious without ostentation. The arrangements of the household were exactly as he liked them; that everybody who had the luck to share them liked them as well, is a proof that his taste and judgment were of the best. His servants were devoted to their indulgent master. He was served from affection rather than obligation.

During these years, Mr. Appleton's brother Nathan lived with him, the affection between them being so strong that each had become indispensable to the other. With the double management of these two heads of the household, there never seemed lacking that feminine influence which is said to be all-important to the proper regulation of a home. But any account of the establishment would be incomplete without some mention of the faithful housekeeper, of admirable intelligence and tact, who for years reigned supreme in her department, carrying out the will, expressed or only guessed, of her chief. Mr. Appleton's hospitality, to which there was no limit, sometimes put the resources of Bridget to a severe test, but she was always equal to the occasion. The latest, least expected arrival at the crowded table was welcomed by her quiet smile, though a slight contraction of the brow might hint her anxiety lest the soup might not go round, but in fact there was never any difficulty on that score.

It will not be easy to forget the charm of that dinner-table, round, well lighted from above, bright with fine damask and tasteful appointments, the host

at its head always genial, never more entertaining
than when he saw a circle of merry faces around the
board ; never less agreeable, however, when the number was reduced to its smallest limit. Mr. Appleton
believed in the gospel of good-eating, maintaining
that the pleasures of the palate were given us to enjoy, as much as those of sight and sound. Marvelous
were the huge turkeys, fat capons, and generous sir-
loins that appeared upon his table ; but the charm
was not in these, but in his own unflagging conversation and bright spirit of conviviality.

Mr. Appleton was an early riser. Even in winter
he was up and out for a little walk before breakfast,
by eight o'clock or half past, often without an overcoat, greeting the letter-carrier, the newsboy, and his
early neighbors, as they went down-town, with cheerful praise or vigorous abuse of the weather. He loved
the eccentricities of the Boston climate, for the very
extremity of it. "The whip of the sky," he called
the east wind lashing the inhabitants into desperate
energy.

"Is it not delicious? Is it not delightfully con-
sistent?" he would exclaim, joyfully opening the door
himself to some wind-blown guest, when the gale was
sweeping gusts of snow and sleet along the avenue.

After breakfast and his newspaper, his custom was
to paint for an hour or two, either in oils or water-

color, enjoying the work for its own sake, and for the
memories of lovely nature it called up. Then he
never failed to start for a walk, often without any
definite object in view. Fortunate was the chance
companion he might invite to join him on one of
these delightfully vague excursions; in and out of pict-
ure-shops, book-stores, carpet-warehouses (if by good
luck Bridget had told him he needed a new carpet).
Everybody knew him. Briggs rejoiced to see him
enter his carefully-spread and tempting snares, and
Doll and Richards pricked up their ears as the light
tap of his cane sounded upon their steps. All the
artists knew him, and each was glad when Mr. Appleton's well-known figure appeared in his doorway,
when he took the proffered seat, and stayed perhaps
an hour, perhaps two, talking in genial strain, probably himself sustaining all the *frais* of the occasion,
after which he rose and took his leave, saying—

"Well, this has been a delightful conversation!"

A cream-cake at Féra's often satisfied him for
lunch, after which he found his way home again,
across the Common and through the Garden, where
he never failed to observe the changing flowers, and
note with pleasure the improvements, and the wonderful growth of the city since his younger days, when
Charles Street was the water-street, and the waves
dashed against its wall.

Then came the cigar and well-earned repose upon his sofa, accompanied, if any listener were by, by the narration of his morning's experiences. He was an ardent smoker. A box of Upmann Brevas stood always in a corner easily accessible ; in this, as in everything else, he used moderation and method, and never exceeded the number of cigars per diem which he found suited him the best.

Reading occupied the rest of the daylight hours. Mr. Appleton read for the pure love of reading, and his taste in books was very general ; serious, gay, heavy, light, scientific, or frivolous subjects all commanded his attention ; he read thoroughly, and seldom forgot what he read, and could give an abstract of a biography, or an exploring expedition, often more pithy than the book from which it was derived. All the new books, all the magazines, all the daily and weekly papers came into that house, and none remained unopened.

Then came darkness upon the short days of winter, and cheerful fire-light in the coldest evenings made the library bright. The dinner-hour was every day a time for enjoyment, prolonged to its utmost by delay and pleasant chat. In the evening, at one time, Mr. Appleton had the habit of dictating his letters to an amanuensis, or the text of the volumes of essays published at that time. For the last few years, however, he preferred, most of all, listening to reading ; and, in the quiet room, when the guests had gone, under the light of softened lamps, the harmonious litter of books, papers, Christmas-cards, invitations, scattered broadcast over tables and book-shelves, how many a romance, how many a biography, he has listened to with appreciative delight !

Mr. Appleton dearly loved a novel.   He liked best a good one, but he was not above enjoying a bad one ; and, with generous sympathy for the difficulties of authors, discovered the merits even of doubtful efforts. In literature, as in art, he was a most indulgent critic, making all allowance for the intention of the workman, tolerating some books which many a reader finds dull ; but a really clever book, with an intricate plot and sparkling conversation, delighted him.

With his convivial habits and gifts of conversation, Mr. Appleton, of course, was much in demand in society, receiving plenty of invitations during the gay season.   He had always liked dining out, which is not to be wondered at, as he was sure to be the life of the table, and he readily accepted the demands made on him by his friends.   In his latest years, however, and especially after his fall on the ice, in 1877, he grew a little weary of so much visiting, and gradually came to prefer the quiet evenings at home.   He enjoyed the theatre, and seldom missed a new play, or an old favorite. He had seen all the great performers of his time, but never spoiled his own enjoyment of the present, by comparing the actor he was seeing with the phœnixes of the past. During the last winter of his life he saw every play, at least once, of Irving and Miss Terry. His pleasure in their performance was just as keen as at the triumphs of Grisi and Taglioni fifty years before.

"Now we are perfectly sure of a good time," he said every night, as the door was shut of the cab which was taking him, through storm and sleet, to the Boston Theatre to see "Louis XI," "The Bells," and all the rest.

Such were the winter pursuits of the last few years. In summer, Mr. Appleton's favorite home was the house at Nahant, than which it is difficult to imagine anything pleasanter, especially during the lifetime of Mr. Longfellow, who shared the place with his brother-in-law. There was a warm affection between these two men, which deepened as they grew older. The death of Mr. Longfellow, in 1882, was a great loss to Mr. Appleton—one more of the events which loosened his hold upon this life, and turned his thoughts, always conversant with the things of another world, more constantly to the life beyond.

At Nahant was the yacht Alice, and the ever-lovely sea, with the town and sunset-view across the water.

The piazza there took the place of the cozy library in town, and there Mr. Appleton passed luxurious hours, with his cigar, surrounded by books and papers. A daily walk, varied by calls upon his neighbors—for in every house at Nahant he was a welcome visitor—and a drive across the beach, or perhaps as far as the Appleton pulpit at Saugus, filled up the day, with sometimes an ocean-bath.

A new generation had come up to claim his attention. His niece, Mrs. Dana, was often with him at Nahant, and her children were a great source of satisfaction to him. The house in town, on Sundays especially, overflowed with children, the two families of his half-brother and sister. These young people reproduced, to his thought, their parents, who also had come about him as children, regarding, as they had done, " Uncle Tom " as a source of manifold blessings.

Once or twice Mr. Appleton was persuaded to leave the comforts of home, to which he was becoming more and more bound, for short excursions not far away. One of these was a trip to North Carolina, in the autumn of 1880, with Mr. and Mrs. F. E. Church and the present writer. The journey was a most agreeable one, the mountain-scenery of North Carolina proving as fine as it had been described. The party spent ten days delightfully at Warm Springs, in a pleasant, old, rambling hotel. Mr. Appleton was as active as of old, and as keenly awake to the amusements of the place. Always a wonderful traveler, his spirits rose with the discomforts of bad inns, bad food, and sleepless nights. He never was funnier than on one occasion, in the middle of the night, when the train was late, and there was nothing to do but to walk up and down the hideous carpet of a dreary hotel-parlor, between one and two A. M., for an hour or more. Mr. Appleton said he enjoyed it ; and, with his gay talk, kept the party not only awake but merry until the arrival of the train.

He kept up his relations with friends and things in New York till the last, generally making a visit there in the spring of each year, as much at home there, in the galleries, shops, studios, and drawing-rooms, as in Boston. These trips were sometimes extended as far as Washington. Two or three weeks sufficed for such absences, and he returned to Commonwealth Avenue to Bridget, to the dogs and birds, with content.

These genial pursuits did not prevent him from maintaining a lively interest in the public matters of Boston. The Art Museum was his favorite hobby ; his walks often tended toward it, and he delighted to show friends and strangers what it contained. He was the best cicerone for the treasures of it ; indeed, he prepared a short addition to its catalogue, full of infor-

mation valuable to the visitor ; but it was far better to
hear him talk about the statues and pictures. He lingered always before the busts of the Roman emperors ;
like the likenesses of old friends, they called up to him
the characters and lives of those whom they represented. He had many a personal anecdote connected
with the objects of art in the various rooms.

It would be too long to enumerate the many objects for the adornment and improvement of Boston
in which he took an active share ; and vain to try to
reveal the countless kindnesses, pecuniary or otherwise, which dropped from his open hand, unknown
and unmentioned, upon the objects of his sympathy.
In that direction no day was without its mark.

CHAPTER XX.

THE LAST.

1884.

In the autumn of 1883 the friends of Mr. Appleton could not have failed to observe a slight change coming over him, which even then seemed to them a faint foreshadowing, not of the end, but of approaching old age. Although he had passed his seventieth year, he had still up to this time been as young in his feelings as any of his circle. Now there appeared a little flagging of the hitherto undaunted spirit. His sense of hearing, always remarkably quick to catch a chance for repartee, the song of a bird, the roll of waves upon the shore, began to fail him, according to his own impression, though others did not perceive it. He was advised to consult an aurist.

"It may be only wax in your ears," said some one, consolingly.

"Ah, my dear!" he replied, "I fear it is not wax, but wane."

How idle to repeat such things as these, which, lacking the manner, the glance, the smile, which belonged with them, convey no point to the reader!

He became more attached to his sofa, more indifferent to the invitations of society, put off demands upon his time requiring exertion, and sometimes sent away the carriage waiting at the door for him to drive.

Yet he never was more genial, more sympathetic, more gentle in his judgment of men and things. In his earlier years, very likely, he was willing to pass sharp sentences upon follies and crimes, even upon acts which did not excite his sympathy; but of late this was changed. It was easy to turn away his wrath, about to fall upon some imagined offender in a torrent of condemnation, by a few gentle words defending the absent sinner. "You are quite right," he would say; "I am glad to hear so much good of him. No doubt he is an excellent fellow."

It would be pleasant to linger over those hours, so pleasant while they were passing; so sweet, so sad, to recall now that they are gone forever. Those who enjoyed them would fain have put forth a detaining hand to check their rapid flight, but this could not be. Mr. Appleton's devoted brother, and the friends nearest him, saw the gradual change with unspoken pain; found themselves, to their surprise, called upon at the bright dinner-table to be talkers rather than listeners, because the host, who once had needed no spur to be the life of the party, now sat listening, though always cheerful and pleased. No one thought of death, but perhaps of long years of failing perceptions, senses dimmed, and activity repressed. Perhaps he himself saw something of this in the future; and bravely, silently prepared himself to play the part of old age, retired from the active scene he so long had distinguished.

From such a decline he was spared. It was better that a brief, unexpected illness, without much suffering, should close a life with which it would be hard to associate the ideas of physical failure and infirmity. His last hours were distinguished by the same bright cheerfulness which ruled his later years. In the full possession of his faculties to the last, it is easy to imagine that he approached with intense satisfaction the portals of the other world — the solution of the mystery of the two lives which had ever occupied his earnest and devout speculations.

No effort has been made in this little memoir to adorn or add to the story of a life spent in the pursuit and use of the highest things. It may be seen, without comment, that, from the beginning to the end, Mr.

Appleton's course of intelligent travel, his search for
the best in Nature and in art, his intercourse with the
leading minds of his time, were fitting him for the
position he was destined to fill—of a leader in artistic
thought and advanced cultivation in his native town.

Since his death it has been frequently said that
there is no one to fill his place in Boston. Truly, the
position he held there, as authority in all matters of
art and literature, foremost in brilliant conversation,
a liberal protector of talent in every line, was not
lightly won. It was the well-earned result of a youth
and manhood spent in wide and liberal self-culture,
resulting in a knowledge scattered broadcast for the
benefit of all who came within its influence.

THE END.